THROUGH THE HEART
OF THE SPIDER

Chip Wright

iUniverse, Inc.
New York Bloomington

Through The Heart Of the Spider

iUniverse books may be ordered through booksellers or by contacting:

iUniverse
1663 Liberty Drive
Bloomington, IN 47403
www.iuniverse.com
1-800-Authors (1-800-288-4677)

ISBN: 978-0-595-48022-7 (pbk)
ISBN: 978-0-595-60124-0 (ebk)

Printed in the United States of America

iUniverse rev. date: 12/16/2008

Evening was just starting in eastern Afghanistan. Mickey Twitch and I walked along a washboard road just outside of Towr Kham, the last town east before the gates to the Khyber Pass. I had a wool blanket wrapped over my nose and up over my head, letting the rest fall down my back, cutting some of the biting wind. My eyes looked straight ahead as Twitch rustled along next to me, buttoned up tight in that long drab-green Russian military coat of his, its collar turned up over mounds of matted hair.

Everyone who knew Mickey called him Twitch at least sometimes, Twitch or Mickey Twitch depending on who it was. He'd picked up the name from an involuntary wiggle he had in his left eye that would do its own sideways twist every now and again. It was something that had started after a two-month stint smoking hashish in the stand-up hookahs in the town of Balkh-e-Sharif, which was ground zero for hashish production in northern Afghanistan. Mickey was something when it came to hashish.

Mickey and I met early one winter in Kabul at a small hotel along the river in old town. I guess you could call it a river. In that part of the city, in the winter at least, the river was more like a maze of open ditches winding in and out of each other. It was forty-some feet wide, with muddy mounds stuck to a variety of broken trash. Fingers of chocolate gray water meandered in mini rivulets here and there under yellow-brown ice bridges that froze up off the muddy mounds from one cruddy frozen bank to the next, weaving an icy web across the river bed. They called it "old town" here where the river ran, which seemed funny because everything was old in Kabul except a few places around the embassy district.

The night Mickey and I met was an awful damn cold and snowy one. I'd found an entrance to tuck into in front of an old hotel while a squall blew down the street. I sat there with my knees pulled up against my chest, squatting and waiting out the winds and sleet. The icy air bit at my cheeks and ankles as I hunkered there. I was wrapped up as best I could in my snow leopard skin coat I'd picked up in the Hindu Kush. I had it pulled up over my nose even thought it stank like horse piss and musty smoke, a real drawback of the tribal tanning process. I'd gotten used to the smell like you get used to most things if you're around them enough. Besides, being wrapped up in a stinky coat was better then freezing to death, which wasn't all that uncommon in an Afghan winter. Right then, up off the street stepped Mickey Twitch.

"Bitter-ass cold, aren't it, mate?" he said through the muffler wrapped around his face. I nodded, not willing to drop my coat below my nose to speak.

"Bugger all, mate, you been in the Kush for sure, wearing that coat. Bloody well warmer in the mountains by a fire than here in the catchway." He winked and shifted his head.

"Come on inside, mate. I've got a stove, some wood, and a warm naan." He held the flat bread up against his cheek and pressed it hard, winking again and with a slack smile, like the nerves in half his upper lip were late he continued. "Well, it *was* warm, so what do you say, mate? Come up and give me your stories?"

I looked up as he held out a greasy bag.

"Kabob meat here too, not dandy sure, but not dog. At least I don't think so." He winked once more. I looked at that cotton bag dangling from his gloved fingers and could smell the meat right through the coat and my own rancid stench. It hovered over me that smell, as close to heaven as I'd been since I'd come out of the Hindu Kush mountains a few days earlier. I let my collar drop, pushed my back up against the wall to keep out of the sleet, and slid up on my feet.

"Sounds good to me, man. Lead the way."

That's how we met on a bitter cold night in Kabul over cold naan and what could have been dog meat or old billy goat. But don't get me wrong—it was good!

After that Twitch and I spent lots of time swapping tales and found we had some common friends not only in Afghanistan, but in Pakistan and India as well. We'd both spent time hoofing between Istanbul and Calcutta, and it was a small world in the Far East then, particularly when it came to our brand of expatriate.

Mickey was trying to figure out the twists and turns of his mystical cosmic epiphanies, and he sure had some! Me, I was trying to figure out how to reenter the world that I'd never trusted much. I'd spent most of a year before we met in the Hindu Kush living with nomadic tribal Kuchi, while Twitch had been in Kandahar and Bamian obsessing over what he called the oracles. For him that was the *I Ching* mixed with various readings of Huxley and Aleister Crowley. We were night and day in that way. Not that I didn't know about all that stuff, but his take on the mystical was mumbo jumbo to me at best. I'd come up on the streets of Oakland in the blues clubs. I'd run into this stuff sure, but my links to San Francisco's flower children and Berkeley's hippie scene were about reefer not metaphysics. I didn't have any real interest in the esoteric or mystical stuff. I'd seen the *I Ching* and tarot cards in San Francisco when I'd spent a few nights with some lovely ladies in their Clement Street flat. There were a lot of topless dancers in the city then, and I'd run into these two on a weed deal I'd done. I was a romantic figure, it seems; go figure. Anyway, we became friends. They'd "do my cards" as they called it and then "throw the Ching" whenever I'd stop by to see them, me sitting on the bed and them serving me tea while they told my fortune. I thought it was silly, but it was foreplay, and that made it OK.

Now Twitch had very strong opinions about the power of the *I Ching* and carried an old leather-bound copy with him everywhere he went. When he first brought it out with his yarrow sticks, I just watched. I'd never seen the sticks before; the girls back in the city had just tossed coins. But with Twitch I learned more about the *I Ching* than I knew about any book. He showed me how to use the yarrow sticks and how to count them and all.

3

The *I Ching* was like a mother and lover to Twitch, and that seemed right even though I didn't really know how that all worked for him. What I did know was that it was a whole lot more for him than for most, and that was fine. I had my own weirdness, and who was I to judge?

Both of us were reeling from relationships that had gone sour or were sour from the jump. Me, I'd left Oakland when my pregnant girlfriend had decided not to come home one night and go live with her latest lover. When I think about it, that was both good news and bad at the time. It was hard, but it gave me the break I needed. I'd had hounds nipping at my ankles for a while by then, and I didn't need the hassle that relationship brought to the table, so I grabbed what I could carry and got out of there.

After an eventful trip through Europe and overland through the Middle East, I finely landed in the Hindu Kush Mountains of central Afghanistan and began living with the Kuchi, a nomadic tribe that held to old customs with just the thinist layer of Islam over the surface. They herded goats, fought dogs, and hired out as mercenaries. But it was a place nobody could find me or would think to look. And it was a place I could trust to be just what it was and keep me awake and in touch.

As for Twitch, well, his wife had dumped him out of the Land Rover in Iran, just outside of Mashhad, in the desert. They had been on a turquoise-buying trip. He'd taken some LSD and—not deliberately or as not deliberately as one can behave in that state of mind—had almost caused a riot. It seems he'd dervish-danced up and down the streets of the little town of Nyshabur, spewing garbled lines of half-remembered poems to the tunes of Stevie Winwood and Traffic until the local police cornered his wife and told her to get him out of town or they'd shoot him. She managed to round him up then proceeded to drop him off in the desert. As he told it, he watched as she disappeared in the dust and never looked back.

Both of us were working out what life was about and whether it mattered. The conclusion after lots of hashish and laughing was that life did matter but not in the way it had mattered in the past. We became good friends. We both figured we might not live very long, but we were clear that we were going to live a whole lot while we did. And it was nice to find someone to speak English with; even if he did have a Birmingham accent thick as clay, it still was English, and Twitch made the English language worth listening to, which was more than I could say about many who speak it.

All the time I'd been in the Hindu Kush, I'd spoken no English. Cut off from almost any thought of my past, I just got through day by day. I'd skated by with a little Urdu I knew, and I learned some along the way. That mixed with lots of hand signals and bluster worked.

Mickey and I did lots of stuff in the surreal landscape Afghanistan offered in those days. We wanted to get all the life we could out of the time we had. I still remember one of the last times I saw Twitch before he died—he told me he'd figured it all out; he'd finally "got" how the *I Ching*, Vedic astrology, the Torah, and god knows what else were all related by some strange mythic numerology. He'd figured out the key; it all finally made sense! I still wonder if he would have made it and not been killed if he'd just been looking over his shoulder watching out for his ass or mine instead of swimming in all that mystic crap. Or at least not killed in the way he was. I still think sometimes, *Damn, if I'd just been there—I should have been there.*

The spring and summer passed slowly in Kabul. We made ends meet by hooking up traveling hippies with whatever they might be looking for. There was a steady flow of Europeans through Kabul; almost always hippie types who wanted something but had no clue how to find it on their own.

Fall came, and we were sure we didn't want to sit through another winter in the city, so we headed north to Balkh for the hashish-making time, which happened in the dead of winter when cold dry air made the resins separate from the flowers better. It was something—hashish making in the north of Afghanistan. Hashish flowers tight full and as big around as a fist and as long as your forearm lay in piles on racks climbing the barn walls. Buds thick with resins sparkling like frost, fragrant and dazzling. The sharp smells everywhere of hemp flower mixed with the sweet aromas of tea and fresh stewed mutton and everyone busy making hashish in the crystalline air.

Their breath would billow like frothy cream in the icy dry air as the batters laid the plants out on woven mats and then beat them with flat sticks. After that the piles of twigs, stems, seeds were removed and the remaining powder was sifted through finer and finer weaves of mat. Then the pressers went to work taking up small mounds of the powder into their hands and kneading it between their palms until it formed an elastic piece of fragrant hashish. It was a beautiful thing to watch a fresh plaque of hashish happen out of all this.

Hashish pressers had a tough job—I knew because I'd done it myself, and not just once or twice. I did it every day for weeks. One trick was to heat the hashish on rocks near the fire with just enough spit to keep it from drying out. You needed to keep it warm and moist to work it. Spit or a little tea helped. But if it got too hot, it stuck to your hands and tore the skin right off your palm. I'd tore up my hands until they built up calluses that would take it. I pressed hashish day after day until the locals didn't laugh at me anymore. I was as good by then as some of them. Still, I never got as good as those ancient babas, those old men who had worked the hashish all their lives and had hands like rhino leather and eyes like a children.

Twitch and I were after what they called number 1 powder, the kind that came from the final sifting. This quality was almost pure resin. Even on the coldest nights, you could stick your hand in a bag of it and between your finger and thumb roll up a spaghetti shaped piece of hashish.

We stayed in the little mud city of Balkh, the last outpost city of Alexander the Great. It was the place where he'd turned around and headed home. Locals knew this history and proudly showed off old coins from Alexander's stay found in the fields when they plowed. In town lots of people had blue or hazel eyes and curly hair, and many men had beards. You could picture them slipping out of a Trojan horse with swords and shields in hand, if they hadn't been in those long shirts, turbans, and baggy pants. Alexander not only stopped here but also left some of his clan behind it seemed. The people in Balkh were different, not like the Mongolian camel-herds and the dark-haired nomadic Afghan who moved in and out in this part of Afghanistan.

Mickey was crazy when he got on the hookahs. With that Birmingham accent of his and as skinny as he was, Afghans would whisper to each other after they watched him smoke. You never knew what they were saying but it was with half smiles on their faces so that was good, at least I guessed it was. We smoked lots of hashish in those dens in northern Afghanistan

We'd smoke all size hubbly bubblys, which was what we called the big hashish hookahs around town. Some were a couple feet high, and you smoked them kneeling. Others—the big ones—you had to stand to smoke. They all held about a thumb-sized piece of hashish that you broke up and mixed with a little charcoal. Twitch and I liked the dens with the stand-ups best, usually a back room or a shed off the street. We'd sit down on the benches that lined the walls, with curtains just behind us and the hubbly bubblys in the center. When we finished smoking, we'd push the curtains aside and spit. That was the custom, you always spit after smoking those big hookahs.

The hookahs always looked like prophets to me, standing in the center of the room with smoke pouring from their heads with one hand stretched toward the sky preaching some fiery truth about a hidden pastel world.

When Twitch smoked, the pipe bowl would go into flames. Sparks and amber-yellow tongues of fire would dance one or two feet in the air as the bellowing clouds of smoke filled the room. His nose would smoke like a steam engine, his chest heaving in rhythm pulling smoke directly into his lungs as a constant flow of hashish smoke poured from his nose and the sides of his mouth. It was like watching him play a flaming didgeridoo. Then, like the custom demands, he'd fall away from the hookah and crouch in the corner, coughing and spitting. Twitch was the John Coltrane and Dizzy Gillespie of the hookah pipe. A one-of-a-kind who, when asked who he was and from what country he came, would burst out, "Ruski, Ruski, Ruski, Ya" (Russian, Russian, Russian, I am) or turn wild-eyed and cry, "Malang, malang," reaching out a cupped hand for Alms. "I am crazy with God; there is but one God, and Mohammed is his prophet."

Hashish season was all but over, and I'd had enough of the north for a while. I was sick of all the Russians we'd been seeing in and around town and wasn't up for anything that smelled of politics or government.

"I'm bloody well racked, mate! You up for a slog?" Mickey said over his morning tea.

"Sure, let's do it. I'm for sun, girls, maybe India?"

We caught a ride south to Kabul with a friend and then grabbed another ride from an Austrian hippie who was driving overland to India. He was a classic, decked out in baggy tie-dyes and blue sunglasses. We took the ride even though I knew riding with someone looking like that could bring trouble at the border. This far out, it was good to look as much like everyone else as you could. Hippie-types stuck out like fires in a lake. So we told him to drop us on the road just outside of Towr Kham on the road to the Khyber Pass.

We started walking up the road, looking around for a place to stay. As far as you could see through the dusty twilight, trucks, buses, and cars were lined up and down the road, parked in a broken ramble waiting for morning. The pass was closed at dusk; no traffic moved through after that. Everything stopped until 6:00 the next morning. The Khyber Pass was all tribal, and they kept a pretty tight control. We figured that at worst some trucker would let us lay our blankets under his axels out of the wind. Cooking fires burned here and there, and Pakistani pop radio stations blasted echo chamber music, one station wafting over the other as we moved past the trucks. That music had sounded like cats with their tails caught in a door at first to me, but after a few months I'd got to like it.

"Hey, you mans," a voice broke through the echo-chambered layers of music. "Landi Kotal, going want come? Dancing man, dancing, yes."

I looked up and saw five men and an old Austin Gipsy with a fifty-caliber machine gun mounted on a turret in the back. All of them were armed to the teeth and wearing clean, well-pressed clothes, right up to their turbans and wool hats. There were two in the front and three in the back. I looked over at Mickey, and his bad eye was twitching so much I couldn't get a read.

The Austin Gipsy had stopped right next to us, so I looked up with the warmest of smiles. "Yeah, man, sure. Dancing sounds good."

They shifted about in the back of the Austin, and I climbed in. It didn't feel like a good time to say no even though I could see that Twitch didn't like this much.

"What the hey, man?" I said, reading the question in his eyes. "You only got one life—live it."

He broke a smile, looked up at the tank hauler, and climbed in the front.

They were a grisly bunch but very clean. The man sitting next to Twitch had twin bandoleers of polished shotgun shells crisscrossing his chest. Hanging from his neck was an elaborately engraved twelve-gauge cut-off double barrel breach breaker, strung on a brightly colored wool and horsehair strap with silver and lapis dangles. The others were dressed to the tee as well, right down to their polished, fully automatic rifles and oiled pistols. Clearly, they were out on the town and dressed for the ball.

No sooner had we sat down then we were off at a clip toward the gates of the Khyber, the dust churning up behind us. Twitch looked back at me from the front seat, and I shot back a short smile. I didn't want to look too uncomfortable. The men with me in the back were looking us over. God knows what they were thinking. Twitch leaned over in the front seat and started a conversation with the man riding next to him. I couldn't hear what they were saying through the road sound so I turned my attention to the two who were standing with the mounted gun, their turban tails flowing out the back of the Gipsy and fluttering in the wind. They looked like high plain Afghans. Those kinds of turbans you only see there, one end trailing off over the shoulder and the rest wound up around their mouth and nose. Another fellow squatted across from me on the bench seat, his knees poking up on either side of his slumping shoulders while his hands hung down holding a well-oiled M-16. He looked me directly in the eyes and smiled a grin that exposed dark brown teeth with several empty spaces and one gold crown. I knew after that smile just who these guys were. They were tribal and from the Kush for sure. I'd lived with mercenaries like these guys when I was in the mountains, but I'd never run into them on the job, and I'd certainly never seen them so well dressed! I figured they must be working for someone, and they were.

I smiled back at my friend on the bench and gave the customary greeting: "Mumkin farta en shala," a phrase that means a whole batch of things. To my friends in the mountains, it meant "I'll live to see tomorrow, Allah willing" or "I may get out of this alive, Allah willing" or the like. Literally, it translates to "maybe tomorrow, God willing." But it takes on a whole variety of meanings depending on the situation. But it was the right greeting here for sure because it drew smiles, and that felt good. Just then, Twitch spun back over the seat and started talking so fast I couldn't understand him.

"Hold it, man. Slow down."

"All right." He leaned over. "Mate, this bloke in front here is bloody mayor of Landi Kotal; these others are personal guards."

"So?"

"Seems we're his guests. We're off into the bloody Khyber, mate. Some dance troop is 'particularly good,' he says. The bugger wants us as his guests, or I think that's what it is."

He leaned closer, speaking softly. "He wants to impress somebody, someone he's got family stuff with likely. Lots of 'big men' to be there, and he figures we look good. We're his bloody foreign dignitaries. Its all bullocks, mate. Way I figure is he wants to impress someone. We aren't tribal or hippies, so we're the guests. That's the best I can make. Can you believe this shit?"

"It could be worse, man. These guys here," I said, lifting my chin slightly toward my buddy on the bench, "are mercenaries from the mountains around where I stayed. I know the type. Anytime there's a choice in the matter, I want them on my side. Dignitaries, huh, well that's fine by me. What's not to be dignified about?"

Mickey almost laughed, and so did I, but we caught ourselves. You only laugh at jokes everyone gets in places like this.

The Austin rolled up to the Khyber Pass gate, and six armed men stepped out in front of us. Then another six or eight came around the back and took up placements.

"Shit, this is not a good thing," I said to Twitch in a whisper.

The men around the car started talking like chattering crows, and then like a light going on, they spotted the mayor next to Mickey and started shuffling like kids. They couldn't get the gate open fast enough. In a minute the Gipsy slipped through, and we took off, bouncing up the canyon road.

As we rolled up into the tribal zone and the Khyber Pass, the dust billowed up behind us in swirling browns on browns against a fading magenta sky. The first star just started to show as the Gipsy slowed down to enter Landi Kotal. We moved at a crawl as we closed in on the center of town, passing groups of men walking on either side laughing and talking with one and other. They were all headed the same way we were, toward the town's center. A major event was in the making—that was sure. I'd never seen so many different clans in one place before. And we were dignitaries? Well, that's what the mayor wanted, and dignitaries are what we would be, for all that meant out here.

The crowd got thicker as we got closer to the center of town. Folks were arriving from all directions on foot, on camels, on horses, and on ox carts. There were a few Jeeps, Rovers and Russian four-by-fours, but we were the only Austin Gipsy and clearly the most formidable of vehicles in the gathering, with the Gipsy's independent four-wheel drive, Rolls Royce engine, and high stacks with the manned gun turret on the back. We were impressive, the proper car for dignitaries in this sliver of the world. It looked like everybody that was anybody in the tribal zones was there and dressed to the nines, including lots of Pashtun in their pressed white cotton and silk, with their white hair and beards hennaed bright red against their dark skin.

As we closed on the town center, Twitch nodded toward a group of very well-armed and clearly underdressed men. They started walking in our direction right as we stopped in the center of town. I didn't recognize them. I knew lots of tribal dress, as subtle as it sometime was out here. But these fellows and their dress, I hadn't seen before. One thing was clear: they weren't dressed for a party. Their faces were streaked with deep creases, the kind you see after a firefight, and their eyes were red and half shut, thin slots like lookouts in a blockhouse. Their guns were blued and freshly oiled with no frills or bangles. These guys were serious, and whatever business they were about was clearly not a walk in the park. War and intertribal feuding was always in the air in the tribal zone. It was a way of life here and had been for thousands of years. The only thing that got in the way of old grudges was a common enemy, and then the revenge for some score old or new was set aside, if only for a while. Confrontation was very real stuff out here.

They walked down the main street, and no one looked them in the eye or entered their path. They moved purposefully with directed steps like a good fighting band does, with no sign of pause. Their intensity was so loud it seemed to stop the air. The men on the gun turret watched their approach with unblinking eyes. There was a silent transformation of the bodyguards into a calico web of demons as surreal as anything I'd ever seen. If Twitch hadn't understood before why I preferred having these hardened mercenaries on my side, he certainly did now. The jolly colors and flamboyant turbans seemed to turn into fiery feathers of fighting cocks, and the golden crowned teeth turned yellow and stained like those of fighting dogs with a taste for blood. Time seemed to slow to a sluggish crawl as every eye watched each arm and hand and the weapon it carried. The slightest move was assessed and understood. Other people in the area turned their eyes and heads down and stepped back. They had their own battles and, like Twitch and me, didn't need to be drawn into this one.

The band that was focused on the Austin Gipsy slowed its pace a bit. It felt like hours. We were outmanned, but they were clearly outgunned and, I knew in my gut, outclassed for downright nastiness. I'd lived with nomadic mercenaries and had heard their stories. I looked toward Twitch to catch his eye and immediately understood what he was thinking. I was thinking the same. This was trouble, and we didn't need to be anywhere close to it.

The mayor sat unmoving in the front seat while his guards like flowing water took up positions all around the car. It was serious business now, and I didn't like being in other people's business. I didn't have anything to do with whatever was going down here. But I also knew that out here you chose your camp or died alone. I was kicking myself in the ass, pissed that I'd jumped into that damn car so fast. But that was wasted thinking. I needed to figure a way out or at least a way to win.

I'd had better times in my life. One good thing, if there was any, was that whatever the problem was, it didn't feel like it could be solved by offering Twitch and me up. And I knew my new friend with the gold crown wouldn't cross the lines of his culture, and that meant fighting to the death for me as well as for his employer. The problem with that was it made my position more complicated. Shit! I hated this kind of crap; the bottom line was that my only option was to go for it, whatever that was going to be. I'd keep an eye on everyone and trust them to do the same for me. What was happening around us was not about Mickey and me, and that was good. We were in the middle of it by chance, what little difference that might make.

I needed to figure a way to count here, not just for my sake but for Twitch too; as strong as he was in some ways, he needed watching at times. Our new friends didn't need to be worrying about guests, but I knew they would. A guest means something to the tribal Afghan, something far more than the word "guest" does in the muddy culture of the West.

I watched as the turret gunner stiffened his legs and relaxed his arms, hands at the ready. His eyes followed the group like a hawk's. The men were fixed around the vehicle, and I glanced at a shotgun strapped to the back seat and raised my chin slightly toward my Kuchi friend. I could see his eyes smile and then shift back to his job. I turned as slowly as I could to position myself for a lunge at the shotgun while Mickey saddled closer to the .38 automatic hanging in a shoulder holster off the front seat. Well, I thought, this was an interesting way to go. But just then, like the plug being pulled from a bathtub, the group spun away and slid off down a side street into the darkness.

A moment or two passed with all our eyes fixed on the darkened street. The tight feeling in my belly softened just a bit as the men's last movements faded in the darkness. Still tight as a piano string I kept thinking they were just out of sight, waiting for our guard to drop. Then like the volume being turned up on the radio, our host went on in a very loud and purposeful voice as if nothing had happened. A smile stretched across his broad face as he went on about something or other. I wasn't hearing it. My heart was still in my throat ready to hear a shot ring out of the darkened street. But as if nothing had happened, he kept right on talking until his words like rain starting on a tin roof rattled through the pounding blood in my ears.

It was hard to tell if he'd felt at risk. From the way he was acting, the incident might as well have been no more than a matter of letting a flock of goats cross the road. I guess the challenge-turned-to-concession was just another day for him.

A surreal edge hung on the world now, and I hoped whatever bad blood was between these folks wouldn't resurface while we were here. Tribal Afghans face off all the time, in feuds, revenge killings, and fights for power. In the tribal zone confrontation and even ambush were not uncommon. Somehow, understanding this made it easier. My attention started returning as the adrenaline flush faded.

Somewhere along the line, our host the mayor had gotten into small talk about Landi Kotal and was explaining all the town's benefits. He praised the chai shops, gun dealers, and money markets. He claimed you could get the best deal in the world on rupees there. If I'd had any money to exchange, I would have taken him up on it.

"You have anything here, my town: opium, hashish, guns, German, American, Russian, tank, rocket." He smiled. "And tea, meat bread, and eggs."

This was a big city as cities in the tribal zone go, with its electric lights and "paved" street. At least a piece of it was paved—a strip in the middle of town. And the lights—well, there were no electrical lines running into Landi Kotal, but there was a generator that powered a few light bulbs here and there and the radio in the chai shop.

A faint dusting of red-gray sky hung over the jagged cliffs that stood lookout over the little city. Twitch and I sat in the chai shop looking at each other as the topic shifted to dancers. You could tell the mayor was very excited. It seemed this bunch of performers got to this area only once or twice a year. They spent most their time much deeper in the tribal zones.

"Hell of a way to come into town, mate," Twitch said, smiling.

"Yep, not my idea of a warm welcome. I'm glad we had the Kuchi in our camp. My money says they made the difference."

"Sure as bloody hell wasn't us, mate."

I stood there at my window overlooking the town center and watched the people shuffle around in front of the chai shop. The fifteen feet or so of hard-packed dirt on either side of the road leading away from the center of town gave space for trucks to park while still leaving wide access to the shops and mud buildings. The mayor had obtained rooms for us on the roof of the chai shop looking right over the center of town. As I stood there, radio music came up through the floor, sounding like it was being played in the world's largest shower. Up it came into the room mixed with the clatter of teapots and plates and the smells of spicy mutton stew.

I could see out on the street lots of men in fancy dress. Some had bodyguards, some didn't, and they came in twos, threes, and occasional groups. They were filling up the street in front of the chai shop. There were no trucks, cars, or carts moving anymore—just a mass of people. I looked around but couldn't spot the bunch we'd faced off with earlier and that was about as comforting as swimming with sharks and a bleeding leg.

The room I had was four mud brick walls set on the roof about waist high, the rest was wood. There was a small woodstove the size of a keg of nails with a couple of pieces of wood next to it. The stovepipe leaned like a windblown tree and ran out through a makeshift tin-can hole in the wall. The bed was like all beds out here, a short, thin, low wood frame with rope netting and no covering. There was a small table fastened with various brass couplings and pins. Setting on it was a kerosene lamp with clean glass and a freshly trimmed wick. Mickey lay back on the bed, his left eye twitching madly and a half smile across his face.

"Bugger all, was that something or what mate?! For a minute there, I thought we were heading for a bloody mix-up that would end us." He turned his good eye at me. We hadn't said much to each other about the ride or the arrival here in Landi Kotal. I could tell he was still rattled, which was no surprise—so was I.

"Yep, shaky for a minute there, for sure. I'm still not feeling great about where that bunch ran off to or if they're still out there and going to keep this shit up, I sure as hell hope if they do it's after we're out of here."

"Me too, mate. I got no bloody interest whatsoever. Not more than once in a lifetime. My stub is in for that stuff as of this afternoon."

"Yeah, I'm on for that. From the sight of everybody down there, I don't think there dressed for it anyway. Look at all those fancy rags and turbans." I was doing my best to smile and let the worries slide.

"Quite right, mate. Tonight's about putting on the dandy. Those buggers would be out of step."

"I wonder just what this is going be like tonight. I've never seen dancers in the Khyber Pass before."

Mickey raised an eyebrow. "I've seen some in my time out here, mate, but I've never seen such a bloody bunch of hard-necked rag heads so dolled up in one spot. I'd wager there's a treat in store, all these big men. Like the mayor said," Mickey said in very proper English, "we are dignitaries invited to the ball."

"So how's your room, man? As nice as this one?"

"The same, mate—a wooden bed, stove window. Bugger all to look at, though. It looks over the back side of some gun shop. I got more wood than you." He pointed at the few sticks next to the stove.

"Pretty uptown to put us in such digs. I mean, two rooms?"

"We're posh, that's why. Besides, there aren't any rooms with more than one bed. I looked. Bugger all, mate, we're bloody dignitaries, remember."

"Oh shit, that's right. I nearly forgot."

We both started to laugh. We couldn't help it after all that had gone down. I didn't want to laugh. The last thing I wanted was someone thinking I was laughing at them and not with them. But Mickey couldn't hold it, and that kicked me off. We roared till our eyes ran. We needed that after the ride.

Night came, and we made our way down to the chai shop. We came around the bottom of the stairs and passed a row of cooking pots boiling on a mud stove. The cook had a long scar down the side of his face that disappeared under his shirt. I wondered how he got it. The room was filled with the sent of boiling mutton and spices and the pungent smell of black tobacco.

Across from the shop in the center of the street, young boys were bringing wood to a fire pit. Some of the crowd sat around on their carpets smoking hookahs in loose circles, and others milled in and out, looking to find friends or good seats. We were sitting right next to the mayor and his guard and a few other important-looking men. We had our own table and chairs at the front of the chai shop. Everyone in the place seemed friendly, talking and smoking. It was nice to feel we had friends in a crowd like this one.

A large circle started to form around the fire pit, ending on either side of the chai shop. It was quite a picture, with all the well-armed and well-dressed tribal folks. Many looked like they'd come from deep in the mountains and didn't have an interest in chairs and tables or, as far as I could tell, even much acquaintance with such. Some squatted while others sat on folded legs on small personal carpets like Bedouins at tea. They were all well dressed in pressed hand-embroidered cotton and silk, clothes you saw only on wealthy men. The older Pashtun with their beards and hair freshly hennaed had boys hovering around them bringing them tea, tobacco, and hookahs. I figured some of the better-dressed for opium or gun smugglers. They usually had lots of money and power and lot of them were Pashtun. They knew how to move things around and survive. Almost all the tribal I'd met in the Kush and the zone were illiterate beyond a few lines from the Koran, if that. Still, their skill in moving people and goods ran deep. They were powerful and influential in their remote communities. I figured many here must have come up from Waziristan and parts between, places where what we think of as the modern world was just a story or unknown.

"The rooms are very nice. Thank you," I said to the mayor.

He smiled and nodded, saying, "I am mayor at Landi Kotal, this is Landi Kotal," while waiving his arm around the horizon. "Dancers we are having this night. Very special coming here. New dancers, best dancers, best singers." He smiled broadly, looking at us both with an almost goofy face. "Famous in all of tribal land! Beautiful, we wish you to enjoy."

He spoke the best he could with the English he had. I looked around to see whom he might be trying to impress, but no one was within ear shot or paying any attention.

"I have a degree, college degree, but not very good English," he said, smiling a bit uneasily. "People outside never get to see here. You'll get now."

He looked at me this time with a kind of wink and a smile. I wasn't sure just what to say. Mickey hadn't said anything to me about his English or that he spoke any.

"Where did you go to school?" I asked, expecting him to say Kabul or Tehran.

He smiled. "In Germany—Frankfurt." Then he said something in German and gave that goofy look.

"When I saw you walking I thought I'd give you a gift of our dancers. You are guests now. He smiled again and waved at the Chai Walla, the man who owned the shop. "Teen-Chai-louw, three chai now," he barked, and the tea maker went to work on it.

I liked hearing "my guests." that meant he'd drawn a protective circle around us. Twitch had been listening to us talk, and I could see that telling look on his face. A sure sign he had a hair up his nose over something, likely something the mayor had said. Luckily, he hadn't stood up and shouted, "I don't bloody fucking believe it! Bugger all, mate, you haven't got any stinking degree from a university!" or something like that.

Mickey did that kind of thing. Right when you hoped he'd let things slide, boom! He'd flash and blow. I'd seen him do it more than a few times. Once he dumped a two-foot clay pot full of hashish powder all over a floor, calling it "trash," and to give him his due, it was. Still, out it went all over the place, and then he spit in it and hollered, "Do you think I am a bloody Frenchman?!" First the guy looked like he was going to have us skinned, but then he quickly lowered his eyes and admitted it wasn't his best product. I thought that was considerably better that getting shot. Once Mickey took two slabs of hashish we'd been offered, broke them in half on the edge of a table, and then pushed them right up under the nose of the fellow selling them and threw them out a window into a courtyard. He did things like that. And out here that could cost you big time if you didn't know what you were doing. Mickey, well, he did know, I think, or maybe he was just "malang," or crazy, as he used to say often. I think both were true, really. He also had an uncanny way of reading situations, and up until now, he had only acted out when he knew the power was his, or so it seemed.

No matter how Mickey felt about the mayor's claim, compared to the norm out here, the mayor was educated and articulate, no matter how he got there. I figured it was smart to recognize that.

"You live in town?" I asked.

"Yes, here and sometime Kabul, Peshawar."

"How'd you get to be mayor—were you elected?"

"No election here, am Pashtun, Patton, my family Mayor always."

"So your first son will be mayor when you stop?"

"First son is dead, fourth son dead too, car hit bus a in Peshawar back five years now."

"Sorry."

"Both good men."

"I'm sure, so you are mayor by family and clan?"

"Yes, clan, Mayor of Landi Kotal like my father before was mayor; I'm choice of all Landi Kotal people." He waved his hand all around. "You ask them."

It was easy to see he was in charge by his confidence, and his first-class bodyguards.

"I'm looking forward to the dancers."

"You will like," he said with a smile, "tonight you dream something."

I had no idea what that meant, but it wasn't worth spending time on.

"Mickey there's from Birmingham, England, and I'm from northern California, America." I said.

The mayor cut in. "You look to belong here so I picked you as special guests tonight. I invite."

"Yeah, we do belong here, thanks, and we are honored to be your guests. The rooms are great, and I wait to see the dancers. May Allah bless you and your family."

I'd learned some things out here and one of them was that it was never a good idea to prejudge, or at least to say anything that way about something, one way or the other, until you had been there and seen or done it. The dancers would be what they would be.

The Chai Walla arrived with the tray and three pots. He smiled at me through jagging-out teeth the color of old yellowed piano keys. He set the tray down and handed us saucers and cups. The chai pots rolled steam out their spouts into the cool air. I poured mine into the cup, and swirling twists of steam rose into the air. I poured a layer of the hot chai onto my saucer balanced on my fingertips and blew to cool it down. The temperature had dropped in the mountain pass, and the steam off the chai was thick as cream. As I sipped, I gazed through the wisps at the pastel turbans and red beards in the background. Above them dark jagged rock cliffs stood against what was left of a red-orange sunset. The smell of cardamom, honey, cinnamon, and buffalo milk circled my head and filled my nose. The chai in the Khyber Pass was the best. It was in the Khyber Pass where you would first find spiced tea. Before you got there, all the way west to Persia and Turkey, the tea was black or green, and you drank from a glass with hard sugar lumps. In the Khyber the chai was made in double-fist-sized pots with spice, milk, and sugar placed directly on the coals to steep. The surface of the pots they made it in were blackened and cracked with years of service. Once the chai had steeped, it was poured from pot to pot to froth it up before it was served. The stories these pots must have heard over the years, tales layered as deep and as black as their patina.

We sat drinking our chai, and I half listened to the mayor talk about the politics in the pass. It was a topic on his mind, but I had no interest in it at all. I knew better than to get cornered there. It's better to just agree when needed. So the mayor went on with his descriptions of who, how, and why as my attention focused on all the people around us. The growing firelight flickered and made the colors jump and fade and blend as the darkness grew. Men milled in and out of shadows, still searching for places to sit. All I could see past the first line of faces in the firelight was motion and a polished gun poking up here and there catching the light. Fine clothes weaved in and out of the dim background. I'd never seen a gathering quite like this.

In the first row faces were dark and chiseled with lots of bright red henna beards. There were Mongolians in their silks, Pamiri tribals from the Yarkhun with curly black beards and long straight noses. There were men from many different clans all spit-shined down to their sandals. There were so many men milling around outside the light from the fire that you couldn't make out who carried what gun. But everyone was armed. Brown to black movements like shadows were visible here and there, just beyond recognition. That didn't make me feel very good, with the light burning behind us and the fire in front setting us up like actors on a stage. I couldn't help think what good targets we were making.

Right then across from us, the circle started to part, and three men stepped into the light of the fire. It was the singer and musicians. The opening closed behind them as they moved into the circle. They crossed the open space skirting the fire. Two of them carried instruments hung across their backs like long rifles tied up in carpets. The old man of the troupe, clearly the leader, carried an old harmonium strung from his shoulders by a woven strap. He stepped up to our table and greeted our host with a respectful nod. He didn't say anything at all but just stepped back a few paces and nodded to his two companions. They all took down their instruments, rolled out the carpets, and sat facing the fire, looking across the open view. There was a drummer and another musician who played some kind of wooden bowed instrument with three strings. They sat to either side of the old man.

The old man grabbed his long white beard and folded it up under his woolen hat. He was clearly not Pashtun and wore his white beard proudly. The other two were younger. The drummer was dressed in a patchwork vest with woolen pantaloons and wore a hat that fell to one side like a jester's. The other player looked like he was from the deep mountains somewhere, with straight black hair tied up in a leather strap and olive skin and Mongolian eyes. A knife hung from his neck and down past his hand.

They settled in to play. It was eerie at first. It sounded like nothing I had ever heard. It was gentle and had no rhythm. Hypnotic as it drifted in and out of melody. Then the drummer started to hold a rhythm, and the sound leapt up and filled the air. Before I knew it, everyone was moving to the music, their hands overhead or reached out to the side like flapping wings and their heads rocking on their necks like bobblehead dolls on the dashboard. I raised my arms and rocked my head, doing my best "when in Rome." Mickey was sitting back in his chair sipping chai and rocking to the sounds with his eyes closed. His matted hair swung back and forth.

Then like an early morning breeze, the harmonium player started to sing in low tones, and an easy yet strained harmony surfaced. Before long, the singing was full and penetrating. The old man's voice surfaced through the strings, harmonium, and drumming like a sunrise melting a starry sky. I had no idea what the song was about; the words just flowed together like water. I could tell it was melancholy—a love story or a legend maybe. Whatever he was singing about, he was passionate.

This first song went on for quite a while, and when it ended, men started hitting their legs and pounding gun butts on the ground. Some stood and stomped their feet. I didn't have a clue what I should do. My first instinct was to stand and clap. I looked over at Mickey to see what he was doing. I knew he'd spent time in the Khyber before and figured he might have a clue. Wouldn't you know it—he was staring right back at me, a puzzled look on his face. So I stood up and clapped as politely and subduedly as I could, not quite sure. Mickey shrugged, stood up, and clapped and then started to call out praises to the singer and musicians. I took his lead and started clapping harder and stomping my feet. The mayor smiled up at us and turned across the table to his friends and smiled. Mickey and I sat back down after the stomping and pounding died down.

The musicians started to play a number of shorter songs. This went on for a while, and then the attention started slipping. Conversations started to pop up here and there, quietly at first, but eventually you could hear talking in the background, and the musicians stopped playing.

In about ten minutes, they started to play again, only this time the music was loud and rhythmic, a driving, shaky rhythm more typical of the tribal folk music I was used to. Like a father calling his children, the singer yelled into the shadows. The circle parted again, and into the light stepped a beautiful young girl in a yellow brown and red layered skirt and a short halter-top vest. Scarves were wrapped around her head and hanging down her back, and bells were tied to her ankles and wrists. She started to dance in circles to the rhythm of the drum as the harmonium and strings started to fade out.

The singer kept beckoning in a chant-like tone as the drum played. Then on the other side of the circle, in stepped another dancer in full tribal clothes: long layered dress, a short vest, and colored scarves wrapped around her head in layers. She held bells in her hands, and others were buckled to her waist on leather straps. She danced round and round, shaking the bells in time with the drummer. Soon the dancers were circling one another. The younger looking dancer started stepping around, one foot over the other, side to side, with her hands held over her head like a Celtic dancer, as they both weaved in and out of each other's circle.

The singer sang, and the drummer laid out rhythm. Every so often, the old man would wave to them, pointing at a man in the circle. They'd turn and dance to these men, smiling and lifting their legs from the hips with slight bends in their knees. As they came closer, the men would take money, fold it up, and put it behind their ears. The dancers would come closer and pluck it away. The bolder men would lean into the dancers and sniff at their bellies and, when the money was plucked from their ears, fall back laughing. The dancers would laugh with them and push the bills inside the front of their skirts out of sight. Some of the men were not so bold. They'd hand the money to the dancers with their right hand, their eyes turned to the ground.

When the dancers got close to the firelight, I could just make out their faces. The younger one was beautiful, fifteen at most, and the older one was maybe eighteen. They both were striking, with long, straight features and clear olive skin.

I knew the Khyber Pass and the tribal zone not just by reputation; I'd been through here more than a couple times. But I'd never seen anything like this. True men here prided themselves on not covering their women like the rest of Islam, but they didn't put them out on display either. How did girls like these get to be here, doing this? What was going on? It was mesmerizing, tantalizing, and loaded with risks. It didn't help that I hadn't been with a woman since I'd hooked up with a German gal on tour in Kabul. I was rapidly falling here but dropped any such thoughts like a hot potato.

One thought that ran through my mind was that they might be sex workers from Sweden or Denmark. European hookers did come out here and could be found almost anywhere the money was deep, and there certainly was serious money around this circle tonight. But we were inside the tribal zone—not a place girls like that went. Besides, these dancers didn't look European.

The music continued, and the dancers joined arms one over the other. They held their hands over each other's shoulders they stepped to the sharp rhythm side by side. The mayor must have noticed how "all eyes" I'd become and took hold of my hand and said, "Beautiful, pretty, don't you think?"

I smiled back and said, "You bet."

Mickey chimed in, "Ay, mate. And these dancers are from where?"

"The players are from Northwest Swat and the Pamir, the dancers Baluchi,"

"They're wonderful, man!" I added. "Are the songs about here, the tribal zone? Are they old, from far away?" It was a stupid question, but I didn't care. I was trying to move my mind off the girls.

Mickey had spotted my interest and was staring at me with a "don't get any ideas that will get us killed" look. I smiled back shaking my head. This was not a time or place to even think what I was thinking, and I knew it. I raised my eyes slowly to look out at the dancers once more, this time committed to being a spectator and guest and nothing more, leastways not in any way that might show. I guess it didn't work as well as I'd hoped. The mayor and his friends thought it would be fun to bring me even more into things. Before I knew it, one of the mayor's friends had slipped a folded bill behind my right ear and patted me on the shoulder, saying "OK, man, OK" before backing off to his seat.

The mayor's friends were laughing, in a friendly way, smiling at me and waiving at me to step out into the circle. I didn't know what it was all about or what I was expected to do. Just then, the old man looked up at the two dancers, who were slowly turning circles on the far side of the clearing. He sang out one of those mournful calls that he used, and the tempo shifted. The younger dancer turned and looked toward him. He raised his eyes in my direction. She spotted the bill behind my ear and started to dance across the clearing. Her eyes held to the bill until she got close. Then they shifted directly to mine. It was like a tight rope—a look I'll never forget, her eyes pulling tightly. My heart sank right to my crotch, and at the same moment, my mind started creating all kinds of bad situations that could come from this. I struggled to keep my thoughts above my belly. Still, I kept having this fantasy run through my brain of living out my life in the tribal zone, maybe a hashish smuggler or the like, with this beautiful young dancer wife who would dance for me when I returned from my journeys. At that point, I almost pulled the bill from behind my ear to offer it by hand, like I'd seen others do. But when I reached back to grab it, I saw the mayor looking at me, shaking his head and smiling. So I left the bill alone, figuring it was the best move. I would let it be and enjoy whatever happened as best I could. Looking over at Twitch, I could see his eye shifting around in his head like a rattle.

The young dancer got nearer and nearer, closer than any time before. I could make out her features framed in the layered cloth falling round her face. Firelight danced across her smooth unveiled skin. There was a brief smile, inviting and sexy. Just then, the singer started to sing louder, drawing the attention of the other dancer. She turned and started to move across the clearing. Mickey was squirming in his chair with a folded bill behind his ear. Someone had brought him into the game. I laughed out loud, not feeling so alone anymore. I looked straight at him for a quick moment. He caught my glance and cracked a smile, though his eye hadn't settled down a bit.

I thought about the power our host had here and hoped that would make all this work out. I tried to relax, knowing that we were guests and that we had a certain rank, and our treatment would be as guests. I didn't really trust this as much as I should have, I suppose, but I did my best not to show how nervous I was. I had to trust the mayor; there wasn't another choice. He'd treated us well until now and had kept us safe, and I had no reason to believe that would change. Still, the idea of getting close and perhaps even more than close with one of these beauties was not bad.

The younger dancer had moved across the opening and up to me, shaking her hips side to side and making her skirt ripple in waves, her hips pointing at me all the while as she stepped forward, one foot skipping over the other to the rhythm of the music. Then every few seconds, she would stop and dance around in circles. All the time, her friend was moving toward Mickey, and I could see his eye twitching madly. As the younger dancer moved closer, I looked at her flat belly covered with droplets of sweat streaking down both sides and then flying in a spray into the air as her stomach shimmied, the mist sparkling in the firelight. Her tight belly moved in and out with the music. It was amazing to watch. Golden skin circled her deep dark belly button where a shadow of wispy hair ran under her belt toward her loins. With each closing step, the skirt would flare out and offer another glimpse of her dark, smooth, and muscular legs. Her hips gyrated in perfect time to the music, and I was caught in her spell. I looked into those inviting eyes so deep and hazel blue; at her nose straight and prominent, set between high, rounded cheekbones; at her small beautiful ears with long flush lobes; and at her tongue just visible as she breathed heavily. I looked at the full ripe lips and was captive. I let go of all my caution, forgetting completely where I was, and looked directly and deeply into her almond eyes. I could feel the spray off her belly hitting my face. I leaned forward to take a deep smell, thinking, "when in Rome" and all that. But right then, I came back to myself. I stopped and looked up before the money was plucked from my ear. My heart was sinking, but I knew there wasn't a chance here really, and it was more than risky. Still, in some weird way, I'd been planning the rest of my life in the tribal zone as I watched her.

Then, like a door slamming in the middle of the night, waking you out of a sweet dream, I felt a surge of confusion. I lowered my eyes and looked again at the layers of cotton skirts over the now clearly straight hips. Then I looked once again at those eyes and this time found them guarded and disconnected. Then like a beacon on a foggy night, it all came to light. There were no decorations on the ears or nose, and there was shadowy light hair on the upper lip—it was a first beard. This was a boy, not a young woman. I looked up at the dancer, this time with very different thoughts. I could see the same reflected in his eyes. I shook my head, not knowing just how I felt, and lowered my eyes. A small hand plucked the bill from behind my ear, and a cheer rose from the circle.

When I looked up again, I saw hands raised in greeting and smiles all around the circle. It seemed I'd passed some test. Friendly smiles were all around. The veil this young dancer had enchanted me with had made me belong. I had become one of them in a way I hadn't been before.

I really had been falling in lust. Sheepishly, I looked over toward Twitch as his dancer saddled up close to him. He glanced back at me with that "didn't you know?" look he would get whenever I went off in my fantasy world too far. I could see now that the other dancer was also a young man. I would guess sixteen, still beautiful and looking as completely female as the other. But like his partner, he had no earrings or nose piercing. Mickey leaned forward into the dancer as he came into reach and took a deep smell off his waist, gesturing with both hands as if pulling in the aroma. Everybody loved this. Even the mayor clapped and cheered as Mickey, as he did lots of times, did just the right thing.

Then Mickey looked over at me again and smiled, calling over, "Ah, mate, ready to settle down in the mountains here, are you?"

"Yeah, sure. I'll get a little place in the hills and raise peaches," I called back.

"I could find you a mullah if you want to tie the knot tonight, mate. Think kids are out of the question though." He laughed.

"Yeah, yeah, thanks for the heads up, man," I shot back.

"Come on, mate; bugger all, it's fun for everyone, even for the dancers. I didn't bloody know you hadn't seen this before, or I would have tipped you, really, mate, but I had my mind on other things. Besides, I wasn't sure just what it was tonight. But when I saw the look in your eye when the little one came out, I just had to watch and see how long it lasted." He winked his good eye.

Twitch was an irritating son of a bitch sometimes, but I could always trust him to be that and honest. And he did have a real sense of humor. So why should I be pissed? Instead I just needed to take a deep breath and know I wasn't alone out here—know that I had a friend with me. "That was a boy" kept rolling through my mind. Shit, I hadn't a clue.

The dancers went on and made a few more circles, collecting money here and there. Then, just like they had come in, they danced out, leaving the musicians and singer playing. I got up and walked out back of the shop to take a leak. I spotted the younger dancer with his partner out there. He was looking over at a man who had been putting lots of money behind his ear all night. Just then, the older boy slapped him on the back of his head and started to wave his hand in his face like a fish. I couldn't tell, but it looked like an argument. I'd heard of love, sex, and even prostitution with fighting men and boys, but in all my time in tribal areas, I'd never seen it.

When I got back to the table, I went up to the mayor, who was having a conversation with one of the men. "I really thought they were girls," I said. "I didn't mean to do anything wrong. I apologize if I did." I hoped that if there was some issue, my apology would put me ahead of the game.

He looked up. "No, no, no, not bad! All here love dancers." He shrugged as if to say, "What's the big deal?" I guessed it was OK. "It's different here," he said, jutting out his chest. "You like it, we like it. No women here, not right, welcome to Landi Kotal, your true belonging here now."

Mickey had been listening in and looked over my way and shifted in his seat just enough to catch my eye. I looked back at him, not quite sure just what I was feeling about his having left me to hang out so far, without even a little heads up, and just shook my head. In a way he was right not to have clued me in; the experience had taken me to places I needed to go, to an image I hadn't settled with yet, of just who I was becoming and where I actually was. I was a man out here with no roots any deeper than a twig in the sand. I was getting what all the changes of the last few years had made in me. I felt like I could dance now in any world, holding my center free, and that felt good.

I had changed over these last days more than ever. I'd noticed it some, but I think Mickey had more of a clue than I did. I'd always been a loner, and these months with Mickey had been good, but they had also been a time of sorting things out for me. Things had a new spin now, and today had brought it all to a head. There were new colors in my mind that I liked. I wasn't sure what it all meant. It didn't matter; I'd been in a shell of my own making for a long time. It felt like now I was free from so much of my past. It was like I could look right through my own stuff like it was a veil; I could watch myself move and speak like I was in a movie. My actions and words fell from some inner place that I could move into and out of as I wanted. It was clear that life was going to be different, very different.

Warning bells rang in my head. As good as it felt now, in some ways my life had been a series of bridges, some burning, some gone. I'd never looked at where I was, or had been, much as long as I could see ahead. That had changed now, and my gut said there were good reasons. Mickey's eye twitched a bit as he caught my glance. I could tell he thought I was thinking too much, but he just nodded and turned back to his conversation.

I wandered up to my room, my mind still swimming in all that had happened—fistfuls of thoughts popping like corn. I was awash with images of the dancers swirling around, the fires lighting up the streets, the men with guns, and the craggy cliffs of the Khyber. I kept trying to convince myself it must be the hashish. My mind was dancing like a dervish, like white water ripping in and out of the rocks. I could feel changes boiling up inside me. I had no idea why or what they were; I knew only that I was feeling them.

Night closed in, and I stood there looking out my window, watching the coals from the fire below glowing up through the wisps of smoke. The sounds from the street were only whispers now except for a laugh or loud word here and there from the few men who were still sitting around. The music and dancing were long over. I looked out over the dirt brick city, and for a moment I felt like I was looking through hundreds of eyes reaching back into a dim past.

This part of the world, these people, their culture—it all felt so old, like a story. But it was also alive and vibrant. It was a passionate reality existing in a time that had passed it by with so many years and so much technology that there was no connection to the modern world just feelings that would rush through you like a shot of tequila on a hot day. I couldn't help thinking about what had happened earlier in the day and if a fight had broken out or what if it had been dancing girls and not boys? This place wasn't just another leg on my journey now; it was becoming a doorway.

I lay back on the bed thinking about all that the mayor had said about belonging here and about how folks managed life in this place. Relationships were so different from any other place in the world here. Why did it feel so familiar to me? I started thinking about how everyone was a guest tonight—not just Mickey and me but everyone. There was a quiet here tonight and laughter even among sworn enemies, here in such a hard place where feuds dominate daily life.

In the end it was like the mayor said: a gift. The dancers were beautiful, really beautiful, and in the end they were my creation. And regardless of who they were or who took whom home or didn't, they were about beauty, about a culture very few will ever know. As the mayor had said, I did belong there, even if it was only to learn something new about what I'd become, and that was that I really didn't belong anywhere anymore.

The clatter of the cups and dishes awoke me in the morning. The day had started in the chai shop below. I propped myself up in bed and looked out the window. I could see the sunlit dust from the activity of the day, a thin layer pushing up into the sky. I spun my legs off the bed and sat up rubbing my eyes and pushed the hair off my face.

The only bathroom I knew was across the alley downstairs, so I headed out. Just out the door, I spotted a water tap on the far side of the roof. It was over a sunken grid that drained into a downspout. I splashed my face and hair and then pulled a hand down off my chin to wipe off the dirt from the day before. Just then I saw Mickey.

"Morning, man."

"Hey, mate." He went directly for the water.

"Wonder if they have a bath in town. I could sure use a wash-up," I said.

"I'd go for a dandy-up myself. They must have—every ruddy goat stop has a bath."

We made our way down the stairs to the chai shop and sat at that same table we'd been at the night before. Before we could order, there were two pots of chai and a hot naan on the table. I asked the boy how much, and the cook called from behind the clay stove, "No money, no money, all paid, mayor pays, mayor pays." I didn't expect that but said thanks anyway and asked where the mayor was.

"Mayor gone to Peshawar, he told me all you need he pay, "

"'He pays, does he? A steam bath, washing, hot water, where?" I asked. He looked like I'd asked for the number of miles around the moon, and then slowly his eyes started to un-glaze as he got it.

"You want bath, OK, bath down street, there, there." He pointed at the same alley where the bunch we'd faced off the day before had gone.

"Over there?" I asked.

He nodded and smiled. "Yes, yes, there going bath, steam hot, good bath good."

"What do you think?" I asked Mickey. "Just how dirty are you feeling?"

He lifted his arm and took a sniff.

"I've been bloody worse, but not a whole lot." He smiled.

"Sounds like the mayor is covering us, so let's do it. I'll even pay for it." I paused a moment after getting up from the chair. "I hope the mayor's greeting party ain't there."

"Me too, mate."

When we left the baths, we headed back toward the center of town. We planned to catch a bus east to Peshawar. We hadn't paid for anything since we got into Landi Kotal, and it seemed that we couldn't even if we wanted to. We had money—the winter in the north had been good to us—but wherever we went, we got the same treatment: "No money, no. Good, good, all good, mayor's friends."

Everyone must have been at the party the night before and seen us there. To be a guest of the mayor was a good thing here. So of course Mickey wanted to get some hashish with his status as guest, but I didn't want to push the hospitality bit. Mickey figured that because the mayor was tribal, hashish would be cool with him, but I didn't want to find out. Mickey finely went along with me, but he was unhappy about it. We kept the gifts to the room's bath and some food. We had the money; I told Mickey that if he really wanted hashish so bad to pay for it. Everyone had been great to us up to this point, and the mayor's generosity wasn't something I wanted to treat lightly.

Mickey could be a real hippie at times. I don't think he really got it. But I knew if it looked like we were using hospitality for profiteering, it wouldn't be good. I also knew Mickey would smoke anything he got his hands on, but most folks here didn't. Hashish was a business out here, especially if it was an outsider buying it. For sure that's how it would look to somebody. I'd been in tribal zones enough to know you needed to be careful about keeping friendship and business separate. In fact, "be careful" was something worth remembering every time you blinked. I might as well have had it tattooed on the inside of my eyelids, but I don't think Mickey ever got that "be careful" idea in that way. If he did, he didn't show it anyway that I ever saw.

Traffic was moving through the pass now, and we were about the only nontribal folk walking around. It was an intimidating place that most travelers didn't get off the buses at. We'd seen a couple of Sikhs at the baths earlier, before the first buses came into town. They must have had business of some sort there. You always knew Sikhs even without their clothes because of their silver bangle, netted hair, and beards. We'd also spotted a couple guys that looked out of place. They were in Western clothes. They'd kept showing up here and there and stood out like a pair of soccer balls on a dining room table. With one wearing a black leather jacket and the other wearing a wool vest, they were an easy make. I figured they were operatives of some kind, from Britain maybe or somewhere like that. They were too scruffy to be FBI or DEA. Even out here, those guys never took off their wing tips. These guys were scruffy but not scruffy enough to be contract operators.

This whole region was wide open, and this town its market. The tribal zones had no agreements with any nation or police of any kind. Drugs, guns, information, money, you name it—it was all for sale here. Lots of different governments tried to monitor it, buy into it, or just understand any part of it. But it was risky for police or military in the tribal areas. You really had to know how to hold your mud in places like this, and most of them weren't much good at that—couldn't get with the program even if you gave them a script. It was important to be liked and if possible respected out here. And police and military of any kind other than tribal were not liked and certainly not respected.

The city of Landi Kotal was the heartbeat of a very large lawless area, a city surrounded by vast tribal territory where you could buy a pot of tea, a flat bread, and an M16 at the same shop and then go next door and grab a kabob and an anti-tank rocket launcher with a kilo of opium. Everything was for sale in this town, everything except women. At least I never saw a woman in town, not even a covered one.

Buses and trucks were pulling into the center of town now, loading and unloading. Dust churned up over the square around all the activity. That haunting sound of pop radio stations wove itself into the dust, one station over another. The rumbling of the diesels and barking voices started to take over the radios as we entered the square. Buses, trucks, and cars were all mixed up and squeezed tight together. No one would have guessed this piece of road had been a dance floor the night before, not even me. It was hard to picture the dancers and music swirling up into a star-filled sky as we stood there surrounded by this herd of diesels.

We wanted to head east out of town, but there was no way to tell which bus was what in the mess. I asked a truck driver, "Which bus is going to Peshawar?" He pointed across the street and waved his hand at the far side of two trucks. I could see a cloud of blue exhaust from the bus pushing through the dust. We zigzagged through milling handcarts and stacks of goods.

As I started to get on the bus, I felt a hand grab my shoulder. I turned, thinking it was Mickey, but it wasn't. I could see Mickey across the way in front of a truck. He was in an animated conversation with one of those Western guys we'd seen popping up here and there earlier. The hand on my shoulder belonged to the partner of the man with Mickey. I hated this shit—I hate having to act out; it makes me feel like an idiot—but there wasn't much else I could do. Without a pause, I spun round as fast as I could and slipped down under his arm and off the bus.

"Who the fuck are you?" I said, standing behind him with my hand on his shoulder now, spinning him around. I'd already made him earlier and had numbers of answers to that question in my mind. But I was wondering just what game he was going to run.

"Be cool man—no problem here," he said, pushing his hands palm out and stepping back.

I looked over at Mickey, who was still engaged in his conversation.

"What's your act, man? Who in hell are you, and who's that bugging my friend?"

He stepped back another pace.

"We just want to offer you two a ride into Peshawar, that's all. The mayor said you would be looking to head that way this morning. He left early so didn't tell you. He knew we'd be headed out this morning, so he asked if we would take you two into Pakistan."

My gut said not to trust this guy or his friend. I couldn't tell if he was carrying a gun, but there was a worrisome lump in his vest, just the same. In this part of the world, if you carried a gun, you carried it openly so that everyone could see. Concealed weapons were a sure sign that these guys were out of tune here.

"You know the mayor?" I asked.

"Not really well, but we are acquainted. It just so happens we had a conversation with him this morning about some business, and he asked if we could help him by giving you two a ride. That was fine with us, but we looked all around trying to find you but couldn't, until we heard you speak. You guys look like you live here—hard to spot."

He grinned. "That's all; we just wanted to offer you a lift."

"So what's the problem over there?" I pointed toward Mickey, who was getting more and more animated.

"Don't know. Let's find out."

He gestured for me to walk ahead.

"You first," I said as I smiled and stepped back.

Mickey looked over and shook his head. I wasn't sure just what that meant, but I knew the guy in front of me had seen him shake his head too. I could run if I had to, but I wasn't ready just then. But these guys had nothing on me, even if they were cops of some kind. I was a guest here, and they would find out just what that meant if they tried to grab us. I looked carefully at his back as we walked and couldn't make out a holster strap.

Maybe he was telling the truth and was just doing what he'd said. Maybe they really had told the mayor they'd offer us a ride into Peshawar. I figured I'd let it play out. We were still guests, and that gave us a level of safety. As long as we were in open view, we were OK.

When we got to Mickey, the other guy looked at me like he knew me and blurted out in a strong Australian accent, "Your mate here won't leave his hashish behind. We don't carry contraband. I could personally give a rat's ass about the hashish, but we don't take anything over the border that's not kosher, and that's sure."

He looked at me with a frustrated expression on his face and then up at his partner.

Mickey started off. "You're a bloody pee hen! It's only half a kilo, and it's a gift! Look here, mate," he said, pushing it under the nose of the guy with me. "It's really good shit. If it were crap, I'd drop it like a stone, but its first–class, mate!"

He looked at me for support. I looked him straight in the eye, the one that was staying still.

"You want to take that shit with you, OK. Say thanks anyway to our friends here, and we'll ride the bus. But I don't know you until we're on the far side of the border and in a hotel in Peshawar. I'm not spending the night in a Paki jail."

"I ain't carrying this on a bus! What kind of fool you think I am, mate?! These guys are hooked up somewhere—we all know that," he exclaimed, pointing directly at them. "If it's so important that we ride with them, then they can tuck this little piece of shit somewhere in that big car of theirs. No one is going to search these guys, isn't that right?"

He looked at the pair. They didn't seem to disagree with him. At least they didn't say anything. Still they both looked over at me like I could do something.

"So what are you guys doing out here?"

I figured I might as well go straight to the trough.

"We work for the World Institute of Genetic studies out of Geneva. We are part of several field support teams collecting information and samples on inbred populations."

"Yeah, right."

"No, really. We are here trying to arrange access to the northeastern areas of the tribal zone where there are villages of people who've never married out of the local population for hundreds of years. We are here trying to get the mayor to help us find some guides so we can collect data from some of these places."

This was either a very good cover story or the truth. There weren't any operative types out here that were so creative. It would take brains to come up with an elaborate story like that.

"Did the mayor offer you help?" I asked.

"He said he would look into it in Kabul."

"Mickey, you believe this?" I looked over his way. "Ever heard of the Institute of Genetics?"

I looked back at the two. "You got any identification?" The one in the vest reached into his pants and pulled out a British passport, opened it up, and unfolded a special visa stapled to the last page with his picture and name on it, Charles Culvert. Sure enough, it was a travel visa for tribal areas of Pakistan issued to "employ" Institute of Genetic Studies, Geneva, Switzerland.

The other fellow was Lawrence Wooddale, and he had an identical visa in his Australian passport.

"All right," I said "They look real. So either you're working out here, or you have real good connections for passports and visas."

I looked over at Mickey. "You going to leave the hashish here so we can get going with these guys or not, man?"

"Aw, mate; it's really first-class shit! I hate dumping it."

"How about you smoke up what you can, and dump the rest before we hit the border?"

I looked over to see if Lawrence and Charles were OK with that.

"If he tosses it at least ten miles before the crossing," Charles said.

Lawrence shrugged and said, "Smoke what you do out the window!" He glanced at Charles and back at me, adding, "We're guests here too, so if you don't want a ride into Pakistan with us, find another way!"

"All right," Mickey said softly. "But your being pee hens about it. What's a handful of hashish out here?"

I could see Mickey wasn't happy about the deal or with them, or maybe even with me—I couldn't tell. But finally he looked up at the three of us and agreed to toss the hashish, or what was left of it, before we hit the border check. For Mickey it all had to do with hashish, the whole damn universe. His life played out through a window of hashish smoke, which for him was a mystic wall that kept him from harm. It was a strange and convoluted thinking, but he believed it, and I'd seen it work for him. He was like a fundamentalist with hashish as his Jesus or Muhammad and psychedelics as his religion.

My world was bigger then the drugs. I felt stronger without them for the most part. Sure, hashish had its place, and I liked it—occasional LSD and good opium too—but my search was connected to something outside the drugs. Things had to have meaning. But for Mickey it was different.

By the time we passed the outskirts of Peshawar, I was ready to get as far away as I could from Charles and Lawrence and their constant jabber about lack of hygiene and health knowledge in villages of southern Pakistan. Apparently they'd been north of the pass for two months. We heard story after story about encounters with the "ignorant and unclean," as Lawrence put it.

Mickey almost lost it at one point and leaned over to me in total frustration, whispering into my ear, "Mate, if I hear one more tale about staff infections, fibrous cysts, mis-set bones, or 'popping the cork before the party, I'm bloody well jumping out of the car."

Charles had gone on about working on a fertility study for the institute, which was one of his pressing reasons for visiting the villages in the north. He was studying sexuality in isolated villagers. Weird but true, I guessed. At some point he said he believed premature ejaculation among young rural Pakistani men was a primary reason for low fertility numbers.

"There must be a viable explanation for the numbers," he said. "I'm sure it has roots in sexual dysfunction. Eight out of ten young men interviewed ejaculate at the mere thought of coming close enough to a woman to smell her. This means when they do marry and actually get wives, the cork is out of the bottle, so to speak, before they leave the wedding. This sensitivity can last for months. It's amazing the young men ever actually get sufficient sperm implanted to impregnate their wives."

He went on about reasons for different fertility statistics between Pakistan and India and how it was due to this problem. Man, these guys were weird. India was growing far faster then Pakistan, sure, and they were essentially the same people, from the same gene pool, but Indians had always been into sex. It seemed to me that was an answer in itself.

Any thoughts of these guys being members of some covert British bunch had long left my mind. It seemed to me they were contestants for the most uninteresting men with the weirdest job. And any competition between the two was a tie. As the Mercedes pulled around a corner into the cantonment district of Peshawar, I said to Charles, "This will be fine for us, thanks."

I didn't want to be in this part of town; it made me tense. The cantonment, or the "cant," was the old British district where the moneyed and politically powerful lived. It wasn't a place I felt very comfortable, and I knew Mickey didn't either. I knew a good hotel in old town, which was more our style. Mickey could smoke his hashish without any problem there.

Charles turned and looked over the seat and said, "You sure you don't want to eat? We know a good place just down the street—it's on our sterling."

"I could eat; what about you, Mickey?"

He looked at me like I'd just given away all our shoes. "Sure, let's eat," he said, and then he turned to Lawrence and asked, "You think this is a good place—not too unclean?"

There was nothing I could do. Mickey was doing his thing, and I couldn't stop it. Luckily, Lawrence was driving and had his eyes on the road. He didn't see the look on Mickey's face when the question was asked. So he took it as straight. I guess there's something to luck after all. These guys had driven us for hours and actually had been better company than the bunch of German and French hippies who inevitably would have been on the bus. And I for one appreciated the ride and the easy way it happened, even with the company getting so boring at times. At least these guys were grounded in something.

I knew Mickey preferred the hippie adventurers that you'd find on the bus. He liked them because he could act out his "seasoned traveler" character. And he could always find somebody to listen to "his" theories on numerology, Aleister Crowley's tarot cards, and the mystic writings of the Jews.

Lawrence chimed back, "Absolutely, Mickey. The restaurant is very clean, and the food is cooked well. I've been in the kitchen and checked it all out myself. They boil the water each day and make the ice cubes out of that same water."

I thought to myself, *Ice cubes—this is going to be interesting.* The only ice I had seen in months was in ponds, dirty rivers, or blocks in some sugar cane juice stop. Lawrence pulled the Mercedes up in front of a one-story nondescript building with plate glass windows all along the front. We got out of the car and walked through doors. We sat down at a table right in front.

Mickey and I never went to restaurants like these, not because we couldn't but because they just didn't feel right. We didn't dress the part either. Our baggy cotton pants and long Afghani shirts, a blanket wrapped around my shoulder and the long Russian coat Mickey wore weren't the preferred dress for places like this. We really did stand out, but I guess that was OK. No one seemed to take notice. I think that was because Charles and Lawrence had brought us in.

We sat there at the window facing the street, traffic going up and down the wide paved boulevard. There was a park-like strip of dirt with skinny trees down the middle and what looked like government buildings on the other side. Edwardian architecture ran as far as I could see in both directions. The restaurant was a newer building tucked in between two of the older buildings. Newer, but still crap. Inside it had loose and crumbling grout in the wall tiles that rose up to the windows from an ugly linoleum floor. There was nothing on the upper interior walls but whitewash and wiring conduit leading to ceiling fans that spun and wiggled like they were ready to fly off their mounts.

The place was a classic attempt to look like someone's idea of a Western restaurant. There were white tablecloths, starched stiff. But they were yellowed from the city water and had frayed corners. The place settings were old worn silver plate with the brass coming through. The waiter wore a white coat that was starched like the table linen and didn't quite fit and a pair of black pants that were about three inches short that showed dry flaky ankles sinking into scuffed patent leather shoes. It was classic; the guy even had his hair lacquered down with some kind of petroleum jelly.

The people walking by all looked in at us or did their best to get us to look at them. Charles and Lawrence seemed to like that. They were poised there like they owned the place, oblivious to anyone. The waiter stepped up to the table.

"Very good to see you, sirs. May I bring you some water?"

"For us all," Lawrence replied, not looking in the waiter's direction but smiling at us.

"So what's good here—they have any fish?" I was in the mood for fish; I hadn't had any for months.

"Don't know," said Charles. "I've never tried it, but it is on the menu, I see."

Menu—now that was a flash from the past. I hadn't seen a menu forever. The thought of eating at some place where I didn't go into the kitchen and point at what looked hot enough and smelled good had become a distant memory.

"You've seen the kitchen here?" I asked Lawrence.

"Absolutely," he replied without hesitation.

"It's absolutely rickety-boo, is it?" Mickey chimed in. I did my best to ignore him.

"So they got rogan josh or kima?"

"Yep, I've eaten both here, they're good," Charles said. "Just don't get the hamburger."

"Hamburger? Come on—you're kidding me. Who ever heard of a hamburger in Pakistan?"

"They have, but let me warn you against it. First, the bun is just a cut above an old biscuit with a small portion of ground mutton molded into a ball, boiled, and placed inside with something that I don't quite recognize. If that sounds bad, well, it is."

"It's not Wimpys that's for sure," Lawrence said, smiling.

I settled on rogan josh and hoped for the best. Mickey got the kima and rice. I almost went for the fish, but when I asked the waiter what kind of fish, and if it was fresh, he looked at me like I'd asked for the drawings of a five-mile single-span suspension bridge. He just stood there, his eyes caught in some imaginary light. Finally I said, "I'll take the rogan josh." He was happy with that.

As we finished up with the meal, Charles looked over at me and said, "Tony, how is it you ended up out here?"

I was struck dumb—nobody knew my name here, not even Mickey. Everyone knew me as Skip. This was not good. I looked over at Lawrence and saw him looking at me with a very wry smile. These guys had been pulling my chain!

I looked back at Charles and said as calmly as I could, "Tony? My name's Skip." I turned to look at Lawrence, and he just smiled at me. This was not a good thing. I wasn't interested in getting into this any deeper; I knew where it could go. I did my best to look dumb, thinking about how to handle it. And right then like a shift in time, I could see myself from above. It was like I was sitting on the ceiling fan watching all three of them looking at me. I could see I was looking honestly surprised and confused; that was positive. *I might pull it off if I can keep this up,* I thought to myself. Then wham, I was back in my chair.

"I'm sorry, Skip, my mistake." Charles said. "Just that I swear the mayor told me your name was Tony, Tony Rice. He must have been mistaken?"

"Yeah, he must have been. I'm Skip, just Skip. I said doing my best to keep up the dumb look. I watched to see if either were letting their game slip. But the faces gave no clue. They just looked back at me like two boring guys who had just made another mistake.

"You mind dropping us off in old town? We'd like to get a room in a place more to our pocket. If that's a problem, we can catch a rickshaw."

"No, that's fine," Lawrence replied quickly. "We would be happy to take you into old town. I need to go there anyway and check on some furniture I'm having made."

He looked over at Charles with displeasure, and right then I knew these guys were not what they had played at.

"I need to go to the institute and tell them we are back," Charles said in a soft, almost apologetic voice. "It's just down the lane here. Lawrence will take you into town."

Charles pulled some bills from his jacket pocket and paid for our dinner with substantial tip. "Good to have met you two. I hope we get a chance to have more time. I'd love to hear how you ended up out here and what you've learned about this place. Sorry about the name mix-up, Skip. The mayor must have been thinking about someone else."

I could tell he didn't believe what he was saying, but I couldn't tell by much—he was good. This was more uncomfortable by the minute. What was going down here? I wasn't sure just what Mickey was thinking at this point either. He knew me only as Skip. He was sure to be clicking through reams of his own thoughts now. Clearly Charles and Lawrence were more than they were letting on. We had made them right in the first place. I felt like a fool, and I had good reason to. Mickey had never really gone for their act, but I had almost given them a little house in Geneva somewhere, with kids playing in the yard wondering when Dad was coming home.

Lawrence said nothing as we drove along. When we got into old town, he dropped us off in front of a tailor shop down the road from the hotel. I didn't want him to know where we were staying. As he drove away, he lowered his window and hollered, "See ya, Tony—I mean Skip" and drove off smiling.

"OK, mate, just what the hell is this all about?" Mickey said, staring at me. "I thought we were mates. Now I find out I don't even know your name? Think you might want to tell me anything about all this-n-that now? Like who am I traveling with?"

"Look, we all got reasons we don't share stuff. I don't use Tony, haven't for a long time. Trust me—it's not a good idea. That name has history, not all of it good. History I'd rather was left back in the States like it should have been. I didn't plan on it following me here."

"Bad planning, I'd guess?" Mickey replied.

"Look, one of the reasons I'm out here is to leave that name behind."

"I'm cool with that, mate, but you need to tell me why. I need to know before it starts to snake around and bite us both on the pecker head, OK?"

P eshawar was the gateway to the tribal zones. Some called it lawless, but it functioned pretty well, just under a different set of rules. It was easiest to see in this part of town, where you seldom saw Westerners, unlike the cantonment. There were no cars on the narrow streets in old town, just three-wheel rickshaws, those little mini-cabs all decked out in bright colors, bells, and bangles and small enough to navigate the maze of narrow back streets and allies. The police didn't come into old town. Folks took care of their own here, and the authorities knew it.

Old town in Peshawar was like what Tombstone or Dodge City must have been in the old days, but here it was all still alive and happening. You could almost smell the blood that had been spilled here over the generations. In this part of the city sporadic gunfire would pop off here and there all the time. There was always some feud, conflict, or political push being played out.

We got a room in a little hotel where I'd stayed before. It was just off the main drag. The hotel was three stories high, higher than anything else around it and had a flat roof that was a nice place to hang out in the evenings. You could look out over most of old Peshawar from there. You could see the low flat roofs in all directions except where the tall trees at the edge of the cantonment district cut the view. On one side, the hotel overlooked an open-air laundry, and on the other side a bakery. From the roof you could watch them hook the flat breads in and out of wood-fired mud ovens. At the laundry a half dozen women scrubbed clothes all day in a long trough of running water that was diverted from someplace. It ran right through the back of the laundry like a creek in a trough. Clothes were drying on lines, hung on walls, laid flat on broad tables, while other women ironed with cast iron irons filled with burning coals.

I sat on the roof thinking about all the life below and what it was about, how it managed to continue like it did. It was so different here, yet it pulled me in so many ways but I was not a part of it. There was no place I belonged anymore really. Not the streets of Oakland, the Kuchi villages of the Hindu Kush mountains, or here in old town Peshawar.

Mickey had gone out to find hashish, and I sat there on the roof thinking about what had happened with Lawrence and Charles. Who were they, and what was the real reason for the ride to Peshawar? I wondered about the mayor, and if he'd actually fit in this at all. But in the end that didn't matter much.

The scary part was that they knew my name; I'd never told the mayor, Mickey, or anyone that name. And why had they waited to play the name card until after we got into Peshawar and not in the car? None of it made sense. It wasn't a mix-up. The way they'd played it right to my face could only mean they wanted to let me know. That meant my old life wasn't so old anymore. I knew I had warrants out for me when I left Oakland but nothing so big it was worth spending money or time on, and it had been some years. It didn't make sense. So why the elaborate story, and how and why did they know me, and how much did they know? In the car I'd kept thinking that these guys were too lame to be real, and I was right, but I didn't expect this. That made me uneasy.

The evening was cooling down a bit, and I went out to walk around and see if I could shake some of what was running wild in my mind. My head and shoulders wrapped in my blanket, I headed toward the center of old town. Shops were busy with the evening market, and the lanterns were beginning to be lit here and there. You could see lights in back rooms and the craftsmen working away. I enjoying being in the city and liked this cool time of late day with all it colors, smells, and activity. I tried to focus on all that and to forget what had happened the last few days

I stopped at a street vendor to buy a cigarette, and when I looked up, just about a half block down the street was a face I knew. It was Tom the Bomb as we had called him—Mr. Super Hippie. He was an old friend from southern Mexico. His face flashed me like headlights on a dark street. I stepped into the first doorway I saw without drawing a breath. It wasn't that I didn't want to see him or say hello, just that I wanted to choose the time and place, and this wasn't it. Tom was anything but low-profile, and I liked keeping a low-profile, especially now.

Tom and I had met in a little village in northern Michoacan a few years earlier. He'd come to Mexico from the Canary Islands recovering from a trailer explosion in the south of France. A propane tank had been set off by somebody in the middle of the night. From what I could tell, it had something to do with bogus American Express traveler's checks. He'd come through it basically intact except that all the hair on his body had been singed off and some slight damage to his ears put him in a hospital. He woke up with the police waiting to talk to him about inks, paper, and pieces of a printing press. His girlfriend Kathryn shuffled him out of the hospital in the middle of the night and onto a boat to the Canaries. Our last conversation in Mexico had been about me joining him and Kathryn on a trip to Afghanistan.

Reconnecting with Tom was a "pick the right time" deal. There were risks. To ignore them you had to be a fool. He lived a life few would ever chance and did it with a kind of strange grace, even a joy. I guess that was why we became friends; he definitely had style. And we were good friends in some ways, and I didn't want to just shine him on, I just wanted to hook up with him when it felt right. But that wasn't now for sure.

This wasn't the first time I had seen him, and I knew it wouldn't be the last. I'd spotted him twice in Kabul. I'd also heard he was around Istanbul having come in from Beirut when I was there. Now here he was in Peshawar, right down the street. He was impossible to miss, stocky and solid as a bull mastiff and all decked out in hippie rags. He was bouncing around like a kid in a candy store like he always did and in conversation with some merchant type in front of a shop. I didn't want him to know I was in town, not just yet, not with all that was going on with Charles and Lawrence.

I slid into a chai shop to get out of sight. As I walked through the room in front I saw men at low tables drinking tea and smoking black tobacco. They were all in suits and those long embroidered coats that rich afghans wear. I headed into the back room to get out of view of the window and the whole scene changed. This room was filled with men from Swat, Hazara, Kalam, Chitral—all the northwest territories, the most remote northern regions. You could tell by their clothes. These places bordered on the northeastern finger of Afghanistan, Badakhstan, and the district of Wakhan. This area was the heart of disputed borders of Pakistan, the Soviet Union, China, and India. Outlanders who had moved around out there and knew this part of the tribal zones weren't many. Those of us who'd been out there called it the spider. It got its name because three of the highest mountain ranges and five international borders all came together up there: the Himalayas, Hindu Kush, and the Karakoram mountains and Afghanistan, Russia, China, Pakistan, India. The eight legs of the spider. You never knew whose military you would run into—Russian, Chinese, Afghani, Pakistani, or Indian, all five nations trying to put some stake in the ground or paint some rock with their colors in this high granite world.

This back room was clearly a hangout for northwest political types. Politics in Pakistan and in particular in Peshawar were always hot and heavy. The walls in the room were covered with posters of some guy in a Chitrali hat and a uniform and the space was strung with party flags.

I didn't do politics. If anything in Pakistan was risky, it was politics. People got shot all the time over politics. Here in Peshawar it was a daily event, in or out of election season—it didn't seem to matter. I wasn't interested in getting caught up in or even tuned into the various factions, beyond what I needed to know to get by. The lines were blurry at best in all this. Everything was corrupt here, and everyone knew it. That much was a given. But the particulars and who knew whom and who helped whom were issues I wanted no part of. The safest political position no matter where you were in this country was ignorance. So I took care to know as little as I could and to like whomever I was supposed to at a given point. It was clear the guys in this room were for someone and something—and against anyone who wasn't on that ship.

I moved to a corner table in the back and slid up on the carpets. The boy brought me a tea and hookah. Everyone was up on the tables here with their legs folded or lying half out on cushions and smoking. In the narrow lanes between the tables, boys ran in and out, carrying tea and small plates of food. This was unusual for Peshawar; most places here, even in old town, had chairs or benches and tables. No one seemed to notice me or care that I was there, and that felt good. The carpets were thick and comfortable. I pulled up a cushion and leaned on it.

At the other end of the room, there were three men engaging in an intense conversation and smoking a hookah pipe between them. Then all of a sudden, in a blink of the eye, they all morphed into some Indians passing a peace pipe. It was like they were really there. Thick tobacco smoke billowed blue-gray, and a dreamlike hue lay across the images. Red-brown colors in the carpets under them had turned to a campfire on the ground. Then, bam, just as quick, I was back in Peshawar surrounded by political mumblings.

I felt like I should be dizzy, but I wasn't. I'd tripped out here and there the last few weeks, but this one worried me. It was more than shape-shifting or out-of-body stuff. It wasn't like watching myself from another spot in the room. I'd been doing that for a while and was used to it. This was some weird kind of hallucination. I figured it had to have something to do with all the hashish I'd pumped into my blood in the last few months. This total fantasy deal was a shift from the norm. I liked being in control, and with this stuff I wasn't.

I woke up bleary-eyed with the sun full in a dusty Peshawar sky. My eyes had popped open and my mind set running by sporadic gunfire a number of times during the night. Patchy gunfire was normal in old town, but usually it was somewhere in the distance. Last night a bunch of it sounded like it was right in front of the hotel. Each time a rat-a-tat-tat of fully automatic weapons sounded off, it was like they were right under the window. It sat me up right out of deep sleep. I had to keep telling myself, "Lie back down. Don't go to the window."

Mickey sat up in his bed and looked over.

"Bloody Chinese New Year, you think?"

He shook his head. It was full on morning, and I was getting hungry.

"You up for food, man?"

"Bloody right, let's to it."

We gathered up and headed out into old town.

"How'd it go last night?" I asked as we walked. "You find what you were after?"

"Bugger all, but I did run into some mates who gave me a slice of their kit."

"Groovy."

"Not like up north, but good enough; and what about you, 'Master' Tony? Did you figure just what kind of crap we got on us from those two slogs yet?"

"Same as it was. They're fishing."

He shifted his eyes toward me with as sober a look as he ever had. "OK, mate, I'm willing, or think I am, to go with all this, but not without some tad of info. How does this Tony you aren't become such a bloody highwayman that they spend royal jewels to look you up? Not to mention how in hell did someone find you out here? I've traveled out here for years, mate. You hold your mud as close to the vest as any bloke I've ever known. You're game is tight and as bloody well unlit as anyone could handle. You've been deeper in the Hindu Kush than most snow leopards and came out alive and maybe even sane. So how did they know you were here? How?"

"I wish I knew; it must be about old shit."

"You think!"

"There isn't anything new. Not with that name attached." I'd never seen Mickey so intense or cautious. "It's no biggie, man."

"No, well, see those buggers over there? What's the wager?"

There were two men dressed in Levi's and button shirts standing on the far side of the street. They looked really out of place and were trying way too hard to look like they hadn't noticed us. It would have been funny had it been any other time.

"This is worse than an old movie. What the crap is going on?"

"That's just what I was asking you, mate."

"Let's go inside somewhere and see if they follow us." I hated being on the defensive; that wasn't my style but I wanted to see their play.

We walked down to the chai shop where I'd been in the night before without looking back. I smiled remembering the back room, knowing that if these two wandered into that crowd, it would be a major mistake.

"Tony, you know where you are, right?" Mickey asked as he looked around.

"Yep, I was here last night. It's as good a spot as any. And listen man, call me Skip—I really mean it. I don't like that name being used."

"All right, mate, sorry."

We sat in front where we could look out through the window. The glass had a blue tint and was rippled and full of bubbles. On the outside its wavy surface reflected light and made it hard to see in. If these two wanted to know where we were, they'd have to come inside.

"OK, mate, if they come down on us like the queen's bloody guard, what in the hell are they going to say?"

"Cut me some slack, man! I don't have a clue. I didn't ask for any of this shit. I'll tell you as much as I can figure just as soon as we know if we need to lose these assholes."

"Sorry, mate, but it's a bit dodgy in this town for me."

"Well, ain't that a surprise. I'm not the only one with history! So there is a reason for your being so weird since we left the pass?"

I hadn't been watching the street while we talked, and when I looked out, the two were on the move.

"Man, they're heading this way."

They were walking straight toward the chai shop but hadn't crossed the street yet. It was hard to tell if they were looking our way or not. When they got directly crossways from us they started across the street.

"Maybe they weren't watching us, mate; look."

They had angled off down the street.

"We've been smoking way too much, man—got us paranoid," I said, trying to crack a smile.

Mickey shot out, "Too much, no such thing!"

The two had headed down the road and stepped into the shop where I'd seen Tom the night before. That was good and felt like one thing I didn't need to think about. Still I had bad feelings about the way things were shaking out all and all. I was getting hit with a whole new set of questions. Rather than sort them out, I figured hell, I'll get out of dodge and leave this crap for another year.

"Mickey, I need to split—could be real soon. I need to move quickly when I do. I need this shit behind me, to get as lost as I can. I'm thinking maybe north. You have your past. You don't need to be carrying more than your own crap right now. And these cowboys seem focused on me."

"OK, mate, I'm down with that. I won't ask. Let's eat and bugger out of here. North is peachy this time of year. Besides all that rata-tat-tat in the middle of the night destroys my beauty sleep and makes my eye twitch!"

As I looked around the place across from us four men sat at a table. They didn't look like they belonged. They were in Pakistani suits with pressed cotton shirts, way too well-dressed for this part of town. I glanced up a few times to see if they were looking our way, but they had no interest. Still, I was sizing up their potential for causing me grief. They hadn't even turned their heads in our direction, and there I was building some story about them that was likely all about me. I started to laugh at myself.

"What's so funny?" Mickey asked.

"Just thinking about what a circus life can be, that's all. What do you make of that table over there?" I nodded at the well-dressed crew.

"Fit for the parliament, I'd say."

Food arrived, and we dug in. Flatbread lightly spiced and painted with a thin layer of peanut oil. The meat must have been lamb or kid goat. I hadn't had such a tasty meal for months. I bit into the naan and chewed on the lamb, and then I got it. The food here was good, better than good! That's why those guys were here, the food. All of a sudden I felt like the fool I was.

I didn't want to leave the city so soon. There were lots of things in Peshawar I wanted, not the least of them good food. This was one of the only places between Tehran and Delhi you could run into European women. Western women were the only play out here, and even then, there was no guarantee you wouldn't get shot. I'd spent too much time in Balkh and Kunduz, where no Western women ever got. I needed to hook up. A secretary from the German embassy, a French hippie chick, I didn't care. That had been a priority in my mind when I headed here, and it pissed me off that these guys were fucking up my game.

"Twitch, when I was back in Oakland, I was what they call politically active."

I figured I owed Mickey some explanation, so I started to tell him what stuff I thought might tie into all this. Just as quick, he put his finger up in front of his lips.

"Look, mate, you're right. We don't really need to know all the bloody details of why assholes might be sniffing our heels. You got stories, and I got stories. That doesn't really matter, right?"

Just as he was speaking, I started to trip out again; his face faded, and his voice started to trail off like he was walking away. Pastel colors started dripping across my eyes and faint words churned together like surf and then no form, no sound—I was freaking out. Then light started coming through a colored fog in my mind, and an image started to form. I thought I'd passed out for a second but then instead of Mickey in front of me I was looking down at an old baba I'd known in northern Afghanistan—a little man who lived in a mud brick shed dug into the wall around the old village of Balkh. His front door opened out on the graveyard outside the city. I could see myself sitting there across from him, just like I was looking through a hole in the roof. I was sitting right there on the edge of his low wooden cot in his little hobbit hole of a home with its roof beams no more than five feet above the floor. Bent from age and hard work, he stood in front of me, three heads lower than the roof beams. Then just like that, I was looking out the door over the graves like I had so many times before.

I'd stayed in his place during a long blizzard once. I slept on the floor and took the whole room when I stretched out. He pulled me in out of a light snow once when I was walking into town. It was just in time. Somehow he'd known a storm was coming. It hit right then like a hammer, and the temperature dropped from freezing to where spit froze in less then a minute after it hit the ground. I couldn't stand up in his little place or understand anything he said, but by the time I left, this man was a friend.

Now there I was. I turned, and Baba looked directly at me and spoke. I understood his words for the first time. His language hadn't changed, but I understood it somehow.

"Life's turning and sometimes sharply. Hold to it even if things are hard and bend you down like me. Let them, but keep standing. Roads are rough and some narrow; walk directly, and worlds will roll out like they should."

Then he turned, bent down, and started to light the little fire in the corner of the room just like I'd seen him do. The icy wind whistled through the cracks in the walls like the first time I was there, and the flames flickered as a fine dust rained from the roof tiles. Then like a sunrise flow of swirling pastel, the old man turned to clouds, and Mickey's face started to form and his words to sound.

"So, we need to get together when this bloody crap is over. What say, mate?"

I didn't know what to say. I hadn't heard anything he'd said. I didn't want to tell him I was losing it, because I really might be. It was too weird. Weirder yet, I knew he'd go with it if I told him what had just happened. I wasn't sure I was ready for that; I wasn't sure about any of it. I needed time to sort this crap out, and I didn't have any.

"Well, I guess that's best. Whatever you think is a way to go."

"What? Have you bloody been listening to me, mate?"

"I thought I was, and then I slipped out, man. Sorry—on edge, you know."

"Did you hear anything at all I was saying to you? Hell, doesn't matter. I'm no Jack the Ripper, and you're not either, right? Not even close, I'd count!"

"Right."

"That's what I'm bloody saying here, no more than that. We know things can slip—I don't want slips, and you don't either."

He sat there looking at me, waiting. I'd missed all of what he'd said. It couldn't have been too long gone though because what he was saying made sense. I had no reason to know any more about Mickey than what I did. He was a friend, and I trusted him, and I guessed that's what he'd been talking about. Making sense out of all Mickey had said wasn't a big deal; we were good. What was bugging me now was my tripping out, that and I still had Lawrence and Charles to figure out.

What did they know beyond an old name? And why would anyone take the time, not to mention money, to come out here and track me down? And now, to top it off, Tom was around and that usually meant weirdness of some kind was going down, and there was this visit from my little Afghani friend with cryptic messages, weird. I might have overdone the LSD or hashish I guess, but that didn't make sense—it was all too real. It wasn't a flashback kind of happening. I was clear on real life and always had been. What was happening to me? There was something else about all this and that was freaky. It was like I was becoming two people; not only was I visiting places no one else could see, but I also knew it inside. I was becoming someone and traveling somewhere that only I could.

Real life, unreal life—shit, who knew? Control is what I needed. I could handle the clear and touchable stuff, but this mystical place bursting into things made it tougher in some ways. Or maybe it was making it easier, and I just didn't know yet. Anyway, right now I needed my head screwed on straight. I needed to own it if I was going to understand it. I needed to have control. That was the only way. I needed to learn about what it meant, if it meant anything.

"OK," I said, "we just let things ride as they are. If and when this wave hits the beach, we hoof it, skate out of here as fast and as quiet as we can without looking back."

"Look, Skip, it seems I smell pretty good right now, but that won't last, not in this town. Trust me, mate. If they catch my scent, they'll bite at my heels for sure."

"Look, whoever's calling this dance figures we know more than we do. But if push comes to shove, the less we know, the better, least ways about each other."

"Tickety-boo, mate." Mickey held up his saucer steaming with chai.

"What's the end run, man? Any ideas? You think we should take separate roads out of town when we go and let the dogs follow the biggest stink?"

"Keep the farts guessing? I can handle that." He winked his good eye.

We finished our tea and food and were tight with the plan. The street was clear, and the guys in suits had left. We headed out through the back room to leave through the alley. Then I started to think about what we were doing, running with our tails tucked. A wave swept up through me like I had slammed a double shot of scotch. This way didn't sit right. It was not how I liked living my life, and it was pissing me off. They could be anybody out here, and I was making a federal case out of it. Nothing was sure; it could be nothing but a trick. After all that tripping out I had been doing, who knew what was what? Even if they were trouble, I didn't see much real chance to shake them, not at this point. I stopped dead in my tracks.

"What say we walk down to that shop where our two spooks went and see what they got to sell?"

Mickey smiled and tilted his head. "I like that idea, mate; see how the dogs feel when they got fleas."

We turned around and left through the front and headed to the shop where Tom had been and where the two we'd seen earlier had gone. It was a small furniture factory with about five craftsmen working. I didn't see our two wing-tippers or the guy I'd seen talking with Tom. I'd kept an eye on the place while we were in the chai shop, and no one had left, at least that I'd seen.

"Now this is something, man. No one left this place, I'd swear."

I wanted to see these guys' faces and how they took us being there. I wanted to let them know I was on the offensive, if they were spooking us. I didn't think it would change much, but we might get some idea of just why they were wiring us up. I had a belly full of good food and felt like I was made of granite. It felt good to feel in control again after the last few days. I liked being back in that place, sure of myself. I was not interested in giving it up all that easily again. I walked behind the stacks of furniture and the workbenches. A workman stepped up and said in broken English. "Can helps you maybe, gentlemans?"

"You bloody well can," Mickey shot out.

"Two blokes, friends, told us they'd be here this morning. Are they about?"

The workman smiled at us and waved his hand to follow. He led us through a maze of half-finished woodwork and then through a side door into another room stacked with furniture. There were men sanding drawers and tabletops and others taping in brass inlay. There was a large sliding door at the far side, open to the back alley. On the other side was another open garage door, and I could make out furniture stacked there as well.

Just then I heard Mickey mumble, "Oh frigging hell."

I looked back as he passed right by me and out the sliding doors. I followed him across the alley into the other warehouse. There sat a Volkswagen van and a Mercedes sedan in various stages of body work. A sinking feeling went through my gut as I looked at the Mercedes. My immediate thought was that it was Charles and Lawrence's. But then I saw it was a different model, and Mickey blurted out, "Piss in hell, mate—it's a kitty-car factory!"

Sure enough, the cars were getting customized for smuggling. Peshawar and Kabul were both spots along the route you could get this kind of work done. Get your car or van fixed up to stash whatever, and drive it back to Europe and a payday. That is, if the job on the car was a good one, and no one sold you out. Otherwise you'd lose the car, the stash, and a few months or years, depending.

All the furniture in the place was custom-made, with hollow side boards and tabletops false drawer bottoms and the like. *What a waste,* I thought knowing what crap Pakistani hashish was and that likely that was what was going into theses pieces. But things started to make more sense now at least. The two out-of-place wing-tippers we'd seen. They might have thought we were hashish dealers. But not me—not in this town, maybe Mickey at some point. I didn't know. We did look the part; that was true. They could have been trying to catch our eye. Like so many out here, they were likely looking for better dope. That made sense, and that felt good for a change. At least I had a picture that worked for these two.

The Volkswagen's gas tank was on the floor getting a false top, and a boy squatted, grinding the rough edges off a set of rebuilt fiberglass wheel wells for the Mercedes.

"Well, Mickey, you finally got the message?" A voice rose over the sound of the grinder.

"I bloody figured it must be you when I saw the shop. Crazy days, Johnny—why didn't you just dandy up and come visit?"

A thin man dressed in well-tailored Pakistani clothes stepped out.

"Things get busy, and time's money." He winked.

"Skip, this is Johnny Johnny, old friend from Rawalpindi."

I could see from Twitch's face that "old friend" was pushing it some.

Johnny Johnny spoke up in a thick Pakistani accent. "Some friends of mine mentioned you were in the old city."

"That right, mate?"

"Yes, said you'd arrived in from the Khyber."

"They did, did they? And who might these friends be, Johnny boy?"

"Men that work for me; you wouldn't know them."

"Friends?"

"A figure of speech. Don't worry." He turned, still talking to Twitch but looking at me. "Would you and your friend like some tea?"

"I see you're doing the same as ever, Johnny boy."

"Actually it's been very successful here in Peshawar, much better than Rawalpindi. As always, our work is the best and our product the finest."

He smiled directly at me and then waved at the shop boy to go bring us tea.

I didn't know this guy from Adam, and I didn't really want to. He had a sticky slick style that put me off at the jump. From the look of this operation, I didn't need to know any more; I'd know even less if I could have. I had no interest in this place or its products.

Mickey jumped in, "Yeah, I know your quality and all that, Johnny, but you were waiting for us to turn up? My friend here and I are not doing business right now, and even if we wanted to, we don't have the sterling."

"That may well be true at the moment, my friend, but it may not always be that way, and you might know others with interest?" Again he looked over at me with a slinky smile. "It could be lucrative for you?"

He turned back toward Mickey and went on. "My intent was to let you know what it is we offer, and then if by some chance you happen to find some resource, or perhaps your friend there does," he said, nodding at me once more, "we might be able to cover a project from top to bottom, for a percentage?" Again he looked directly at me. Who was this cracker, and what did he think he knew about me? It was like he had an image of someone stuck in his head, and he'd decided it was me. Anyway, I didn't like it.

"What makes you think that I would be any more able to take up your offer than Mickey? Or that I would have any interest in it? I don't know you, and I'm not sure I want to."

"Oh, I don't think that—please don't take my attention to you in that way. I only use you as an example of someone Twitch here might know or run into."

The tea arrived, and he offered us both a cup and saucer from the tray.

"Sit?" He motioned toward a table and chairs at the side of the room.

We sat, and Mickey's eye started to hop around a bit faster.

"Still have that eye, do you? You should really see if they can fix it. I have a very good doctor here in the cant. Trained in London."

"No thanks, I'm used to it, and if I didn't have the eye, how in bugger all could I ask for alms?" They both laughed.

Who was this guy, and how did Tom and Charles and Lawrence fit in here? I sat drinking tea while the small talk poured out across the table. It seems Johnny and Mickey went back years and more than a few deals. They talked about Peshawar, Tehran, and Lahore. I kind of enjoyed it. It was the first time in a while I didn't feel like the focus was on me in some way. Then someone called over to Johnny Johnny, and he left. Just as soon as he was out of sight, Mickey started in.

"This is one of those things I didn't need to tell you earlier, mate. Johnny and me go back years, maybe five. We were teamed up for a while and sold hashish to a host of buggers. The deal was that we delivered in whatever country they wanted. Johnny's family is big in rugs, and the father is some kind of diplomat—travels all over Europe. He made it happen. The problem comes with his gear, his excuse for hashish. He deals Pakistani hashish, real crap, and it always is. He stays in business because he buys from these particular blokes, so he's not about to change. And it's a family biz along with the rugs. It all goes through Lahore and some government connections.

"Anyway, it all went bloody south with me, and I got some serious trouble in Glasgow! What arrived wasn't right for my lads—good lads too, wharf rats. So I went to Johnny for a fix-up to keep my blokes happy, and he said, 'Do with what it is.' Well, that didn't cut shit with me or the lads, so I walked. That was more than two years ago now."

"Interesting," I replied, "but I think this guy's about more that that. I know these operations, and I'm not a mark, and you aren't either; he knows that. Two years is a lot of air, and now this Johnny Johnny is looking you up, all buddy buddy and old friend."

"And where are the blokes that came in here, and why all the war stories and nothing about why I walked? Bloody weird."

"Who knows, man—it's all too weird; I don't know what he's about except it isn't tea and a smoke. And if I had an interest in taking a load of hashish overland, I wouldn't be doing it out of this town for Christ's sake or working with a sleaze like your friend there. No offense. But I'd bet dimes to donuts he knows all that."

"None taken; and for the chart, mate, we did business—we aren't friends!"

This was too much: Charles and Lawrence, Tom, and now this. It was really tilting my scale. Even if this Johnny was just fishing, I had absolutely no interest in doing anything that would give anybody reason to look my way. I'd made a point of living out of sight, and now here I was spooked from the Khyber Pass into Pakistan. This Johnny Johnny guy trying to sell me an overland package—that wasn't for real; it was too clean. All I could do was wait for what was next.

I got that this wasn't easy for Mickey, sure, but it still seemed a bit funny. We'd walked right into this mess, thinking we were in the lead and going to take charge, and then bang—this Johnny Johnny character, a real piss bucket, turns it back on us. We needed to get out of this warehouse. But one thing was for sure: I wasn't interested in going anywhere out of sight now. There was no point or any place to go. What I needed was to know where all this crap was leading. There was just too much energy in the air around us for all this to be accidental. Someone had tags on the both of us; the question was why? It felt like we were being kept in reach, so it didn't matter where we went. The game now was to figure out what they, whoever they were, were looking for and go from there.

I needed more information. Who were the two we'd seen come in here, and what was their game? On top of that there was Tom. The more I thought about it, it could have been Johnny Johnny that Tom was talking to last night. And if Tom was involved, anything could be going on.

Eventually Johnny came back and right off offered to put together a road trip, car, hashish, and all, to Switzerland for a percentage. It was hard not to laugh in his face. This was way too good to be real, and I knew it. This type of deal never happened. There was always some hitch.

Like Mickey had found out. But it was hype anyway and I knew it as well as Johnny did. He was pitching me for some other reason. He knew I wasn't about to take on a bogus deal. I'd been very clear I had no interest in going west. Anyone who knew anything about me knew that.

I played the game to see if I could learn anything, finally telling him I'd see if I knew someone in town who might be interested and then get back to him. It was a way to get out of there at least. I could tell Mickey wasn't easy with what I'd said, but he hadn't got us any closer to the door, and I wasn't interested in hanging there any longer. We left Johnny's with nobody, including him, believing any of the come-on glad-handing and bullshit.

Mickey was looking at the ground after we exited. "You understand, mate, that this is Johnny Johnny's town, right? His family is big, real big shit here, in Lahore and Rawalpindi. He's not a bloke to be nonchalant about. Bullshit him, and it can be bloody bad!"

"Look, Twitch, this guy is not interested in working with us. He's working with someone who wants to know where we are. If he gets us involved in his game, then folks know where to find us, or at least they think they do. That's my take. Remember, he was expecting to see you. Why did he expect that, unless someone clued him in that you were in town? Someone put lots of energy into this, and it ain't my good looks or yours that's fueling it. You got history, and so do I—what pieces of that brought this shit down? If we can figure that out, we might figure the reasons for all this and maybe a way out. The good thing is that it seems we're not at risk, least not yet, with Johnny Johnny's doing that song and dance."

"What I know, mate, is it can shift like a bale on a bus with these Pakistani lads—they're serious game. I hope you figured this right, mate. I don't want Johnny Johnny feeling like he's been snookered by me or my friends. These blokes can be bloody bad news. A bad cricket match can switch them on."

We walked around old town not talking much. I turned the day's events over and over in my mind. I'd learned a lot about Mickey listening to the conversation with him and Johnny. Clearly the trouble in Scotland had been enough to push Mickey out—a good decision as far as I could figure. But still, Mickey's history with Johnny didn't clear up what all the rest of this was all about.

The next day was moving like molasses, so I decided I'd go see a tailor and get a new shirt. Both my shirts had been washed on rocks so much that they were coming apart. Mickey had headed downtown to meet some Germans he knew figuring they had hashish. I didn't want any more new faces. All the cloak and dagger bullshit had kept me up most of the night as it was. All this crap had really cut my style, and I liked my style as it was. I missed simple day-to-day living—new places, food, and getting laid now and then. I didn't want to lose the easy style of life I had managed the last few years or, more to the point, admit that I already had.

The tailor told me my shirt would be ready in the morning. I headed out to the street, and just then two women wearing head scarves were starting to come into the shop. They paused and stepped aside to let me pass, but as I stepped by them, they turned their eyes up, smiling. They were not Pakistani, and standing so close to them, I could smell coconut oil, from their hair, I guessed. I stopped mid-step and smiled back my best smile. I'd been smoking black tobacco and hashish for months and was sure my teeth were stained, but I kept smiling anyway. Their eyes glanced at my tarnished pearly whites. One asked in a deep, rich French accent, "English?"

"I speak English. I'm from California."

She was beautiful, her deep green eyes looking into mine.

"American," the other said in an accent that was French too but a bit different.

"Well, Californian."

That had been a golden word for European women before; I hoped it still was. So I slathered it on: "San Francisco."

They were both wearing the long pants and dress-shirt tops typical of Muslim women. One had a bright green scarf over her head, and the other wore a multicolored hat pulled over a pale silk scarf.

"You getting clothes made?" I asked.

"We look for old stitching and shirt fronts."

"You find that kind of stuff in here?" I glanced at the shop door. "You guys know about the thieves market in old town, don't you? Lots of stuff like that there. You been?"

"No, we don't know this place. Is it safe for women?"

I spotted some tattoos on the shorter of the two, just under her sleeve. Maybe she was French Moroccan? But she had no tattoos on her chin or face. One thing was for sure—they were both beautiful, and I hadn't been this close to a woman in months. This was unreal. I wasn't in Milan or Barcelona; this was Peshawar.

"What do you do with old stitching?"

"We design clothes and use old embroidery, stitching, appliqué—stuff like that—in them."

"And this tailor has stuff like that? I never figured him for old clothes."

The tall one laughed as she said, "You wear them though."

She pulled on the front of my shirt.

"Yeah, I know, that's why I'm here—I need a new shirt."

"We can make you a shirt, if you take us to this thieves market."

"Sure, I can take you."

The thieves market wasn't a good place for women, especially not alone—a street full of vendors selling stuff from everywhere that was stolen, collected for debts, or pulled out of dowries. You could find anything there on a given day, from kitchen appliances to jewelry, anything. Even hookers would show up there now and again—both local and European—and that made it a real issue for a woman without a man in tow. Solitary women, especially if they were Western, would be immediately pegged as prostitutes. This market was filled with some of the sleaziest merchants in the city, and lots of money changed hands. But it still was the best place to get off-the-wall old stuff.

"You really don't want to go there without a man, even dressed like you are. Believe me."

"You mean they might think we were prostitutes?" the little one with the tattoos said with a smile.

"Yep, that's what I mean. So what are your names?"

The taller one answered. "I'm Cecile, and this is Amber. And you are?"

"I'm Skip. People call me Skip."

"Skip," she said, with a slight question and smile. "Well, when we can go to this thieves market—tonight?"

"Nope, can't do. It's only in the mornings. They pack up and are gone by noon. We can go in the morning. How do I find you?"

"If we are making you a shirt, you should come to our house so we can measure and fit it. You can stay the night. We can go to the market in the morning?" Amber looked at me for a response.

I wasn't about to turn away from this. If they wanted to make me a shirt at their place, I was there for it. I'd been in the mountains and in small villages so long, I couldn't tell if my mind was running wild or not. It didn't really matter. They were inviting me over, and I was not about to say no.

As we talked, the tailor came out. He'd obviously been expecting them. He had in hand a basket full of old embroidery, some of it very nice. Cecile looked at the basket with a passing glance and averted her eyes toward the ground and spoke in very soft Urdu. I couldn't understand. The tailor answered politely and stepped aside, inviting us in with a wave of his arm.

Now this was a new twist. These two were at home here. Cecile leaned over and said softly, "Follow our lead, and sit down when you are offered."

Weird. This guy knew me—I'd just been in the store, and he'd just measured me for a shirt—but he didn't even give a sign. I figured if I wanted to stick with these two, I'd better just follow directions, so I sat when the tailor offered me a seat and didn't say anything.

"You friends," he said, looking at them and then me. "I give you best price on shirt, half money now, thanks please." Then he smiled at the girls. I was willing to pay what he had asked but thanked him. "Very good."

I sat there watching as Amber looked through the basket, pulling out pieces of fabric and speaking a soft Urdu dialect. Every so often, she would hand a piece of cloth to Cecile. They had ongoing business with the tailor from the looks of things. I was impressed with the quality of embroidery he'd gathered. For all I knew, it was good enough for what they wanted, but it wasn't what I knew was available at the thieves market. It was a sure thing he knew about the market, but maybe he didn't like buying there; lots of people didn't feel safe there. Finally they finished and negotiated a price, and we left.

"Where is it you two stay?"

"We have a small house in the Cant," Amber answered.

"Nice neighborhood."

Cecile started to laugh. "You know the neighborhood, do you? You stay there?"

"Nope, I never stay there, but I have friends who do now and again."

"Like us," Amber said, winking at me.

"Well, not quite like you, or I'd spend much more time there."

They looked at each other and said something in French and then started to giggle. Cecile stepped out onto the street and flagged down a little three-wheel rickshaw cab. They were all over the city, decked out in bright colors with bells and banners all over them. Some of them were covered with political posters and slogans, and some displayed scenes of tranquil forests and peacocks standing at ponds, but most were painted in gold and silver on black, with geometric designs and quotes from the Koran. The one that pulled up was the peacock style with a couple political posters stuck over it. We buzzed off toward the cant like riding on a big sewing machine. Coming from this direction, when you went into the cantonment, there was a large stone gateway. As we were heading toward it, I asked Cecile, "Where'd you learn to speak Urdu?"

"I grew up in Paris," she replied, like that was an answer.

"I didn't know Parisians spoke Urdu."

"Most don't, but I'm not Parisian. I just grew up there."

Amber broke in. "She's fluent in five languages: French, English, Spanish, Italian, and Urdu. Her father was a linguist for the French University in Lebanon. She went to school in Paris."

"Good school," I said.

"I'm jealous." Amber looked over at her friend and smiled.

Cecile responded, "Amber speaks Urdu as good as I, and Hindi, English, and what else, Amber? Bengali? And French of course."

"Don't listen to her; I'm only good in English, French, and Urdu. But I can get around in Turkey and North Africa. At least I know enough to find the bathrooms, even if I wish I hadn't after seeing them." She laughed.

I liked these two. They were beautiful, smart, and fun. Most women out here came East with boyfriends and various dopers of one kind or another, and they almost always had a sad story, that and a handful of give-me. Boyfriends would run off or disappear some way, and there they were, shit out of luck. Some European women lived pretty OK out here, working as live-ins with local dealers or pharmacy shopkeepers. Fair-skinned, light-haired Dutch and German types commanded good prices as domestics as long as their work included sex. I had nothing against working girls, but out here, they tended to be pretty dim lights for my taste.

I'd struck gold here with these two, and I knew it. Better than that, they had taken my mind off all the crap that was going down. I hadn't been around anyone, especially not a woman, who was just fun for a long time.

I could feel their bodies pressed up on either side of me as the rickshaw turned. With the smell of Amber's hair right under my nose, the coconut oil brought memories of lying on the beach in southern India. It had been way too long. I just leaned back and took another deep breath.

"You feel happy?" Cecile asked.

"Yeah, I am."

"We're not dragging you away from something?"

"No, god no. You're like a day on the beach."

"We're that nice?" Cecile spoke softly and grabbed my arm and snuggled up closer. "I guess we'll have to try and live up to that. What do you think, Amber?"

"We'll manage." She smiled and laid her head on my other shoulder.

I hadn't felt this good in months, years—hell, maybe ever. I could fall in love right there. But then a little voice started to laugh inside as I remembered how I'd felt in Landi Kotal at the dance.

Seemed life was heading to good places with these two showing up. Mickey would have said I was "bloody dim" to think it was coincidence. But he thought everything was a plan and that it was all either kismet, or some kind of scam. I'd been around Mickey too long. I couldn't help thinking, *What if these two are part of Charles and Lawrence's dance?* That bummed me out big time, so I let it go.

I was never one to think things were driven by fate, karma, or kismet whatever that was anyway. Thinking that way was like a mangy dog, something I didn't want to touch. But in these last few months, I was beginning to like the way I felt, letting stuff just be in the hands of whatever, hopefully luck, until this crap with Charles and Lawrence came up. But the question of trust wouldn't leave now, and that was a pisser. Could I even trust myself really, without questioning my own sanity?

These women were beautiful, funny, and here! Was there some hidden hook? I was seriously horny, but I needed to keep a grip. Things were just too crazy to be laid back in Never-Never-Land too far, no matter how good it felt. Things had been tense, but I wasn't about to ruin how nice I was feeling now. The world had shifted under me for sure, but that was no reason not to enjoy what was good. And this was good. Hell, if there was some plan to resurrect my old life floating around out there, why not get it delivered by these two?

Just then, the driver started yelling out the window. I sat up like a stick and leaned over, looking out the rickshaw. We were heading down the main road into the embassy district, just about five blocks from the gate. Three blocks up or so, there was a crowd making its way toward us, chanting and waving banners. It was some kind of political rally. The driver came to a stop, and two young men stepped in front of the rickshaw while another looked in from the side. He was shaking his finger and screaming at the driver. When he saw me, his attention shifted, and the two started pointing at me and yelling. Up the street, the crowd was moving steadily forward, and I was beginning to hear chants.

"What's up?" I asked the driver.

Amber grabbed my shirt and pulled at me.

"What's going on?" I asked.

"We ran into a political rally. The driver is arguing politics, I think."

One young man leaned into the rickshaw and saw the two women and then leaned back out immediately and directed his words to me.

"You go now. Dangerous for you. We kill you."

"Kill us, why?"

"It is against you; this is demonstration."

"Me?"

"Go now before coming here—dangerous for you!"

Before I could ask any more questions, Amber was yelling at the driver, who it seems was set on going straight ahead and winning his argument. The crowd was moving closer now, and the chanting was louder and louder. I reached up into the cab and grabbed the driver by the back of his neck and turned his head toward me and looked him dead in the eyes.

"Turn around and go the other way now!" I pointed in the direction we had come from. "Now!" He got it. I let go of his neck, and he turned the rickshaw around, mumbling under his breath and then yelling out the side at the three men as he sped off. Cecile had watched as the driver and the three students had done their thing and was very nervous, I could see. I took her hand and said, "Don't worry; we're on our way out of here."

The rickshaw was heading full-speed back in the direction that we'd come. I looked back to see the crowd start to run down the street after us. They knew they'd never catch up, but all the threatening made them feel big, I guess; some things never change. The driver was lucky that I'd pushed his ass to get us out of there. I don't think he got it. He may well have ended up beaten half to death on the street or worse. I don't even want to think what could have happened to Amber and Cecile. But there was no way they could catch us now, nor would they have any interest to. Cecile didn't say a word as we rolled away; she just grabbed my arm tightly and sunk her face into the side of my chest. I looked over at Amber, and she was smiling a grateful thank you and settling back down on my other shoulder.

"Are you sure you want me along?" I asked after a few minutes. "They don't like Americans much in this town, you know? They weren't after you—you know that, right? They figured me as an American, or at least English. They wouldn't have hurt you or Amber."

I knew that was bullshit, but it felt like the right thing to say. She looked up at me with wide eyes and gave a little nod.

"That's the kind of trouble you run into when you pick up refugee Americans," I said, laughing.

"I'm glad you were with us," Cecile said softly.

"Me too," Amber whispered in my other ear.

I knew lowland Pakistanis and the hill or tribal people had some similarities, but there were huge differences too. What was common in all lowland Pakistani political stands was some identification with Islamic social and community structures, which got translated to "anti-Western"—British and American mostly. Community leaders would demonstrate against the godless West with all its sex, alcohol, and broken families and then after the rally and the hype would go out drinking with their buddies at the local moonshiners and buy a hooker, if they could afford it. Or go home and slap their wives around for not acting like the girls in their western porn magazine. This town was full of that kind of stuff for sure. Not everyone was like that, but enough were to make it a very sleazy place. The politics here was about control of a huge uneducated population. And the power was held by perpetuating that undereducated mass. Not nice, but hell, it was Pakistan.

Tribal folk hung around the city in small enclaves in old town. They held to their own ways and were not really accepted in places of political power. The city was very different in their barrios. Pakistani authorities stayed out of tribal areas and conflicts and let them settle stuff themselves. When situations did cross the lines, there were problems, often big ones, and lives got lost. Now there was a growing political face from the tribal community in western Pakistan. For the most part, politics in tribal culture was about managing arguments, keeping balance in family and clan, and getting debts settled. Getting larger political support of tribal folk was a dance only a few better-educated with savvy knew how to swing. These "Khans," tribal political figures also protected market share in tribal commodities, hashish, opium, guns, betel nut, and the like. They used the larger national political world to keep their lands and ways as undisturbed as they could.

After about a half hour and a series of back roads and narrow dirt paths, we came into the cantonment from the other side of town. We turned up a paved two-lane road lined with tall trees heading into the embassy district.

I hardly recognized myself sitting there between these two and was still thinking about what had happened and how different it could have been if we hadn't gotten out of there. The driver could be dead by now or wishing he was, and the two of them—well, anything could have happened. Cecile reached up and grabbed the driver's shirt, pointing at a gated courtyard along the road. "There," she said. The rickshaw came to a stop at the curb, and we got out.

I followed them into the house where they invited me to sit down at a small table with four chairs. Cecile excused herself while Amber took a seat on the other side of the table. "I'm so glad you were with us and got that driver going. He just wouldn't listen."

"Yep, stubborn. A fool too. None of these guys are the brightest candles on the cake. He just didn't get what was going down."

Cecile called in from the other room, "Me too, Skip. Thanks for being there with us and doing what you did; it was scary."

"Good reason to be scared. Political crap can get ugly in this town. I've seen it. Yesterday one of those rickshaw guys was beat to death on the street—ran into the wrong bunch. You'd think they'd get the hint."

"I read that too but never thought we would be in such a place!"

"No one ever thinks this shit will happen, but it's good to remember it does. If it looks weird, or sounds like stuff is getting sticky, get the hell out, and think about it later. I would have felt like crap if either of you'd got hurt." I stopped talking as quick as if I'd stepped on a rattlesnake when I heard the words come out. "I know, I know," I blurted out before anyone could say a word, "you two can take care of yourselves, I know. But crowds around this town aren't good to fool with, and if you see it coming, head the other way, and fast."

"I like what you said about not wanting anything to happen to us," Amber said. "I hope you mean it. There's nothing weird about that; it's nice."

Cecile called in again from the other room. "Don't feel bad, please. It is nice to hear that after so many months here—someone actually saying we matter to them and acting like it, right, Amber?" Cecile walked back into the room and sat at the table looking at me.

"We are fine. Does that work for you?"

Amber stood up and headed for the kitchen. Looking over her shoulder, she said, "I think we should have something to eat and get to work on Skip's shirt."

It was a little house behind a larger one that faced the street. It had three rooms, including a living space with the table and four chairs and a few cushions around. There was a scalloped archway leading into the next room almost as wide as the room itself but with built-in bookshelves on both sides, with spools of thread, ribbons, and folded pattern paper on them. There were piles of clothes and fabric everywhere, folded and stacked on the layers of old rugs that covered the floor. Next to the window was a foot-operated sewing machine. The other side of the arch was the kitchen, with a long counter, cupboards above, and a window in the middle looking out across a courtyard. There was a doorway to the bedroom off the kitchen that had a brocade silk cloth pulled back and tied up. Amber was in the kitchen, and I saw her pull out a small jar and then pull out an Italian coffeemaker.

A basket of fruits, vegetables, and a few eggs hung in the kitchen right behind her, and a large clay water cistern sat on the counter next to her. It looked like a scene from some sexy Italian film.

"Coffee?"

I hadn't had real coffee for I couldn't remember how long.

"If this isn't heaven," I shouted out. "I'd love coffee. Where in hell did you get coffee out here?"

"It comes from Italy. Our friends know we can't live without our coffee." She lifted both eyebrows. "They send it to us each month. You like espresso?"

"Like it? I was raised on it."

"An American, raised on espresso?"

"I'm from northern California. We're not as simple as the rest of the States."

Day turned to evening as we talked. Amber made a great meal. I don't know how she did it, but she had red wine and a cream sauce on meat. These two were more interesting every hour. They'd been collecting out here for over eight months. Cecile was a seamstress and Amber a designer. They both could do either, it sounded like. The clothing business was centered in Italy. With old materials mixed with new designs, they had a hit. They had come out to buy up all the old embroidery and cloth they could find before others got hip and jumped into this market. Their business was centered in Milan, and they had clothes in boutiques in Paris, London, and Amsterdam. Their partners back in Europe were all women too, as far as I could tell. They did ask if I knew anyone in San Francisco with a clothing store, maybe in the Haight-Ashbury or North Beach areas. Exotic dancers around the city loved ethnic-type clothes, but I said no and left it at that.

Evening passed quickly, and it started to get dark. Cecile suggested they get started on the shirt, and Amber lit the kerosene lamps and took my measurements. I told them I didn't need them to make a shirt and that I'd be happy to take them to the market just for the dinner and company, but they insisted. They wanted me to have one of their shirts, and that was that. I asked if I could use the washroom while they worked on the shirt. I didn't want to put a new shirt on a dirty back. They laughed and pointed me out back toward the bathhouse.

I had to go through the bedroom to get out back. There was one large bed in there with multicolored covers and throw pillows. Lots of neatly stacked clothes were set to one side on a box, and next to them was a full-length mirror. I hadn't seen a mirror in months, and one glance made me wish that I hadn't seen this one. The bathroom was in the back in a separate little building. It had running water, a stand-up privy, and a place to wash up. There were soaps and shampoos that all looked like they were from Europe and smelled like it too and scrubbing things—at least I think that's what they were. In the kerosene lamp light, it all looked like a Van Gogh painting. Best of all, it smelled good! It was the nicest bathroom and washroom I'd seen in months.

I scrubbed with various tools and soaps, also the best wash I'd had in months. The pine branch scrubs in the steam baths were fine—with scented oil and all that—but they didn't do the trick like this. This was like a three-star hotel in Lahore. I scraped my teeth with my knife and brushed them with one of the toothbrushes.

When I walked past the mirror on my way back, I took a look. My teeth were almost whitish, but the clothes were still raggedy. When I stepped into the main room, Cecile said, "Try this one," holding out a beautiful raw silk shirt with fine old polished cotton embroidery down the front.

"You just made this?"

"No," Amber said. "We have lots of shirts we are working on all the time. We just tailored one to fit you. We thought this one would look nice."

"We think it's a good look for you," Cecile continued. "It's a very old Afghani front; you can't find these any more. Try it on. See how it fits. "

The cotton shirt front was hand-stitched to a jallaba shirt made of the softest raw silk I had ever felt.

Amber reached over and lifted my old shirt up and off my back. It shocked me a little at first. I felt her breath on my chest as she pulled the shirt up and over my shoulders. She was so close that the heat of her body hit me. As she pulled my shirt off, my stomach flip-flopped like a fish. I hadn't been so close to a woman in months. She stood there looking at me.

"Boy, you are clean," she said, smiling. "You must have taken off ten layers."

"I used those dried-up things you have. I didn't want to dirty a new shirt."

"You clean up very nicely," she said, pushing her fingers through my damp hair.

Feeling a bit awkward and bare, I slipped into the new shirt. It fit like it had been made for me; I suppose it had been.

Amber stood back looking at me. "Just like I said. Turn around."

I turned a full turn as Cecil and Amber both passed in front of my eyes.

"You agree, Cecile?"

"Yes, new pants."

Amber had already gone over to a pile of clothes near the sewing machine and was bringing over a pair of raw silk pajama pants. She handed them to me.

"Try these."

Before I could move toward the bedroom to change, Amber had dropped to her knees and was taking my pants down. I didn't know what to do. I tried to think about the wall and the garden out the window, anything but how I was feeling. I tried talking silently to myself, repeating over and over that fashion was their business; this is how they did it. But the issue wasn't about how they acted. I kept looking across the room thinking and doing my best to keep my mind on something else, anything else. I did everything I knew how, but I had no chance. It all happened so fast that I couldn't do anything. Before I could react, she had my pants down and was asking me to lift my feet.

She looked up. "Step out of these rags and try those."

I looked down at her and then over at Cecile, who was looking where I had hoped no one would. I didn't know just how to act. I looked down at Amber and shrugged my shoulders, trying to smile. She turned her eyes away, which was kind, and smiled. Then she reached up and took the pants out of my hand. She tossed them back on the pile and looked back up into my eyes and said, "It's fine, Skip. It is nice, really."

She took my hand and put it on her cheek. I tried to relax, but it wasn't in the cards. Cecile stepped over and took my other hand. Amber leaned over and gave me a kiss on my leg and stood up. They took my arms and led me into the bedroom.

Amber pulled my new shirt off as Cecile let her dress fall, kicking it out of the way. She stood there looking at me in her velvet skin. She had small breasts the size of champagne glasses, and firm like a Greek statue. She was gorgeous. She moved forward, and I felt the warmth from her body surge over me as she came up against me. Her skin felt like fine silk sliding along mine as we fell back onto the bed. She crawled up and straddled my leg, moving up and down and looking at me with those deep brown eyes. Then she slowly closed them and hummed softly.

Amber pulled her long shirt up and off and looked at me as she dropped her pants and stepped out of them. Shivers ran right up through my loins as I watched. She was as exotic a beauty as I had ever seen. She had full rounded breasts with dark cherry nipples set above a perfect pear-shaped belly on strong hips and long sculpted legs reaching down to fine ankles and feet with skin the color of coffee and cream. Celtic-pattern tattoos ran down the outside of her arms, from the tops of her shoulders to intricately woven patterns around her wrists. There were orange, red, and yellow stars that got smaller as they moved up from her loins and encircled her belly button; above her left breast was a crescent moon, and above the right a sun. More matching patterns ran down her thighs, and as she turned to pull the curtain at the bedroom door, I saw on the small of her back a winged scarab in the same rich colors as the stars on her belly. She was a work of art.

Amber slid down onto the bed across from Cecile and slowly leaned over, kissing me softly on the mouth. Cecile leaned down and kissed her on the neck and Amber snuggled up against us and whispered in a very soft voice, "Relax. It's fine." Cecile kissed me as Amber's soft hands squeezed and her lips wandered the side of my belly. It was a wonderful night, and in the morning we woke up tangled and laughing.

I finally got out of bed, which took real focus, and tried the pants. They fit fine. I hadn't had such a nice set of rags for years. It couldn't have been finer, and we even had coffee!

The market was about five blocks of vendors with piles of stuff strewn down the middle of the street. There was everything from old shoes to fruit bats. You could find ivory, silver, gold, gems, and buckets of everything in between. I had Amber and Cecile walking behind me so close that everyone was clear I was with them. Once that was established, I could let them dig through whatever they wanted. They dug through all kinds of stuff like kids in a candy store. Eventually we hit the far end of the market where the embroidery and clothes were. There weren't any prostitutes down at this end, but there were several opium sellers, so while the women haggled over a trunk full of old embroidery and ivory jewelry, I sat down and had a pipe. It was good clean chandu, opium prepared for smoking in a Chinese pipe, very unusual in Pakistan. Chinese-style smoking is not common anywhere in Pakistan or Islam. The smoke was good, and it relaxed me a bit, and I started to rethink the reality of what my life had been these last few weeks, not adding in yesterday and last night.

I was thinking about how to get a message to Mickey without putting Amber and Cecile on front street. I didn't want to mix them up in any of the crap that had been going down. I figured I'd go back to the room on the off chance he might be there. I could lose any tail that hooked me up in old town if I kept a sharp eye out. I knew how to move around old Peshawar better than most.

The girls finished up at the market just before the sellers started folding up. We loaded baskets of stuff along with a trunk they'd bought into a cab and headed toward their house. We put all the stuff on the floor in the middle of the main room, and Amber and Cecile started to go through it right away, pulling stuff out, setting aside, sorting, and laughing.

"You were right, Skip," Cecile chirped like a songbird. "That was the best market I have ever been to."

Then, holding up a hand with some cloth in it, Amber said, "You see what we got?" She was holding up a roll of old sari ribbon that had been buried deep in the trunk. "Cecile, look at this—it's unbelievable." They kept looking through the stuff, laughing and talking about how they could use it.

"I have to go out for a while," I said softly. Their chatter stopped abruptly.

"Go? Where?" Amber asked.

"I have a friend that I need to see. He'll be wondering just what's up with me by now. I don't want him to think anything happened, anything bad."

"Bad, I hope it hasn't been bad." Cecile said and smiled.

"God no."

"If it was up to us, we wouldn't let you leave—you're doing just fine so far, and we like it!" Amber smiled to let me know she was kidding. "But you need to see your friend. We'll be here." She smiled again and then asked, "Will you be here for dinner?"

"I'll try."

"I hope it's a he, your friend?" Cecile chimed in.

"Yep, we are traveling together right now. I'd introduce you, but it's a bad time now.

"You can bring him for dinner," Amber offered.

"Maybe, but not likely—we just need to talk so he knows I'm OK. You go ahead and eat without me if I'm not here in time. I'll be back tonight." I reached over and kissed Amber softly.

"You're wonderful," I whispered in her ear. She smiled and kissed my chin. I turned and kissed Cecile lightly on the mouth, saying, "I love the way you smell."

"You too," she answered.

I got back to old town mid-afternoon and went up to see if Mickey was at the room. He wasn't, but I could tell he'd been there—and with friends, by the look of things. There were empty pop bottles and half-empty tea cups sitting around, and the smell of hashish hung in the air like spicy mold. *Must have had quite a night,* I thought, *but not as good a one as mine.* I grinned at the thought. I didn't know where to find him. He could be anywhere. I gathered up the stuff I had there. As long as I was in town, and Amber and Cecile were willing, I was staying with them.

I sat down on the bed and looked around. Amber and Cecile were wonderful and all that, but they would head back to Italy at some point, and what would I do? I wondered how long I would be of interest to them. I was out here for the long run and knew that. I didn't want to think about this. Why couldn't I just enjoy it, just take it hour by hour? I could do that, but did I want to?

I needed to see Mickey and see what he was thinking, if anything. I wanted to know if he had any news. I knew he wasn't about to go to Johnny Johnny's, and I wasn't either. I swung my bag over my shoulder and headed to the chai shop on the chance he might be there.

I walked through the door, and before I could turn and walk out, Charles called over.

"Skipo!"

"It's Skip."

"Sorry, friend. Come over and sit down—have a tea."

"I'm looking for Mickey. Have you seen him?"

"Actually, not for a few hours. Sit down; join me."

"You saw him today?" I turned a chair and sat.

"About noon, I think, with a couple Germans—at least the accent sounded German. Friends of yours?"

I looked around to see who else I didn't want to see. "I know lots of people, man. Where's your other half, Lawrence?"

"Should be here soon. Just trotted off to get some cigarettes; can't stand black tobacco."

"Don't let me interrupt you." I spun to get up.

"No, no, don't go. Lawrence would be unhappy if he missed you."

"Well, as much he might, making Lawrence happy is not big on my list at the moment. I don't know what it is with you two, and I'm not sure I want to, but one thing is sure: I am not interested in games. You seem to think I'm someone I'm not, so what is it that you're after? We clean that up and then I'll decide if we are going make each other happy and be friends or something else."

"Well, Tony," he said slowly. "Can I call you Tony?"

"This is bullshit!" I shot out, half for real and half-posturing, kicking myself for not making the real part more convincing. "Call me Tony if it makes you happy, but my name for the record is Skip. You'd better have something good to say or know where I can find Mickey, or this conversation ends."

"Look, I'd hoped this relationship wouldn't have to start the way it did. We're not about trouble, though it might seem so at the moment. You need to listen. Everyone can win here, Tony; believe me. We have absolutely no interest in any other outcome."

"Stop talking in riddles if you want me to listen. I don't have the time or interest in puzzling out your shit. I'm off to see if I can chase Mickey down. See ya."

As I was heading out the door, a hand came down on my shoulder. I turned slowly and deliberately, trying to look tougher than I was. It was Lawrence.

"Hey, Skip, good to see ya."

He had a Marlboro hanging from his mouth, and set on his nose was a pair of $200 Ray-Bans. He reached out a hand. After a pause, I took it with a pasted-on smile.

"You know in old town here, those Ray-Bans of yours could get you dumped in an alley."

He smirked and looked around the room and said, "Nobody around here knows what they're worth."

"Yeah, whatever, that's my point."

"Some grip you got, Skip. You pickax lapis in that Hindu Kush all summer?" He rubbed his hand.

"I play guitar. Thanks for remembering my name. Better than your friend. I appreciate that. Sorry if I hurt your hand."

Charles called over, "Skip there said we could call him Tony if we liked, for the sake of discussion."

"Not shouted across the fucking room, I didn't!"

"Right on, point taken."

"That's a good start," Lawrence said flatly. "So should we get something to eat? I'm starving." He led me back to the table..

"You guys go ahead. I'm not hungry."

I hadn't planned on this, but what was new? In fact I hadn't planned on anything that had happened in the last few weeks. Still, I'd figured this sit-down was coming at some point after the "See ya, Tony" bit the last time I'd seen them. I'd still wanted to choose when, but there was no chance of that now. I wondered about Mickey. Charles wouldn't have said he'd seen him unless he had; there was no reason to. It was me they wanted to talk with.

"OK, let's talk," I said. I shifted in my seat, leaning forward. "Suppose I did know this Tony and had a way to him. Why it is two field workers in sexual dysfunction got an interest?"

Charles started to laugh, and Lawrence shook his head, looking at me with a grin that reached ear to ear. "We really had you going on that one, didn't we?"

"You got Twitch so sick of your drool, he was ready to jump out the car and walk. Me, I don't like walking all that much. So let's cut to the chase or at least the starting line—where's Twitch, number one, and two, who are you, and yeah, third, what's it you want?"

In a bad Texas drawl or something akin to it, Lawrence said, "Whoa, Nelly, hold on there. Charles and I need to know a couple of things before we go sharing here."

That was enough. I didn't have the time for or interest in this crap. I stood up. "Cut the bullshit. Is it genetic with you Aussies to want to be John Wayne? Get real if you want me to stay in this conversation. So what do you two know about Mickey? Where is he? I'm walking if I don't hear something that makes sense."

Charles cut in. "Like I said, I saw him earlier with two Germans. When they came in, I invited them over for a tea just like I did you. The Germans were loaded on something—morphine, I think, or it looked that way—and Mickey's eye was twitching so bad, he had a rag tied over it, and he wasn't very understandable, high on acid maybe; I couldn't tell for sure. He was looking for you though—had some idea we might have done something with you. Strange.

"He seemed to get more and more irritated each time I told him that I hadn't seen you, which I hadn't, as you know, but he continued to ask anyway, at least four times, as I recall. I don't think he believed me. Well, Lawrence came in about then, and the Germans with him were starting to nod off at the table. Lawrence doesn't deal well with that kind of stuff, something in his history, I think." He glanced over at Lawrence, who nodded back.

"So Lawrence picked up the two Germans by their arms and walked them out to the street. Like I said, he doesn't like to be around junkies. Mickey, well, he got up and followed after them, saying something I couldn't quite understand, except some bit about drilling holes in my 'bloody knees caps' if I'd done anything with you. That was the last I saw of him. You know any more than that, Lawrence?"

"Nope, not really; I was instructing the Germans about not coming back in the restaurant—I really can't stand slobbering morph heads—and Mickey came out just then and grabbed me by the arm, saying something about Johnny Johnny and that we better have you back or let you go, or some absurd rattle. He was not real clear. Pretty high, I think."

"You see where he went?"

"Down the street to Johnny Johnny's, but the two Germans didn't go in—just sat down on the curb and puked, as I recall. I couldn't really tell. They didn't go in, at least while I watched. OK, our turn now."

"Turn for what?"

"A question. Have you made a deal with Johnny to do business in Switzerland?"

This was thick. Who were these guys? "Hell, I thought you were going to ask a hard one. That's easy—nope, I don't fix watches. Gave it up for Ramadan. And I don't know who you think I am, Tony, Skip or Santa Claus, but I don't work for sleazy types, and if Johnny doesn't add up to that in your book, you guys are missing numbers."

As they looked at each other, I could see another ball was going to drop. I jumped in right then, figuring it was a good a time to grab the tiller. "So go ahead and ask me whatever it is you are itching to. It's the only way you'll get an answer, even if you don't like what it is. And my guess is you won't."

Lawrence looked over with a very serious face. "You aren't in a deal with Johnny Johnny?"

"I told you I wasn't, and unlike the rest of the table seems here, I'm mostly honest. Johnny may think I give a shit about his line of bull, but he's not too bright, and we all know that, leastwise you should if you've actually ever met him. Take my word—I got no interest."

"We have," Charles said plainly.

"Interest in what? I told him I'd look to see if someone might want to take him up on his offer as a way to get the hell out of there so I didn't have to listen to anymore of his sorry-ass bullshit. I got no interest. Zero. And for your information, I know this guy Tony has zilch interest in anything a sleaze ball like Johnny Johnny can offer. And myself, I'm not in the game and never have been. So it's my turn now."

"OK, ask."

"Who are you two, and what is it you want with Tony, assuming I can get to him?"

Charles looked at Lawrence with a questioning glance and a half smile.

"Look, I'm going to skate right out of here and find Mickey if you two keep doing this mother-may-I crap. Look at me and talk to me, or I'm gone." I responded.

"You can't work with Johnny," Charles started out, and I pulled my chair back to get up and leave. "No, wait—let me finish," he continued. "You can't because we want you to work for us. We are what you might call associated contractors with an international organization. What we do, among other things, is locate individuals who we believe have special skills and abilities we need. These can vary given time or place, depending on situations. We want to find Tony Rice. We were led to believe by several sources, which we trust, that you are him. We still believe that but are willing to play this stupid game a few more minutes if you wish. If you want to know what it is we are offering, then let's get to it and be straight about it."

"Is there a 'but if you don't' part to this offer?"

"Well, Tony—it's OK to call you Tony, right? Just what do you think—do you really need an answer to that? We should try to trust each other here and figure out how to be friends, or at least friendly. That question doesn't sound trusting or friendly to me. It really is a good thing we're about."

"OK, I'm listening, but there'd better be something good."

Lawrence spoke. "How does a new passport sound, a clean one, from the United Kingdom, that gives you tidy accesses world round and out here in the East—no visas needed or time limits? Plus all the sterling you need to do the work we hire you to do and then a substantial purse above that? And if all goes well, a clean slate back in the States."

"What do you mean, 'clean'? And how do you two have any pull in the States or know shit about my 'slate'?"

"You'll have to just trust that we do. We're honest mostly too, Tony. Look, you'll know all that you need to about us soon enough. We need you to agree to work for us. Can we get that far yet?"

"Shit no, what job do you expect me to do? I may not be who you need for whatever this job is, even if I am who you think I am. I won't commit to something I got no chance at succeeding with. If I see a chance of doing whatever it is you need and, most important, see a chance of coming out of it so I can use what you're paying, you may get me closer to a yes. But for all I know, you might want me to fly, and I never learned. Look, I need more. I can't give you a nod without some idea of what I'm being asked to do."

They both looked very different now, no longer like bumbling field workers. I hated to admit it, but I'd gotten myself in now. If I got up to walk, who knew what Lawrence might do. He was sitting right next to me. We both knew more about each other than enemies should know at this point.

Well, you really blew it, I thought to myself. There was no walking now. I had to find a way to move through and come out on the other side. What I did have that might work in my favor was that they didn't know I wasn't the same person I'd been when I used the name Tony—or at least I didn't think they knew. My past felt like ancient history to me now. My life had changed so much. I wasn't the same. Who I'd been was all but gone now. I still knew how to act out if I needed to, but I didn't own it anymore; it was all a game now. There was real power in getting that, in understanding that piece of who I'd become. Somewhere along the way, it had just kicked in.

"OK, I'll work for your, what, bosses, if it works for me too, as long as we all remember that I may not be the person you want, and if I can't do the work, we part friends, and I don't see you again, and you keep your passport and all. I'm not the same guy I was four years ago, but I still have the chops. So here's the deal: if I take the job, when my work gets done, you and your friends give me whatever it is I want."

"They said he'd do this," Charles said to Lawrence.

I didn't like the feeling at the table now. I scoped all the exits and visualized the layout of the back room. If I could get there before I got coldcocked, I had a chance. These two wouldn't get any help in the back, and with luck I might. They might even risk getting their throats cut back there. I was on the edge of my chair ready to jet when Lawrence grabbed my arm and looked me dead in the eyes.

"We offer what we said. We aren't offering anything more. We can't. If there's more bartering to be done, it's after the agreement that you'll take the job. You will just have to hope that there is room there." His grip was solid.

"OK," I said, "it's a deal. Do you tell me now what you want me to do, or does that come after you chain me up someplace?"

"You don't catch up quickly, do you?" Charles looked over. "Tony, we really want to work together with you. Our people thought they gave us plenty to offer for you to come over. Were they wrong? Knowing what's to know about your past and all, I don't think so. Is there no room to negotiate? I can't say, I don't know—not our job. What I do know is, if you're interested, there could be long-range relationships in this for you. I can't offer you more than that and what's approved. Our job's to get you to meet with our people for what we offer. The rest of the conversation, you have with them. So if you decide to bolt out the back here, I can't say how that will affect our relationship, truthfully, but I'm certain it will.

"I won't make this offer in this way again, you can be sure. What I can say is that there are no chains involved other than ones you drag with you. Like I said, we can make some of those go away, and will, if we come to an agreement. That is sure. Are you with us, or are you heading to the back room where you know we won't follow?"

"OK, I'm with you; you have my word. And if you know anything about me, you know that's good."

"That is quite good enough for us, 'Skip.'"

I walked along the back roads in old town thinking about all that had happened in the last few days. I needed to find Mickey and let him know. I had no idea what the future held, but I was sure I had to do it alone, at least for a while. I'd agreed to meet with Lawrence the following afternoon, and I needed to see the girls before that too. I had no idea if I would be around after noon tomorrow.

I wanted to let Cecile and Amber know that I was going to be gone soon and that it wasn't about them. If I drew good cards in this one and got through whatever it was and back, I still might be able to spend more time with them. I liked that idea. But I was now looking down a road not knowing where it would take me or if it would point back this way, at least anytime soon.

I stepped up over a mound of dirt and trash that blocked the alley and out onto the main street and headed toward the hotel, hoping I'd find Mickey there. I needed to tell him I was going. I knew if he'd gone to Johnny's, it would have been just to see if I had been there. I had to tell him what had happened. I knew he'd never believe anything Charles or Lawrence told him. I had to find him.

I got to the hotel and went up to the room. There he was, sitting cross-legged on the bed, taking a deep pull on a hand pipe full of hashish.

He looked up and saw me and exhaled a huge plume of smoke. He coughed and then grinned. "Well, fancy seeing you, mate. Where the hell you been?"

"I hooked up with a couple women."

"Go away, a couple? Way-laid were you. And nice rags too, mate." He smiled.

"They make clothes. Look, I talked to Charles and Lawrence."

"Shit, mate, they bloody got to you—I knew it!" He sat up straight and looked at me like I was dying from some disease.

"Bugger all, I seen them assholes this morning, and they said they hadn't seen you, bloody, lyin' sons-a- ..."

"Nah, that's right, man. I ran into them after you left the chai shop. I was looking for you."

"I was down to see Johnny to introduce him to a couple of German blokes looking for gear. Thought it might settle the water a bit. We stopped at the chai shop, and those two were there."

"I heard Lawrence didn't take to your friends much."

Mickey chuckled. "Yeah, they'd been in the cooker right before we met up. Morph heads the both, but OK, just Germans."

"Yeah, look, Mickey. I had to make a deal with Charles and Lawrence today. I'm going to leave for a while—don't know just when right now, but my guess is soon. That's how clear it all is. I'm not sure just when I'll be getting back. I may be around town for a bit—I just don't know—but I'll be gone at some point, and I can't tell you where. Would if I knew, but I don't."

"They bloody got to you. Bugger all, mate, we should never have took that ride with those slogs. I knew it. And you were spot on about Johnny Johnny; he is a worm. He told me you'd been booked up by someone. This shit's all hooked up like bananas on the arm. The good news is that Johnny seemed OK with the customers. They were looking for a package deal. Just an introduction and I was out of there with a fistful of German marks, mate."

"Be careful, man. That guy's a real sleaze. You were right—Lawrence and Charles know him or know of him. They thought I'd made the Switzerland deal. Don't know how they got wind of any of that conversation, but it wasn't a little bird that told 'em, that's sure. Anyway, the deal I made was to do some work for them and get some stuff cleaned up. Couldn't say no to that, and I don't think if I tried, it would have flown. It sounds like they want me someplace I can go and they can't. But I can tell you for sure it's got nothing to do with sexual practices of inbred villagers!"

He laughed and winked his bad eye. "Look, mate, be careful. I don't bloody well claim to know what they expect from you, but it's sure to be dicey. I had a few words with Johnny about his go-around with you—not willing to manage a load an' all. He tossed it off like it was nothing—said you were 'booked up.' That means someone got to him, someone in a bigger pond than his. He's a team player, so it's sure to be big dogs putting him off. That can mean serious shit, mate."

"They all know about each other for sure; I got that much from Lawrence. Didn't seem like they thought much of Johnny—just another buffalo fart from what I could tell. They work out of some other camp for sure. The offer tasted British intelligence, like you said, or could be contract work for Interpol—can't tell. One thing's for sure: you don't want to be anywhere around it. If I had a choice, I'd be dust in the wind right now. I'm moving over to the cant tonight, man, and that may be the last we see of each other for a bit. But it's not something I can change."

"Hey, mate, I might be helpful. I got tricks too."

"I know, man, but I'm doing this to get crap off my back, not to put it on yours. Believe me, you don't want to get hooked into this deal. It's bad to be traced down out here. That takes money, time, and people. I'm not worth that, so there has to be some catch, and that freaks me. I have to go alone, but I'll be back, I hope. I think, anyway. I'll meet you in Goa—in Margao—and we'll split a bottle of fenny and chat up all those French hippie chicks."

Mickey looked at me. "You remember that kabob meat I had the night we met?"

"Yeah," I answered.

"I think it was old horse. I just didn't want to say—thought it might put you off." He smiled. "You looked so bloody hungry and cold, mate, I figured sharing would make it taste like kid goat."

I couldn't help but laugh. I'd figured it was dog or old billy goat.

"It was good that night, mate." He smiled again. "Good stories worth a bit of horse meat. I've known crazies, outlaws on these roads, but you're the first had done wild-ass things in the Kush, mate." His eye started twitching fast. "Shit, this bloody thing will get me killed some day." He started rubbing his eye until tears were dripping from it.

"You OK, man? Can I get you some water to wash that thing out or something?"

"It's fine, mate, just a bother. So we meet up in India. Got any idea when to expect your bloody person in Margao?"

I lay back smoking opium while all the stuff that had happened in the last few days rolled around in my head. I couldn't decide just how much to tell Amber and Cecile. The last thing I wanted was to get them mixed up in this shit. It had been so good with them that I didn't want to cut their waves. I might be back sooner rather than later.

I flagged a rickshaw and headed to their place. I kept thinking about just what to let them know. I didn't want to get them hooked up in any of this. I knew it was a long shot that I'd get back before they left town but I wasn't going to discount the possibility. The rickshaw pulled up, and I stepped out and found myself stuck there like a fence post. What was I going to tell them? Hell, I shouldn't go in—I should just turn around and leave and let last night be what it was. I stood there like a rock. I felt like a goose with its legs frozen in a pond, my thoughts swirling round like a flock of pigeons just out of the coop.

"Pay, mister, pay." The rickshaw driver reached out, rubbing his thumb and fingers. "Money, yeah."

I gave him a ten rupee note, twice the fare, and sent him off.

I had to tell Cecile and Amber why I was leaving; I couldn't just walk away without telling them something. Thoughts were pouring through my head, but none of them were helping me much. Finally I turned, walked into the courtyard, stepped up to the door, took a deep breath, and walked in.

"Amber?"

"Skip, is that you?" Cecile called from the bedroom.

"Yep. I need to talk to you two."

Just then, Amber walked up behind me with a basket of fresh vegetables and some bundles wrapped in newspapers. She set her basket down in the doorway and pulled me over for a kiss.

"You don't get it all!" Cecile said as she came up and kissed my neck.

"Nice to see you two, too," I said, stepping back and looking at them both.

"I need to tell you something." I could see their smiles start to fade.

"You're leaving?" Amber said flatly.

"Is that true?" Cecile asked.

I didn't know what to say. It was true, but it wasn't true. I had to do whatever I was told. I didn't have a choice anymore. But I wasn't sure I was leaving—at least I was hoping I wouldn't need to. But in the back of my mind, I was sure it was going to be part of the deal. It was confusing. I had no words ready; all I had planned to say had somehow blown out the side of my rickshaw on the way over.

"No, I'm not leaving. I just have to go do some stuff." That was the truth, in a way. I didn't know how else to answer. I turned away and shook my head. "No, that's not what I mean to say. I do need to go away for a while, but I'm not sure when, and it has nothing to do with wanting to leave you two—that's what I mean. Does that make sense?"

Amber sat down, her long shirt pulled up over her knees, and looked me straight in the eyes. Cecile sat down at the other end of the table and leaned back in her chair. I could tell this was going to be hard.

"OK," she said. "We're here; tell us."

I wasn't sure just how to start. "We don't know a whole hell of a lot about each other. You really don't know about me. My life right now is not all mine as much as I wish it were. I really want to be here with you both, but I can't make a decision like that right now. You two happened in the middle of some crazy shit. If I'd known I was going to run into you, I'd done the last few months differently. Today I found out I need to pay some debts, and I have to do it now."

"We can pay you for your help with our business—pretty well—if you need it."

"No, Cecile, it's not money. I know how to get that. I have to head out of town for a while at some point; I'm not sure when. Lots happened today. I thought about not coming back, but I want you both to know I don't walk on people I like, and I really like you two. I wish things were different, and I could stay, if that's what you wanted."

I wasn't sure what I was saying now. I heard that last line, but when the words hit my ears, I didn't know how I'd let them get out my mouth. I sat there gun-shy, saying nothing and not knowing what might come out. Amber was the first to speak.

"Skip, we are as confused as you sound at this point, I guess. First, was last night all you needed?"

"No, last night was not all I needed or want. I don't want to leave, believe me. I really don't, and I don't want to leave here tonight, but I will if you want me to." I looked at her and Cecile.

Cecile spoke first. "First, we don't want you to leave, right?" She looked over to Amber.

Amber looked back and nodded in agreement.

"I'm not interested in leaving, but I don't have a choice. At some point I'll be gone at least for a while. I don't know when, but soon is my guess. My friend—remember I told you about him? I just told him the same thing. The bottom line is there's a job I said I would do to pay some debts that I can't hold back any longer. I don't know when or what I'm going to be doing. It may be a week or may be tomorrow—I don't know. And how long it will take, I got no idea. If you two want, I'll be history in five minutes. Just ask."

Amber had been looking at me all this time, with an expression I couldn't quite figure. She turned to Cecile.

"Do you believe this guy? Comes in off the street—for all we know some white slave trader—spends one night with us, and then wants to know if we will wait for him?" She looked at me blankly.

They looked at each other for a long moment, and then Amber turned back to me, with a slight twinkle in here eye. "We might be interested in waiting, depending on what that means and how long."

Cecile spoke up. "Just so you know, this is not how we do things. We're very happy with each other and have been for a long time. These last two days have been more of what we want in our life, so that's good. We talked about you while you were gone, and we both felt that you might have to leave. We could tell something was up in your life."

Amber joined in. "We decided it was such a new thing that we could just consider it on hold. What we didn't know was how soon it was going to happen. "

"If I could change things, I wouldn't be leaving. I'm not sure just how soon I'll have to go, but likely soon."

"Why don't you know?"

"No one told me, so I just don't know. Maybe tomorrow. What I know is that I will be gone at some point. For how long, I'll tell you when I know. That's how it's going down."

I rolled over and the sun was shining through the window, a morning breeze was moving the curtains. Amber and Cecile lay there folded together like marble halva. I slid out of bed, went to the kitchen, and put water in the teapot and lit the kerosene stove under it. I turned to head back to bed and Amber was standing in front of me, sleepy-eyed.

"I thought you might be leaving."

"No, just heating up water. I wouldn't leave without telling you."

I kissed her as she put her hands around my waist and molded into my body like a warm sea. My heart felt like it was opening to the sky. I could see in it an image of Amber, Cecile, and me all seated together in a lotus flower deep inside my chest. I shook my head and laughed as the image faded. "You are the best."

Amber and I walked into the room where Cecile was lying on the bed smiling.

"I like your heart," she said. "And I particularly like that I am in it."

I lay down next to her and felt her skin, like Amber's, as a warm sea cascading over me. We lay there for a while just enjoying being with each other. The pot started whistling, and Amber got up and headed into the kitchen to make the tea.

"Skip, would you rather have coffee?" she called through the curtain.

"If it's easy, sure, but tea is fine too."

I leaned over and kissed Cecile's belly and rolled out of bed.

"Are my old clothes still around?"

She looked at me with a puzzled look.

"I don't want to damage that beautiful shirt and pants you made me."

"Why do you want those old rags? What do you expect to be doing, fixing the rickshaw?"

"I may be going places where I don't want to stand out. Old clothes help."

If I was going anyplace in or near tribal zones, I needed local clothes. It was a good bet clothes would be as important a part of how I managed as anything. I didn't know how Cecile would react to that detail, so I didn't tell her. She didn't even blink but called into the next room, "We need to put together clothes for Skip that will keep him from standing out."

Amber called back in French. I couldn't understand it.

Cecile started to laugh and looked at me with a playful smile.

"She said she likes you when you stand out. I do too, by the way."

She giggled, and they called back and forth in French and Urdu or something. Finally, Amber came in with a coffee for each of us.

"OK," she said.

"You need people's clothes, like the ones you wore when we met you? Those are long gone, sorry. Burnt up, I hope. We tried to wash them, but they fell part." They both laughed.

"So should these new clothes for you look 'old' or just typical?"

"Either or both would be good," I said.

"How soon do you need them?" she asked.

"Soon. I have to meet with folks today."

"I think we can do this for you with what we have here. Not falling apart, but worn. If you need them more worn, we can do that, but we need an hour to do it."

"What you have will do fine as long as they're tribal clothes."

They fitted me out, and when they were done, I could have gone anywhere in the territories and been taken for tribal.

"Does this mean we won't be seeing you for a while?" Amber asked in a soft voice.

"I'm not sure. If I don't get back tonight, it's because I can't. If that happens, and it might, I'll try to send someone over to let you know as much as I can."

"OK," she answered.

Cecile reached up, turned my face, and kissed me on the mouth. "Be careful!"

I was scheduled to meet Charles at a government-run inn, a guest house, they called it. It was in an older section of the cant. You found them all over Pakistan and India, simple places but clean. They were set up for government officials' bureaucrats, for when they traveled around the country. The one I was heading for was a mile or two from Amber and Cecile's.

I needed time to think, so I headed off on foot. I felt uncomfortable in the new clothes. The pants were looser than I was used to, but they were tribal and looked worn. Pakistanis in suits and ties didn't take a second glance. That felt good. The clothes were working. I was checking out my reflection in a window along the way, and a merchant came out babbling at me in some dialect I didn't recognize. I smiled, hooked my thumbs under my ears, looked up toward the sky, and cried out, "Malang, malang," which loosely translated means "Crazy for god, crazy for god," a trick I'd learned from Twitch. I turned and kept on walking.

It took me about an hour to walk to the guest house. I wasn't in a hurry. I stood out front for a good ten minutes. If I went in, it was a done deal. I stepped up to the door and knocked; nothing happened. I stood there for a few minutes and then knocked again, this time harder and longer. I wasn't interested in hanging out in this part of town dressed like I was. I had no idea what the clothes said about my politics, and that made me uneasy. I certainly wasn't dressed like any government official. And standing there, pounding on the door, I stood out like a fire on a moonless night. Just then, Charles stuck his head out of a door two rooms down.

"Hey, Tony, over here."

The room was empty except for three men sitting at a table and Charles.

All three men tracked me with their eyes as I scanned the room to see if there were any others, but I didn't see anyone. There was a large manila envelope on the table and nothing else.

These guys were all Westerners, judging by their clothes. And there was no tea on the table, which was a sure sign. There was nothing else in the room—just three empty chairs at the table and a woodstove in the corner and no bed.

"Sit down," the man seated in the middle said. I looked at him, scanned the room once more, stepped up, and sat down. Charles sat down next to me.

"We're happy you agreed to work for us, Tony. This will make both your life and ours much better, I assure you. I'm sure you're waiting to know what it is we want you to do, and I'll get there, but first the limits. Lines are drawn in this negotiation."

He reached over, picked up the envelope, and poured its contents on the table. He watched me, reading my reaction. I stared right back into his eyes as the contents fell on the table.

After a long minute, I looked down at the table. There was a large packet of Pakistani and Indian rupees banded on top of what looked like a quarter-inch pile of hundred dollar bills. Next to the money was a United Kingdom passport.

He watched me look at the pile on the table and then shook the envelope as if to say that was all there was. I looked back at him and smiled and then in turn looked at the other two. I wasn't up for this kind of bullshit. But I was in the room now and with new players. Looking around, I could see I'd only get out if I were let out. I had to play the hand; I had no choice. Then the man with the envelope fumbled in his pocket and pulled out a folded set of papers.

"Oh yes, and this, these papers are from the federal courthouse in San Francisco, signed by the honorable Judge Lynch. Papers that acquit you of all charges related to activities … activities that we need not discuss since you didn't have anything to do with them? Maybe? These papers are all signed. All that's needed is my John Hancock, and I file them with the right people."

"And just when does that happen?"

"As soon as you bring back a report and we log it."

"I'm supposed to trust you?"

"You can trust us, Tony. You'll find we are good to our word. The concern is, are you?"

I looked in his eyes. I wanted to feel OK about all this, at least sort of OK, not that it mattered much. I had to swim or sink at this point; there wasn't a choice I could see.

"Look, I haven't got any idea what you want from me. But you keep trying to get me to say yes, to what? I've said yes to as much as I can. I'm here. I can't say yes to anything more if I don't know what it is. That's honest. If I say I'll do something, I'll do it if I can, but there are things I can't do and things I won't. I won't say I'll do something if I don't know what it is. I don't work that way; besides, I may not be able to do it or be willing to when you finally tell me what it is. How in the hell do I know?

"So until I know what it is you want, I'm not saying yes to anything more than I have already. I said that I would meet with you and work for you if the job you want done I can do. I would really like to take what's on the table. We all know that. I'm hearing, and I'm listening, but I'm not saying yes until I know what you want. And I still may say no."

The man who'd been talking looked over at Charles and said, "You're right—he's the one we need." He turned toward me once again.

"OK, Tony, here's the deal. We represent a team of independent contractors who gather information for various clients. In order to do that, we need people who can move around and listen and spot things without drawing attention. What works best for us is having someone from the West who we can relate with in that way but who also feels at home in whatever context we put them. If we find them, we hire them. You are the person we tagged for a particular job we need done.

We need you to gather information for us. That's it. You don't have any other responsibility—just go, look, and report on what you find out. That's the job, and for that you get everything on the table."

I was getting a picture now and liked what they were offering to a point, but I still wasn't quite at ease. They hadn't said where it was they wanted me to go, and that was a big piece left out. I still didn't know just who these guys were and if they could actually do what they said they could. The money looked real enough, but I hadn't looked at the passport. I reached out and picked it up. Sure enough, there I was, smiling on the front page. It looked like the real thing.

The guy across from me on the left raised his eyebrows, smiled, and then said, "Yep, the real thing. Not a bad picture, what? It was hard to get that one. It would have been easier to take a picture today, but time wouldn't allow. It's good though, don't you think?"

I liked this guy—something in his tone and eyes, nothing hidden. I had a good feeling about him. I smiled. "Yep, not a bad picture, but I don't remember ever having it taken."

"You shouldn't," he said, smiling. "I took it over a year ago, maybe two by now? You've been out of sight for a while, Tony." Then he went on. "The stamps are there to make it look like you've moved around out here. I find it keeps questions down. It might be good to check out the dates and places, but nobody's ever checked one of my passports as far as I know. Even if they did, it is all legit—that book's been to all of the places it says it has and on the dates it says; it just had a different person taking it on tour." He smiled again, looking very pleased with his work.

"You likely won't need to use it anytime soon, but it's good worldwide, and with a UK passport, I'm sure you know, you don't need visas out here. It signals you belong here—at least between Turkey and Hong Kong. And there are plenty of clean pages. Oh yes, it's a lifetime passport, no expiration; that's a bonus, one of the benefits of the United Kingdom. But don't lose it—it might be tough to get a counsel to replace it. I don't know it's ever been tried."

"So just how long do I work for you to get all this?"

"Good question," the guy who had emptied the envelope on the table answered. "We give you the money and the passport after we make our deal today. The paperwork, we fill out and file when we're satisfied that the work has been done to the best of your ability."

"How do you know my ability or that the work I'll do is done? Seems to me you can't do it for yourself, or you wouldn't be talking to me. So how will you know?"

"It all has to do with how well it sinks with other information we already have. You are not the only person we have on the job for this piece. There are other parts we wish to know about. If your information tracks, we'll know it. That's our job. We look at a big picture, see the information mix, and see if it tracks and raises the right questions—we'll know. We aren't doing this just to help you out; we know enough to tell if you're playing us. And believe me, you don't want to do that. If you plan to, it would be much wiser for you to just walk right now. We will give you two hours."

He looked at me in a way I hadn't seen yet. It was nice to have the cards out and in sight, to get all that nicey-nice stuff put where it belonged, off the table. I had a clear picture now, and I could work with that.

"Just two hours! But I thought we were friends?"

"If you walk or play us, Tony, we don't send off papers, and you watch your back forever." He waved the papers like a fan over the table.

"These papers are your friends; it would be a shame if you left them behind."

"Who is it you work for? How do I know you can do what you say you can and this is not just a scam to work me?"

The guy who had done the passport work and taken my picture wrinkled his brow and pulled out four identification documents: a U.S. Air Force ID, an Interpol team investigation badge and ID, a Secret Service firearms division ID and badge, and a U.S. Army intelligence ID paper in leather flip case. All of them had his picture with various names.

"They're all good, though I don't expect you'd know what they actually looked like, until now. But believe me—they are all good and will get you through the doors. The bottom line is that you need to trust us, or at least trust that we can do what we say we can. We can tell you that we are whoever we want and give you all the evidence to back it up. As you see, we are whoever we need to be. Right now, we need to be able to do all we say we can for you, and we can. That's who we are; trust it."

What could I say? I sat back in my chair and shook my head.

"OK, I guess we really do have to be friends. Still, this doesn't sound all that good to me. I don't know what it is you expect me to bring back, or from where. How do I know after I finish whatever it is that you won't just say it's not good enough?"

The man in the middle sat back in his chair, his body language reflecting mine. "Another good question and here's the answer. We will tell you just what it is we need, and if you get that for us, then the job is done. If we want you to do anything else, then we will renegotiate. What we offer you here today is for this job alone. You could do worse than working for us, believe me, Tony. We do have things that no one else can offer. Think about that. We are trustworthy, and if you prove to be, this could be a very good relationship and in the end even a kind of friendship. We don't make this offer to very many folks, and when we do, we make it once. We don't have time to waste. So are you in or not?"

I wasn't comfortable with all I'd heard, I didn't have much choice. I still had no idea what information they wanted; hell, I didn't know if I could do the job. I hated this kind of situation, but the only way over the wall was to take the rope these guys had thrown. In the end it was going to be up to me to make it work. I'd better grab hold and climb. Hell, in the end it was better hanging on their rope there than left on the ground with some hungry wolves.

"OK, I'll do the one job for you. You file the papers, and then we'll see." I reached across the table and offered my hand, and we shook.

"In one hour, Charles will meet you at the chai shop where they talked to you yesterday with all the information and tools you will need. We'll talk again when you get back, Tony. You can trust us to file the papers if you do the work. Good luck." Then all three stood up and walked out of the room, leaving the money, passport, Charles, and me behind.

"That's all yours," Charles said, pointing at the table. "Pick it up and tuck it away."

I grabbed the money and passport, slipped them into my pouch, and headed out. I turned toward Charles. "See you in an hour."

"See ya."

I headed to the street and caught a rickshaw. My mind felt like it had gone over a waterfall and was swirling around in foam and rocks at the bottom. I still didn't have any idea what I was going to be doing other than gathering information, and that could be anything. What did these guys want, and just who were they? Who did they work for? I was no closer to that than before I'd met them. A team of operatives, right! I was sure that they weren't freelance; I'd known too many of those types. These guys didn't fit the shoe. Besides, no freelancers could do what they said they could or come up with that much ID. They had to be government somehow and at least some ties to the U.S. government or military, I'd bet. Not that any of that mattered at this point.

I couldn't turn back, even if I wanted to. They knew where I was, and I'd said yes. Who, I wondered, was the guy who hadn't spoken? He never said a word—just sat there. A bodyguard maybe? The bottom line was, could I trust them to come through? I just didn't know. I'd have to wait and see and live through whatever came between.

I didn't have anything to do now but wait for Charles, so I figured I'd go to the chai shop and have a tea and some food. I had a fistful of rupees thanks to my new employers and an empty stomach to help burn them up. When I got there, I went straight to the back room where I felt more relaxed. I sat up on a table in a low corner of the room, where I could see everyone with my back to the wall. No one gave me a second glance. I ordered chai and a plate of rice and boiled mutton. I poured the steaming tea into the saucer and watched the misty dance rise up. Tribal folk didn't bother with cups; the tea went straight from the pot to the saucer where it could cool down a bit quicker. I smiled thinking about the tight-ass Brits sitting around with their cups, saucers, and biscuits as I enjoyed my chai.

The food came, and I dug in. I hadn't had a full mutton and rice plate for a while. I usually ate kabobs and naan because they were cheap and everywhere. I never had lots of extra cash. When I did, it seems like it always got spent on hashish. The first mouthful sent me leaning back, my eyes closed in ecstasy. Fingering my pouch and all those rupees, I sat up and called to the boy for another piece of meat. My life had taken such sharp turns in the last few days, and my mind still hadn't caught up with it all. It was going to be different traveling without Mickey; I'd gotten used to sharing the world with him. But now when I thought about sharing my days with anybody, it was Cecile and Amber, not Twitch.

Well, times change. I wasn't going to be sharing my days with anyone. I was going to be like I used to be, responsible to no one but me. The only difference was that now life mattered; it was important for some reason. I didn't understand exactly why it had come around that way. It wasn't just the girls—I knew that—but they had certainly helped. I'd been feeling things shift for months now. But those days in the Khyber and then the time with the girls had been the trigger. I was clearer now.

I sat there sipping my tea remembering all the times Mickey and I had shared. I set down the saucer and started cutting down a matchstick to pick my teeth, my thoughts wandering. Then the next thing I knew, I was looking at a drawn knife being pulled along a log. Then the log turned to a lintel over a low door. Hell, it was happening again. I looked across the room, and there was Baba bent over his fire, sticking short twigs in the flames.

"You're back," I heard him say.

Like before, I understood him even though he spoke that language of his; it was like being in a dream but I knew I wasn't sleeping. I looked around, and there I was, right there in his little home again.

"Come and sit."

I felt myself stepping over the bed and sitting down. "What's going on, Baba?"

He didn't say anything—just kept putting sticks on the fire.

"Baba, what is this? Am I really here, or is this me slipping off the bench?"

"You are here, and you are not. You know many don't or would not care. That's why you keep coming, I think.

"I keep coming? What do you mean, this is up to me?"

"There are veils some never see but seems you never miss. Some lean this way now and then, but you push. You decided to step across."

"I just wanted to pick my teeth."

"Chai?"

"No, I want to know what the hell is going on. Is this some acid flashback or what?"

Then in a wink, I was sitting in the rafters looking down, watching myself on the bed while Baba stoked his fire, his house no more than a mud pouch and me like a raven looking down at the two of us talking there. I heard me say to Baba: "I'm sitting in a chai shop in Peshawar."

Baba turned and looked at me sitting on the bed and then turned his eyes up and smiled. Then just as quick as I'd found myself looking down on us, I was back on the bed looking in his eyes. I could see deep into his eyes, like shadows rolling back into an evening forest, and then the room faded. I thought I must be dreaming, in the chai shop, have fallen asleep and was waking up.

"You're not sleeping," I heard Baba say. "You're searching." Just then I was back up in the ceiling beams, looking down again.

Baba looked up. "I could tell you what you want to know, but I might be wrong. I can tell you that you have a long way to go. Life is growing. Watch the ravens. Listen to me—watch the ravens and keep your heart free. Are you sure you don't want any chai?"

"No, not really. I'd rather know what's going on."

"Come, have some chai."

I reached down and saw my arm and hand in rich pastel colors breaking through a crystalline Van Gogh–like air. I reached to take the cup and saucer. My arm and hand stretched out shaking like a plucked guitar string to grasp it.

"Skip, wake up." Words crept into my ears like small flies buzzing louder and louder. I opened my eyes and sat up. Charles was standing over me, pulling on my arm.

"Skip, come on out of here, out front. I don't feel easy back here. I've been waiting for you for a half hour. I thought you got hung up somewhere."

"It's OK here. Don't worry—no one is going bite you." I sat up, trying to get my mind back to where I was as thoughts of Baba and his little house and all he'd said kept running through my mind.

Charles leaned over and looked me straight in the face. "I don't feel good about talking back here."

Still half-asleep, I looked around and saw where I was, and my mind slipped into place like a river otter down a muddy slope into the cold water.

"Look, Tony, I have a job to do, and I do it the best way I know how. This is not the place I want to be talking about what we need to talk about, trust me."

"OK, OK, I got it." I slipped off the table, and we went out to the front. He had the table right next to the window. This guy had a strange sense of privacy. But it was his show. We sat down as he looked around the room and out the window and then back at me. "Skip, or Tony—ah, shit, it's all right to call you Skip, right, Tony?"

"Sure, so you finally get that one now, do you? Whatever makes you easy, man. Doesn't matter much now. Either one you like."

"You see the leather shop over there on the corner?" He nodded out the window. "He has a pouch for you. You need to pick it up as soon as you leave here. You'll find all you need in it. You get on the bus in less than an hour. You will meet Ameed in Malakand, and he will tell you how to locate Peter."

They were sending me into the Northwest Territories. I'd thought that might be the deal, but hoped not.

"Peter—who is Peter? And who is Ameed?"

"They're your touch people, the nearest in the loop to you. It will likely be Peter you'll see the most. If you need anything for any reason, they are the ones to talk to. Peter is a contract worker out of Canada and a good man to have on your side. Ameed is a local who works for some of the same people we do. He can point you in a right direction."

Before I could ask how to find these guys, Lawrence came through the door and sat down next to us.

"What's up?" Charles asked.

"We have a twist. Seems that the cargo was not in the rig, and there are lots of eyes gathering around, hoping to see something." He looked over at me, "How's it going, Tony?"

"Just like Easter in Allahabad!" I shot back. "Sounds like you're having a happy holiday too?"

He smiled and shook his head. "Good to see you haven't lost your sense of humor. Glad to have you with us."

I could tell he meant it. Lawrence was a sturdy man, and it felt good to have someone like him on a team.

"Anything I can do to make your day a little easier." I smiled.

"Just do your job and do it quickly, Tony. We will deal with this twist."

Charles broke in. "Tony doesn't have all the information yet, Lawrence. Considering that, I think we should just deal with what's come up after we get him on his way as planned. OK?"

This felt like I was being talked over, and I didn't like it. "Look, we are working together, right? Or am I pumping gas for you two and all of your puppies? If there's something I need to know, tell me now!"

Lawrence had let some cat out of the bag that was troubling, and Charles wasn't interested in me knowing. I looked at the two of them until Charles spoke. "Skip, we need to trust each other above all the rest we do; that's how we survive. Each of us gets work that helps support the other, or at least that is how it's supposed to be. But you know how things can get; there are always bumps in the road. There seems to be a bump, but it has nothing to do with your job. Lawrence and I will smooth that out. That's our job. Concentrate on your piece. OK?"

"OK, I don't care what it is you two need to do; just do it well. Make sure that it doesn't get in my way, whatever my way is. You said I had a bus to catch? You two can worry about your problems."

Charles went back to what he had been saying. "Peter—use him in support if you need to, but remember he is not super quick, pretty basic as they go, if you know what I mean. He's solid and knows the terrain, but figuring and tight planning aren't his game. Go with your instincts, not his. When you get to your area, find out all you can about any truck traffic and rail traffic, both cargo and passenger, and note how many and what languages you run into that aren't local. Locations, those you'll get from Ameed and Peter both. Be back in no more than five weeks with as much information as you can get. Note anything that looks out of place. Don't come back to Peshawar. Meet Lawrence in Rawalpindi. He'll be there three weeks from today and will stay until you arrive. He'll find you; just get a room at any truck stop. And yes, If things look squirrelly out there, that's all the more reason to hang in. The more info you bring back, the better all around. Don't waste time; focus on what's out of place, understand?"

"I understand. Just be sure that those papers get signed and sent off. It's the paperwork that got me here; we all know that. I gave my word, so I'll do the work and do it well. I'll bring you all I find and likely more than you want. You knew that, or you wouldn't have smoked me out. You two are my solids in this. I need to trust you to do what you said you would, to clean up all that shit back in Oakland. I'll do my end, and I'll do it right, but you do the same; make sure it happens. Don't let me down—deal?"

"We'll handle everything on this end, Tony. Don't think about it. Just figure it's done and concentrate on what you need to do."

I still wasn't sure I could trust them. They had run their health workers game so well when we met. I just didn't know if they were being square or not. They were professional that was sure. I had to trust them and their friends. Hell, I had one foot in the wind already, so if things went south, I knew how to play that game. I just hoped it was all going to go smoothly, or as smoothly as things can out in the Northwest Territories.

"OK, see ya'll in Rawalpindi."

I headed off across the street, trying not to look too focused, and stepped up to the leather shop. There was a little guy setting rivets in a saddle bag. He spotted me as I stepped up but continued to work the saddle bags on his bench. Without a word, he reached down and pulled out a scuffed leather pouch with a shoulder strap. He slipped it onto my hand.

The bus ride to Mardan was hot and dusty. Holes in the floor let the dirt and exhaust swirl up in a dingy gray-blue mix. It wound around like milk fat on a cold chai and then snaked off out the window. Third-class buses in Pakistan are a journey through another time and way, but you have to go with it if you want to stay sane. They stop at every town, person, and chai stand in route. They pick up everyone that waves an arm. Old and young, mothers with screaming babies, everything from bales of cotton to goats, chickens, baskets of grain, and bolts of cloth and the sewing machines to sew them up. The working poor ride the third-class buses; I was the exception. I was sitting there with more money than most these folks would see in a lifetime, tucked just out of sight in my money belt. A few months ago, the only thing separating me would have been language, but now the distance seemed like light-years.

The bus rolled along, tires slapping, then humming, and then growling as the road underneath went from cracked asphalt to gravel to washboard dirt that shook me to the teeth. I'd eaten a little opium before boarding the bus, knowing the trip I was in for. I was drifting in and out of thinking in a kind of half-asleep, half-awake way. Each time the seat shook under me, my eyes would open just long enough to tune into the road or some little town along the way.

We arrived in Mardan in about four or five hours. It felt like I was in some kind of dream. It was mid-afternoon, and I wasn't in the best mood, with road dust caked up in my nose and still feeling cloudy from the opium. I stood there wondering just what I was doing. Was it worth it? I'd left Peshawar, the best friend I had, all that good food the city had to offer, and two really nice women that liked me. What in the hell was I doing? To top it off, I had to catch another damn third-class bus to Malakand. At least a bus went to Malakand, but why a damn third-class bus? Shit, I had a fistful of rupees. They'd handed me four thousand dollars, and I was supposed to take these crappy buses? Hell, there must be some reason for these tickets, good or not. I settled my mind for another slow, hot, dusty trip.

The bus depot in Mardan was a plot of dirt just big enough for buses to turn around. I walked up to a bus driver sitting on the steps of his bus, smoking. "Asalam Aleykum —Malakand bus?"

"Good, very good, I'm showing you." He grabbed my right hand and started to lead me toward the first-class buses that were parked across the way.

"No, not first-class." He dropped my hand, looking puzzled like the world was not right somehow.

"Ticki, ticki." He stuck out his hand, and I handed my ticket over.

"You my bus ride, my bus; come on my bus!"

He grabbed my hand again and led me back to his bus. By then there were a dozen people standing and waiting to get on. He pushed his way through, with me in tow.

"Sitting, sitting, you here." He dusted off the seat right behind him with a cloth pulled off the steering wheel, his head swaying side to side all the while.

"Thanks," I said, doing the best head wiggle I had. Most people never learned that or got why they should; they just stuck with words. Words are nice, but to connect out here—make friends or just making people comfortable has a lot to do with how you act. The little things matter.

Dusk had turned to evening as the bus pulled into Malakand. I liked this small stone village on the bank of the Swat River. The town seemed to almost hang there, its buildings strung together like card houses. Single-story blue-black shale and rough wooden plank buildings were perched along the river. Shops and other buildings cantilevered out over the river. Some were touching others, and some were leaning away, all set on stilt leg timbers hovering together like daddy longlegs above the swirling eddies and white foam. The rest of the town pushed up the steep hillsides on both sides of the river. There were two old wooden bridges crossing it, one for foot traffic that looked like it could have been woven by the ravens that had built their nests in its ropes and timbers. Down a ways was the other bridge, underpinned by a much larger structure that could handle a small truck or cart. The whole town could be seen in one turn of the head, not more than half a mile, all hanging there in the gray granite foothill canyon.

Malakand was beautiful. I'd forgotten just how beautiful. I stepped off the bus, and when the cool fresh air with that smell of cold churning water hit, a real smile swam across my face for the first time since I'd left Amber and Cecile's. Up the river canyon in the last glow of daylight, I could see the clear waters of the Swat River running quick and cold.

Below me fish as long as my arm were holding behind the rocks in the icy blue pools, waiting for a snack. I kept thinking just how good they would taste with cumin, rice, and tea. The water of the Swat River was clean and clear here. It came down out of the mountains in the northeast, the Pamiri, and the Himalayas and eventually merged into the Indus River. What stories this river could tell I thought drifting off into thoughts images, sounds, and scents. Then another thought shook me out of the daydream, and the smile fell off my face.

I was where I was supposed to meet up with Ameed, the problem was, who the hell was Ameed? I didn't know how to recognize him. All I knew was that he was supposed to be on my side, whatever side that was. I still couldn't figure that one out: English, American, Pakistani? It didn't really matter, I guessed, as long as they could do what they said they could. I just needed to find this guy Ameed or be where he could find me. Still, all in all, I would have rather just sat and watched the river flow.

The problem now—the first of a number of them—was how in the hell I was supposed to locate this guy. How was I going to know him when I found him? As far as I knew, he didn't know any more about me than I knew about him. How was he going to know that I was who I said I was? Up till now, I hadn't thought about these pieces. I'd been focused on just getting this over with. Looking through the stuff Charles had given me by way of the man in the leather shop, I found no help, no pictures or descriptions, nothing that would give even a hint as to how to locate him or recognize him. I was supposed to meet someone I wouldn't recognize? How was I going to know if he was the real deal or not? I didn't like this; it didn't fit the picture. Or maybe it did. Shit, with these guys, who knew?

Charles and crew weren't slouches—that was sure. They had the savvy to have papers that were as good as they get and had spooked me from Afghanistan to Pakistan and for all I knew from Turkey to India. They hooked me to information no one should have known out here. Then they sent me off with a fistful of money and a new passport without telling me how to recognize my contacts? Except that Peter, whoever he was, was a bit slow? Shit, there must be something I just didn't understand to the way they set this all up. Meanwhile, I was stuck trying to figure out the next move.

It didn't fit a good plan, at least not one I'd draw up. That made me uneasy. But this was a small town, and I was going to be noticed. Maybe that was it; if not, it had better become it. I had no interest in flagging myself by asking lots of questions about people I didn't have a clue about. The one thing I knew was that Charles and his crowd was not comfortable doing the work themselves, or I wouldn't be here.

I wanted to keep my presence here simple and clean for as long as possible. I had no idea where I was going to end up, and it could be here. I didn't need anyone thinking I was something more than just a traveler.

I'd forgotten what being alone in a small tribal town was like. I'd traveled with Twitch so much over the last months. Two men traveling together didn't stand out like a single stranger did. There was a difference in how people saw you. There was less curiosity when there were two of you.

I needed to find a place to stay, so I started down the street as the bus driver called, "Gentleman, gentleman, you, thank."

"No, no, thank you. Very nice ride, very nice." I bowed as he shook his head side to side, smiling. It had been a long time since I had been alone on the road. This little thank you reminded me of why I liked it.

I went looking for a place to eat and get a bed. I wound my way up the hillside on a path just wide enough for a man and pull cart. I came to an open door with a sign overhead shaped like a teapot and painted with red lettering. I smelled food and heard voices, so I went in. I slid up on an empty table next to a window that looked down on the river. I pulled up a cushion as the boy came trotting over with a hookah on a brass tray. I nodded, took hold of the mouthpiece, and sat back as the boy lit the pipe. I drew a deep lungful of the hot smoke, trying not to cough. Black tobacco's nasty stuff and I never smoked it if I could get away without, but I needed to look at home here, so I paid the boy for the pipe and then ordered chai and kabobs.

The little Urdu I spoke was not of very much use here, but thanks to the British, there was always someone around who spoke at least some English and usually more than one. After I'd eaten, the boy came for his money.

"Rooms? Have you rooms here?" I asked.

He looked at me and said something I couldn't understand. I shook my head and put my hands together and tilted my head on them like a pillow.

"Rooms for sleep—sleeping—room?"

He just looked at me without a clue. Then someone spoke to him from across the room, and he smiled and turned back to me.

"Hautch rupees, hautch." He pointed at his palm with one finger and then rubbed his fingers together in that universal sign. "Hautch rupees, sleeping, sleeping."

They had a bed, and that was good. I could use some sleep, but I also wanted some time alone, one of those Western traits I never lost a feeling for. These places usually had three or four beds in a room, and it was common to sell a single bed. That wasn't all that bad when you didn't have much money, except for the smell at times. Most truck drivers wore strong-scented oils, and that was OK, but others just plain stank, and that wasn't.

I jumped right in, looking at the boy and the man who had spoken to him. "You have one bed, one room?"

The man sat up and hung his legs down off the table's edge and bowed his head in greeting. "No English the boy is having. You like me ask something?"

"A room, with a stove and door, with one bed. I want a room alone."

He turned to the boy. After some animated conversation between the two and input from the others sitting around, he turned back to me. "No rooms one bed. Having room alone, you pay two beds. Room two beds and stove?"

"OK, I will pay."

The boy led me out the back to the room. It was at the end of a long line of low cubicles that shared a stone wall. The room had a shuttered window that looked out the back and down the hillside to the river. There were two beds and a small woodstove. The building had a black shale roof laid on striped saplings that made the space smell like a quarry. It felt a little like a chicken coop with its shed roof and low walls. I stepped into the room, ducking so as not to hit my head. It was high enough for me to stand just inside, but one step further and I had to bend over. There were two beds on either side of the room that reached the full length of the wall. The stove sat to one side of the little shuttered window. I handed the boy a five rupee note and pointed to the stove. Off he ran to fetch wood.

It gets cold in the mountains at night. I sat on the bed pulling my blanket up around my shoulders, waiting for the boy to come with the wood, and looked out the window as the stars reflected in the still pools settled along the banks of the river below. Out in the middle, the water was running fast, and the reflected starlight shattered into dancing patterns of silvers and blacks.

The bus ride had been just about all I could take of people for the day. I needed a rest. Peshawar was a frantic place, and the third-class buses were worse. This little room felt like a fortress. I hadn't been able to think much in the last few days; things had happened so fast. This room, with a fire cracking in the stove now and the stars glinting on the water below in the crisp night, was the first space I'd had to myself in a long time. All the months I'd spent with the Kuchi and then Mickey were falling off like maple leaves in late October. The thought of losing Amber's soft lips and Cecile's warm smile began to sadden me.

What if this job did lead to stripping all that ancient history of mine? Could I go back to Oakland or San Francisco? Could I really return, or were those places like so much of my life now spent and gone? Did it even matter that I ever go back? So much had shifted. My landmarks had too. Maybe this was about freeing up my old life, or maybe not. It could be making more knots to deal with, even tighter ones than I already had. I could do the job, sure; I didn't really worry about that. But did any of this really matter beyond liking a challenge? Pushing myself like I'd always done? I knew this type of arrangement. Tom and other friends had done stuff like this and acted like they were free to choose, but I knew they weren't. I guess the question really was freedom—was there any, really? Or is it just a matter of what camp or cage you tie your hope to? I could get up and walk. I had a passel of money and as good a passport as I'd ever need. I could sell or trade it. A clean United Kingdom passport would bring a good Italian or even German one in exchange, with some coin in the offing.

But who was I kidding? I knew I couldn't just walk off, and I'd said I'd do the work, so I'd do the work. Besides, if they had tracked me down out here, there wasn't any place to slide off the radar.

I woke up with sunlight coming through the window. I had fallen asleep with the shutters open and the fire going. The mountain air was crisp in the room, and there was frost along the window sill. I sat up and wrapped my blanket tightly around my shoulders and reached up to close the shutters. Fumbling with the stove, I got the fire going, and things started warming up a bit. I grabbed the bucket under the foot of the bed and splashed some icy water on my face, swiping it off onto the stone floor.

The fire started to snap and pop, and the room continued to warm up. There was a knock on the door. The boy must have seen the smoke. He stepped in with a pot of chai and a small round loaf of brown bread. I took the tray and gave him a ten rupee note. He bowed, thanking me over and over, holding his ears in that way mountain Muslims show gratitude.

I knew the tea and bread had come with the room, but the kid didn't have any socks, and he couldn't have been more then eleven. I could see the calluses on his feet through holes worn in his sandals. They were blue-brown and cracked. It was hard work running up and down the hillside from the chai shop on those rock streets in the cold and ice. I could afford a good tip with all that money in my belt. Hell, I'd done it even if I didn't have two rupees to rub together. I could always get more money—I knew how—but the life of a serving boy in the Northwest Territories was hard at best. They often had no family other than the shopkeeper who ran them ragged for a bit of food and a hole to sleep in. He backed out of the room, and I said, "Get some socks" and pointed to his feet. I knew he wouldn't and likely didn't even understand me. Still, I had to say something so that he knew the money was his.

I walked into town as the morning sun came up over the mountains. I stopped on the street and turned my face to the sun to let it soak in. Jagged peaks covered with snow shot up in the distance, like white-gloved fingertips holding up the sun. I stood there watching as the morning sounds grew louder around me.

I headed into town and life in the village had started to warm with the sun. Trucks were idling now, and carts were chattering along the cobblestones. The sounds echoed off the canyon walls, mixed with Pakistani radio stations layered one on top of the other. The town was fully awake now with the sun shining down on its river heart. Walking along, I looked into the shops, hoping to see a sign with the name Ameed on it or some clue to my next move.

I started across the footbridge, and it swayed like a swing to the rhythm of my steps. When I reached the middle, my stomach was queasy, and I stopped and leaned over to spit. I watched the water running under me and took a few deep breaths before finishing the crossing.

It was like being in a different town on the other side. There was no traffic, and most of the buildings along the river were homes, not businesses. There was just one radio playing, and it was high up on the hillside. There were no cars or trucks, just handcarts. People were sitting around in front of their houses talking and having tea. Kids were playing in the street and laughing. The whole feel was different. I'd never been on this side of the river before, and I liked it.

I stepped up to one of the shops along the road and looked in to see what it was selling. Along the back wall were racks of guns and shelves of ammunition. On a low shelf in front of them were all the tools and molds for making bullets and shotgun shells. There were ingots of lead and large baskets full of brass shell casings, cans of powder, boxes of firing caps, and all the rest. Along the side walls were buckets, cooking pots, and metal utensils all tied together and hanging like popcorn strings on a Christmas tree, all of it kitchenware as far as I could tell. A man sat in the middle of the floor on several cushions smoking black tobacco in a blue glass hookah on a low table to his side. He nodded at me and smiled while taking a long pull on the pipe. His arm rolled out an open upturned palm, and he flapped his fingers, inviting me in.

"Asalam Aleykum. "

"Aleykum Asalam," I replied.

I pulled up a low wooden chair that stood along the wall and sat down.

He looked at me without a word for a long few minutes and then smiled and said, "Guns," lifting his hand up and pointing to the back wall.

"Very nice," I said, admiring all the antique guns that were hung around.

"Very old, very good."

"I see."

"Tea?" he asked.

I nodded, slipping off my shoulder bag and setting it at my side, a sign that I was interested in his wares, accepting his merchant hospitality. I settled into my chair. I knew I'd be expected to look at his guns and drink tea with him, and that was just fine. If I played my cards right, maybe I could get some information on this guy Ameed. There were some beautiful old rifles on the wall, and I didn't have anything better to do. And where there were guns, there might be information, and I was out to gather information. The more I got, the better. That's what they had said. Besides, I hadn't seen a collection of old firearms like this anywhere. There were old guns around in the Khyber, but nothing like this. The big market there was for the newer stuff.

Tea arrived, and the merchant had the boy bring down a beautifully engraved shotgun. I took a drink of my tea and sat back as he laid the gun on the carpet in between us. Setting down my tea, I picked up the shotgun. It looked a hundred years old, if it was a week. The stock was worn and shiny where hands had gripped it over the years, and the trigger was worn in the center from being pulled. The stock was dark rosewood or something like it, with a rich deep patina that comes only with age and handling. The grain was tight and quilted. The barrel was engraved with grape vines that ran the whole length and down around the trigger guard. I looked for a maker's mark but couldn't find one. The merchant smiled and reached out, and I handed the gun to him. He opened the breach and handed it back. On a metal plate was a signature, a number, and a date. The signature looked Russian or Greek, and the date was 1897.

"Beautiful," I said and handed the shotgun back to him. "I am Skip."

"Good to make your acquaintance, Skip," he replied in very good and proper English. "I'm Ameed."

Before I could say a word, he went on.

"I was going to come to your room this morning and introduce myself, but Mamude, the boy who brought your tea this morning, said you were still shivering when he got there, so I decided to let you warm up. Then when I saw you heading over the bridge, I figured I'd see how long it took you to find me." He smiled.

"Charles might have told you where to find me, but normally he doesn't give out that information. Did he tell you?"

"Nope, you were just the first shop on this side of town. But seeing how I landed here by chance and not direction, just how are you going to convince me you are who you say you are? Not that I don't believe you—it's just that I have no reason to yet."

He laughed. "Well, Tony, if I were to have gone to your room this morning, I would have said, 'Hello, I'm Ameed, the guy Charles and Lawrence told you to—how do they put it?—hook up with. They want you to know that Twitch is still in town, and so are Amber and Cecile. They are working on your paperwork and expect to see you in Rawalpindi in a few weeks. Don't spend all the money in one place. And ...'" He paused. "Is that enough, or do I have to get into the passport and all that?"

He reached out to shake hands. I took his hand and smiled.

"So you are supposed to introduce me to?"

"Peter," he replied.

"And I am supposed to do whatever this Peter says, right?"

"It's your life, friend, but Peter is not what you would call quick. If I were you, I'd follow my own head. He's strong and a good man, someone you would want with you in a pit fight, but I wouldn't take his advice on long-term investments." He winked. "We OK now, Tony?"

"Yep," I said, and we shook hands again.

While we sat and drank tea together, Ameed told me about his family, not an unusual topic for tribal men. It was customary to share this kind of stuff when in friendly conversation with someone new. Family and history were important. This way you cleared the roads. It helped keep stuff from surfacing later that could cause problems. Conversation was needed before a friendship or other kind of relationship could happen. Some friendships just couldn't happen because of family histories. It was a ritual exchange I'd engaged in many times.

Ameed was an interesting guy. He'd been in Pakistan since the partition from India in 1947 when he was fourteen. More than half his family was still in India. He'd gone to school in London, which accounted for his good English, and had been living in Malakand for ten years. What I couldn't figure was what he was doing hooked up with Charles and that group? Or why did they need someone like me when Ameed could move around with ease out here? I decided to keep quiet on this one—to keep my mouth shut and ears open for a while. Things may get clearer. When he'd finished, he asked, "Who are your people, Tony, and where do you come from?"

I was a bit on edge with a question like that. "Ameed, I would think that you would know. At least Charles, Lawrence, and all their company do. Why do you ask?" I replied as politely as I could.

"I understand," he smiled. "You think that I should have your file. Isn't that what they have on you? Well, no, I don't, and I don't care to actually. What I know about you is that you come recommended highly, that my friends Lawrence and Charles both know how touchy the work I do is and would never send me anyone that might cause an incident. At least they don't believe they would. But they have no idea how it works in tribal relationships; they are not like us. We will be working together, and I have told you who I am. So tell me who you are."

I didn't know where to start, or to end for that matter. I understood the need for him to know, but my life and my reasons for being out here were so different. Still, this dance needed to be played out. Besides, I liked him; he was clear and honest and reminded me of tribal friends I'd had in the Hindu Kush. Ameed was tribal Pakistani, and regardless of his education, that meant something, and I knew I had better have as good a relationship as possible with him.

"I'm from California, the eastern part of the San Francisco Bay area. My family is all there. In a city called Oakland. I have no wife. I'm a musician and a poet there, like you are a gun merchant here. And like you with the partition, I had to leave my home in America because of politics. I came here because I was no longer welcome there. I don't have the same opinion about the war they are fighting. I chose to leave rather than kill people I had no fight with. So I have lived all over the world now. I have been in Afghanistan, Pakistan, and India for the last few years. Out here in the Hindu Kush with Kuchi people up the Yarkhun to Chitral and Kurram. I have no ties or enemies, that I know of, in tribal Pakistan. I do have strong ties with Afghani Kuchi and Poshto by friendships, not family. I find myself here because Charles and Lawrence approached me when I was in Landi Kotal and hired me in Peshawar to work with you."

"Someday, Tony, perhaps you will be less cautious. I choose my friends carefully and over time as well. Maybe someday we will be able to be friends as you say you are with the Kuchi. I too have Kuchi friends, and they are honest and honorable, like we are in Swat. But our river has bigger fish, and our snow leopards whiter, softer belly skin!"

How much I was willing to tell about myself was directly related to how much people needed to know. It was a habit I'd acquired over the years and one I couldn't shake or didn't see any good reason to, even with a guy like Ameed who seemed honest enough. Charles and the gang knew plenty. I didn't need to offer up anything they might have missed.

"I'm a very private person, Ameed. If it seems like I am discounting your courtesy and openness in any way, I'm not. If I have made you feel unequal in any way, I offer my apology."

"I have children. Do you have you children?"

"No" I replied

"He barked proudly, "I have two sons and one daughter."

You are blessed." I answered.

"Yes, I am!"

I had agreed to meet up with Ameed the next morning on the main road north of town. I paid for my room and walked down to the shop and was drinking chai and looking out the window at the gray fingers of morning sun on the mountain tops. The stove crackled. and the smell of hot bread filled the place. I watched as morning rolled down the granite and shale like thick cream and hit the river. I still had no idea where I was headed, and that was bugging me. But my mind had bought fully into the game now, so it really it wasn't all that bad, just a day waiting to happen. Ameed hadn't said anything other then "up North" when I'd asked him where I was going. Hell, I knew it wasn't south.

I finished up my tea, stepped out the door, and just stood there for a minute. I hoped I wasn't going to be walking all day. There were no buses north from here; Malakand was the end of the line.

Heading out of town, I passed the last building, and then rock walls and small gardens started. As I headed north out of town, I spotted Ameed about a quarter-mile up the road, sitting on a rock wall with a larger man next to him. It looked like they were talking and laughing. As I got closer, I could make out English. Ameed looked up and waved his hand and called, "Good morning, Skip."

"Salaam alacume."

"Alacume asalaam," they both replied.

"Skip, meet Peter."

"Hey."

Peter was about six-foot-four with dirty blond matted hair. He was clean shaved or didn't have much hair on his face; I couldn't tell. He wore a jallaba that was tight across his chest and baggy pajama pants and those cross-top Pakistani sandals. The muscles stood out from his neck like roots on a banyan tree and ran down under his shirt. His shoulders dropped downward slightly, no wider than his hips, and the veins on his hands stood out like ropes. The guy was as hard as a rock. I reached out a hand and met a grip like a vice, and he wasn't showing off.

"Peter, I guess we are working together? I didn't get a whole lot of details from Charles beyond that. Do you know where we are going?"

Peter looked over at Ameed and said, "This is what they send us, not even a ranger? They really don't get it, do they?" He turned and looked me dead in the eyes. "Don't get me wrong, Skip—it is Skip, right? I'm sure you've been around town and all that, but up here's a whole different circus. My job is to get you where you need to get and then back out. It's more like I take you to work, understand? We're tied at the hip, sure, but the rope is long. Understand?"

"Not really. Like I said, where are you planning to take me? I got no information other than what I'm supposed to look for when I get there and that you've got my back." Peter looked at me deadpan, eyes open and empty.

I went on. "I need to find road houses, places and people, foot paths, horse trails, camel routes, truck and train traffic, if there is any— I want to see who's out here and where. Hell, the Yarkhun, Chitral, Kurram, Mastuj, Wakhan, it's a big place; shit, I don't know—you're supposed to tell me. I only have a few weeks."

Peter shook his head. "Well, shit, you don't want much. The Yarkhun? You want me to take you up into the Yarkhun? Damn, I should have got another job." He winked. "Yea, I know places out there where folks pass. There are some routes that can handle small trucks and at least one railroad track, maybe two that still might get traffic—don't know. I can get you in there, show you where, but I can't go in with you. It's hot as purple chili peppers for me."

"What's this tied-at-the-hip stuff then?" I questioned.

"The rope has to be long, like I said. If Lawrence wants info from the Yarkhun and up round Mastuj, you'd better be good. It's no city park out there."

Ameed cut in. "He's good, Peter; they know what they are doing. He was in the Hindu Kush with the Kuchi and was recruited out of Landi Kotal."

I broke in. "Wait a minute—that's not how it went down. I wasn't recruited; I was negotiated. I'm up here for two reasons: first, because I gave my word, and my word's good, and second, because I needed what they offered me. Now, Peter, if there's bad blood between you and someone up where we're headed, you'd better tell me about it. I don't mind you dropping back when you need to, but I need to know where you are going to be. If you and Ameed are my ropes over the wall, I need to know where you are and aren't. I need to get my info and be back in Rawalpindi in a month or less. So you both need to be in this until then. And Peter, as for the Yarkhun, I've been up there before. I know how it works. I hope you do. Now what's it going to be—we do this together or not? And just who is it that is after your ass?"

Peter looked away like a scolded kid who hadn't been listening. "Shit, Ameed, I could sure use some R&R time out of here. Everyone knows I'm dead meat in half of section 2. Can you get to Charles and let him know I need some Katmandu time?" He pushed his hands through his matted hair and looked up at the mountains in the north, shaking his head.

"Peter, you know I haven't any pull with what group 2 does or doesn't do with R&R. I don't work for them, and they don't work for me. I will, however, inform Charles of your request. Whether it gets answered is something entirely different."

Peter shook his head and took a deep breath.

Group 2? This was inside lingo, and it made me uncomfortable. I didn't like being out of the loop, especially if it meant more risk. But I didn't want to know any more than I needed, just enough to get out with what I had bartered for. Friends like these were two-edged, both edges sharp. I knew the more information I had, the harder it would be for me to walk away, if I was going to be able to walk away at all. Still, the more information I had, the better chance of getting through without something nasty happening and more than just a belt full of rupees and a clean passport. Even if there was a rope with my old life tied to it, it could be completely out of my reach if I didn't get this job done. If I wanted to get through this, I had to bottle up and go.

"All right, guys, I understand you have your issues, and that's fine. I get that you two aren't on the same payroll, OK. So who is it you work for and why?" I sat up next to Ameed and looked down at the ground, waiting for a reply. It was a long few minutes of listening to the river. Finally I spoke up. "OK, I'll go first. I'm out here 'cause Charles and Lawrence offered me fistfuls of money and a promise to get some dogs off my back. Why are you two out here?"

Ameed spoke first. "Skip, if you are worried that Charles might not fulfill what he said he would, don't be. I've worked with Lawrence and him numbers of times, and they have always been straight in their dealings, at least to this point. They're a bit more 'American' than I would care to bring home to meet my daughter, even though they're English and Australian"—he smiled at Peter, who returned his look with an agreeing nod—"but they're honest as far as I know. As for me, I work for what you would know as the Pakistani fish and game ministry; I am what you call in the United States a game warden. I also sell guns, as you've seen, and work as a hunting guide in Swat. I know a few people in government, and that helps at times. I get paid well enough to send my children to school in Europe. Most of that money comes through Charles and Lawrence. As for Peter, well, he can tell you why he's out here if he wishes to."

"All right, all right," Peter said. "I'm out here 'cause I like the place, and I need the money both. I'm getting paid from the same bucket as you, Skip. I'm not complaining, not really—it's just that it's a bit touchy for me since I screwed that chick up in Chitral some weeks back. She had a husband. How was I supposed to know?" Ameed just grinned as Peter stared down at the ground.

"Shit! You screwed a wife? Who's her husband, and how many brothers does he have? Have they killed her yet, or are they waiting to kill you first?"

"Don't know. All I know is that it took me two weeks shrugging through the mountains to shake the six of them that were on me. Never had so much fun." He chuckled. "Except for the bits where I almost got washed away. The rivers up there are big." He nodded toward the mountains. "You ready to travel?"

Ameed hopped off the wall and said, "See you two when you get back."

"Peter, you're a crazy motherfucker," I said.

"Never said she was a mother, Skip, just cute and married."

It worried me who might be up ahead of us with their fingers on the trigger, just waiting. At least the sights would be on Peter, leastways I hoped so. Could be he'd been with an old-school tribal gal. Some tribal folks up in the mountains had old ways very different from the normal Muslims. If he was lucky, she'd been old-religious, and the family was just pissed that they hadn't gotten payment or something and would give up on the whole deal given time. Whatever—you take what you get, so my eyes and ears were open wider now.

"OK, Peter, let's book. Point me in a good direction. I need to go where I need to go and get what I need to get, and get the fuck out. And please don't tell me we're walking."

P eter had an old short-wheelbase Land Rover, old enough to still have a gas-burning heater. You could just make out the military green under flaking black paint that someone had brushed over it. The British had sold lots of surplus stuff to Pakistan rather than part it out or trash it. This Rover must have come from them. Peter spotted me eyeing his car and said proudly, "It works. It also crawls up rocks and hills like you wouldn't believe."

We headed northwest toward Kurram, and I kept trying to keep my mind on what I was doing out here, trying not think about who might be gunning for Peter. We were going to be hooked up in one way or another for the next few weeks, and I still didn't know shit about him. Who was he? I knew he was Canadian—Charles had told me that much—but why was he out here?

"What brought you to the Northwest Territories? How'd you end up working out here?"

He shifted his eyes off the dirt road for a split second. "I'm from Quebec. My family's all climbers—father, brother, sister, all my uncles. Papa died out here on K2. I was on a canoe trip with friends in the Yukon when it happened. I never got to see him, the body. I heard about it a month or more after. He's still up on the mountain—it was too hard to pack him off. So I gathered up my kit and came here to see if I could find him. That's how I'm here.

"I gave up looking—just got OK with it all finally. I didn't have any need. I was broke and hanging around Rawalpindi looking for trekkers that wanted a lead climber. I ran into Lawrence hanging around the office where you get trekking permits. He said he'd heard I was good and had a job for me if I was interested. I don't know who told him about me, but I wasn't keeping it a secret. Whatever. That was two years ago now, and I still got the job."

"So you climb for Lawrence?"

"Not only. I trek too. I tried to map all of it up for him once, just to show him I was on the job, but he burned it right there—said he didn't want it on paper. Job security's what he said. OK by me. He pays my account every two weeks like the clock; he's never missed it once. Nowadays, I just climb stuff that looks fun and check in on the birds that are about and interested." He smiled. "I got lots of time. I don't ask why. It's a job, and it's out here. I don't have to pay to go trekking; they pay me. I'm good, Skip, very good, and worth it. And I know they're government boys somehow, Lawrence and Charles and the rest, but shit, the work is good, and the money's better than bad. I don't ask why. I'm just happy to be working out here."

He knew what was up, so that was good. He may not be the brightest light on the street, but he sounded together to me and knew what end was up.

"You take others like me out here before?"

"No, not out this far. I've scouted around out here but stayed clean away like I was told to. Lawrence wants nobody to see me, leastways not to notice anything but a trekker—that's my job. I find roads and buildings; I find them and get out as quick as I can. Now I'm supposed to take you up and point, wait, and then get you out."

It seemed that Ameed had put Peter on the track, and then he'd trek through the high valleys finding out where stuff was. There were no maps of this part of the world. At least nothing that showed anything but mountains and rivers. They were putting me in now. I was the next piece in a chain of information with some endgame I had no idea about or cared to know about. I was heading up into the spider to find out what and who was moving and stopping, that was all.

It was no spot to play out there. I'd been in the deep territories before, and I knew the place, but I never felt very good or safe. We called it the spider for a reason. The only place on the planet where five international borders came together. And none of the countries liked each other or agreed on just where the borders were. It was rough high country with the Karakoram, Hindu Kush, and Himalaya mountains all converging. There was only one good route in from Pakistan: the Yarkhun River Valley and its fingers. So I was heading into the heart of the spider with all its eight legs and lots of eyes. A spider that was known to bite.

At least things made a little more sense now. They were covering bases. For sure, it was some government game, but just what camp they were in wasn't clear, and I wasn't really interested. The mud was deep enough as it was—any deeper, and it would be just that much harder to pull my feet out.

India, Pakistan, Afghanistan, Russia, and China were all out here, with borders drawn by opinion. There were no maps, no surveys, of the terrain; it was too hard and remote. A mix of five nations that didn't like each other in three of the most formidable mountain ranges in the world—well, I might get lucky.

"Peter, we have any guns in this ride?" I asked.

"Sure, I got a 306—take a crow's head off at 350 yards." He reached over behind my seat and pulled out a canvas bag and handed it to me. "This is for you." Inside wrapped in an oil cloth was a very clean Walther 32 in a black leather slip holster with two boxes of shells.

"It's from Ameed; he told me to tell you Charles shouldn't know."

Ameed knew the game here and I was happy he did. The pistol was just small enough to keep out of sight if I wanted to and not so big to intimidate or call too much attention if I needed to wear it openly.

"Nice. I feel better now."

I tucked the gun into my pouch as we bounced along. I closed my eyes and slipped off into a restless sleep. I woke up to Peter pulling on the front of my shirt.

"Wake up, Skip; you might want to see this."

He had pulled up behind a rock about fifty yards from the road. Coming down the road ahead was a heard of goats with one man in front and two trailing them.

"Goats? You think I haven't seen goats before?"

He just put his finger to his lips and then reached behind the seat and brought out his 306. He slowly pulled open the window and took an eight-inch silencer and fixed it to the barrel with a single twist. He raised the rifle out the window.

Shit, I thought, *he is going to shoot one of those guys! Maybe they're the ones that gave him all that grief in the mountains?* Still, shooting one from the side of the road seemed a bit over the edge, not to mention fucking risky. I didn't need more trouble than I already had, but before I could say a word or grab his arm, I heard the hiss from the 306 and saw his shoulder snap back. I turned my eyes down the road, but nobody fell; nothing was different. The two in the back just kept right on walking the herd ahead of them, and the man at the front kept going like nothing had happened.

"Right in the stinking eye."

"What the fuck, Peter? What in hell are you doing?"

"Bagging dinner and getting a little payback," he said, laughing. "Those assholes chased me through half of Chitral. I figured they owed me at least one good meal."

The men and their flock had turned up a path on the other side of the road now with no idea anything had happened. Just off to the side and down behind a rock, a stocky kid goat lay still. Peter had dropped it so clean and quiet, no one had noticed, not even me. He was right about what he'd said—that was a shot few could make, and he had done it as casually as pulling over to take a leak. As much as it steamed me how he did it, I had to be glad about his skill and the fact that he was on my side. As soon as the flock and men were out of sight, we pulled down the road and picked up the goat, cut its throat, and tied it off on the back bumper to bleed. We continued north for another hour or so until he pulled down a dirt road along the river to a rock wall in front of a small shale house. A young girl, maybe fifteen, in a long, layered tribal dress, with beads woven into her hair, came running out.

"Pitri, Pitri, here! Coming here!" she called into the door of the shale house.

"What's all this, man?"

"This is where we get dinner and sleep. From here on, it's your game. I watch and get you out."

The girl ran over, and Peter pointed to the back of the Rover where the goat was hanging. She took it giggling and ran off behind the house.

"This place is a road house. There's one near every village. They have food and a bed if need be. Money doesn't work so good here; bartering works better for some things." He winked and nodded in the direction where the young girl had headed. "Places like this are where you'll see who and what's about. I got a bed here; this will be base camp. Tonight we'll talk about getting you into where you need to go first."

"Go first—how many places are out here?"

"A few. First, let's get you a bed. I got one regular here, myself"

I figured we must be close to Kurram; we'd been traveling all day. There were a few stone houses and a couple outbuildings around that I could see on the road going north, but no other buildings in sight, just foot paths up and out in various directions. A steep rocky bank fell off down to the river, and a series of poles ran down to the water with pulleys and a rope so that you could bring up water. Next to that was a narrow pathway that wound down to the water and a rivulet off the main flow behind a big rock. This was the privy, I figured, and I headed off to use it. When I got back, Peter was waiting, smoking a small pipe and sitting on a chair he'd brought from somewhere.

"Nice up here," he said, nodding toward the mountains. White craggy peaks stuck up in the sky in all directions. They must have been fifty miles away or better, but they looked like you could touch them in that crystal air.

"Yep, pretty for sure. Is that K2?"

"Nope. Don't know what they call that one, but they're all high, all of 'em seven thousand meters and up. The hills there to the west and north are lower, five thousand or so. The trails are a bitch."

"Never been too far off the road out here, Peter, but I can move OK in high country. I was in the Kush a long time."

"Good. You'll need the lungs."

"Some place around here I can try this Walter out?" I patted my pouch where I'd stowed the gun.

"Sure."

We walked down the road about fifty yards to a pile of old rusted thirty-gallon drums. Several had circles drawn in red paint, and all of them were riddled with bullet holes.

"Give her a try."

I took the little Walther from its holster and filled in the clip. I raised my hand and sighted. Pop-pop-pop-pop-pop! The Walther fired smooth and balanced, leaving five holes in one of the drums. The pattern was the size of a large dinner plate. *Not bad,* I thought, looking over at Peter with a half smile.

"Guess that's OK for people, but I wouldn't want to get a goat that way," he said.

"It's for looks, really." I held the gun up, looking at it. "But it's good to know it works. Might be able to trade it for a car or horse down the road."

"You want a horse?"

"Am I going to need one?"

"Shit, I don't know. But I can get you one if you want."

I liked Peter; there was nothing there that didn't fit; he was simple and straightforward.

After I'd got my bed, I headed into the main house to eat. The sun was setting, and the evening sky was shot full with salmon and reds in the high thin clouds that sucked up the falling sunlight. I ducked through the low doorway to avoid hitting my head, and across the room Peter was sitting in a low chair in front of a small table, knees tucked up.

"You don't quite fit, man."

"They're small here. Visitors are mostly Japanese trekkers, some French and Swiss. Go figure."

"What do they think I am?"

"I told them you're on official business from Peshawar, doing a fish and game count. That you work for Ameed. They know him and like him. He guides hunters out here sometimes."

"You think they would bring us some carpets to sit on instead of this dollhouse tea set?" Just then, the young girl brought over a platter of dark rice and a bowl of yogurt. I could see she and Peter were well acquainted. She smiled while looking him dead in the eyes. Out here that was a sure sign that they were more than friends. He nodded at her in approval, and she set the food down and went out the back again.

"It's good to keep the serving girls happy; that way, you get good food and a warm bed." He smiled. "Shit, I forgot to ask about the carpets."

"I'm fine. You just looked like you were folded up, that's all. Keeping the serving girl happy—that's cool, I guess, as long as she doesn't have a husband, brothers, cousins, or big dogs. Shit, man, she can't be more than fifteen;"

"So what's your point?"

"Come on, man, it can't be about the conversation. Awful risky, no?"

"Not with these tribal. This little one, I call her Sally, she's a no-touchy. Locals here don't want to know. But she's a real go-getter, I tell ya'—likes my blond hair among other things. She's not family here, at least not directly, but she's related in some way. Never could quite figure out how. She can't marry around here. She screwed her brother or something and had a kid. Problem was, kid died. So no one will take her for a wife. She's got her sights on outsiders of some kind. That means anyone ten miles away or more. Malakand or Canada, same to her."

"Not Muslim?"

"Not many here are—mostly some weird mix of old-style tribal."

I knew folks out here had strong ties to the old religion, but they kept it in house. I never saw anyone play it out openly; that would be too risky. But I knew that didn't mean it wasn't happening.

"Whatever, man. Just keep an eye on your backside—I might need you."

"Not to worry. Still, the sooner I can get some time in India, the happier I'll be, and that's not happening till I get you out of here with your pouch full of whatever." He reached over and took a handful of rice.

"So where you want to go first?"

"Wherever traffic is happening."

"Traffic in what—food, drugs, guns?"

"Shit, you know where all that is moving through?"

"Just pulling your chain." He kind of giggled. "I know where people show up and where some trucks and railcars move, but I got no idea what they're up to, not my job. I am guessing it's yours?"

"I need to go where the people and any traffic out of sight of the main route happen—camels, horses, trucks, railroads?"

"You got a year?" He took a mouthful of rice. "Just kidding. I can tell you where to go to see most all that in a day's walk."

Just then, the girl came over with a hindquarter of the goat on a clay platter, cooked to perfection, slipping off the bones. Peter took the platter, put it under his nose, took a deep snort, and smiled at her before setting it down on the table.

"Like I said, these folks aren't Muslims like your tribal types in the eastern Kush—much closer to roots here."

The girl giggled, and her breasts bounced under her little worn top. It was very sexy, and I could see what Peter liked in her. What I gathered about Peter was that he was attracted to anything that didn't have a prick and was interested—and maybe to some who did? That was fine with me as long as it didn't cause me any grief.

From then on, we ate without much conversation. After dinner we sat by the river while Peter smoked his pipe and filled me in on the spots he thought I should take a look around.

In the morning the sky was filled with shifting clouds. I could see a shower here and there in the distance as patches of blue kept peeking through. We headed north, and with each mile the road kept getting thinner and rougher.

"It's walking time soon; best get your gear in order," Peter called out over the sounds of the road.

The plan was I'd walk into town. The village of Mastuj was about as far up in the spider as anything you would call a road went. Peter said he could drive up, but I'd decided we had better not. For all I knew, he could be screwing half the women in town, and that was an issue I didn't need. Mastuj was going to be my hub. Peter had said there was a lot of activity around the hills there.

The wet granite gravel crunched under my feet as I stepped out of the Rover. "See you in two weeks, man."

"You're on."

As I walked into town, the weather got even more pissy and gray. Before I got halfway there, it was pouring rain and cold. I got into town dripping and shivering, and I walked straight to where Peter said I could get a room. The man there put me in front of the stove with a pot of chai first thing. That was a good thing because if he hadn't, I'd have been pounding the streets for the first car to drive me to India!

It was cold and wet, and I had money in my pocket. But eventually I warmed up, dried out, and remembered I had a job to do.

The weather stayed crappy, with a steady rain and biting wind. The river swelled and spit out foamy gray balls that filled the little village, floating up the banks like tiny storm clouds; water was everywhere. My little room sat just above the river bank, and the wind blew cold drops up from below and down from above and through every crack.

I burned damp wood day and night; nothing had time to dry before it was burned. I huddled around the little stove, watching it push out puffs of smoke each time the wind blew down the stovepipe. I sat there, staring at the rain and wind and thinking about my life and how it had changed, and so fast. I'd never thought I'd end up here, cold, wet, and not very happy, working for somebody I didn't know or cared to have even met.

I knew now that somebody could find me no matter how far off the beaten path I might go. Shit, right here in this little room, I was as far off any path as most folks even thought existed, and I'd been sent here because I'd been further out than that, and they'd known it. As I thought about it all, I got more and more pissed. I hadn't been out of sight. I just thought I had. The only way I was going to get out on the good side of all this was to play out the cards I was being dealt and bring my new associates what they wanted.

I knew there was an opium den in the road house where I was staying; I could smell it. So after about a week of wringing out my mind in a damp, cold room, I went in for a smoke. It was a typical Muslim den where they smoked opium in long, thin hand pipes, sepses some called them. They made the opium up into tiny red-black pea-sized balls to smoke—threads of opium like a black-red cotton candy—in a process that took hours.

As I sat down, I noticed a set of Chinese opium pipes and lamps set aside. They weren't being used. Seems the owner had traded for them but didn't know how to use them. Chinese-style opium smoking took a whole lot of paraphernalia, and you had to know how to do it—it was very different from the style of opium smoking you'd find in Pakistan. Chinese-style smoking was an art and a craft both. "Chandu" liquid opium prepared for the pipes was made right there in the pipe bowl, right as you smoked. You could smoke this way yourself, but it was a style developed for dens and having someone make pipe for the smoker. Still, you needed to know how to do it. It was a craft. I knew how to make pipe this way and liked smoking Chinese-style myself. I made a deal with the owner that I'd teach him how to use the pipes if he let me smoke with them. I'd learned Chinese-style pipe making in Bombay. Not a common skill, but it was work at the time.

I lay there smoking and thinking about how weird the world had shook out. There I was in the Northwest Territories of Pakistan gathering information for a couple English spooks, making Chinese pipe in a Muslim opium den on the Yarkhun River in Swat.

On the eighth day, the rain paused for a few hours, and it looked like it might start to taper off. I walked into the den, there was a man I hadn't seen there. He wasn't Pakistani or Afghani, and he was wearing Western clothes. I couldn't tell if he was from Europe or the States. I lay down as usual and started trimming the lamp. Without a word, the owner handed over the small platter with three little brass cups of chandu. I took them and filled up the lamp with fresh peanut oil.

"How much for one of those?" the stranger asked in American English, pointing at my opium.

"Five rupee, one cup," the owner answered.

"OK, I'll have five."

This guy didn't have a clue. Chandu was two rupees a cup, and I was paying half that, but I kept my mouth shut. He could afford it; that was clear. But I was the only one there who smoked Chinese-style or who could. I don't think he got that I was a customer. As soon as this guy got his five cups, he turned and lay down across from me, looking up and waiting for me to make pipe for him.

"I don't work here, man; I'm a friend of the family." I said.

"Damn! You're an American?" He almost sat up.

"No, just went to school there—San Francisco. Subject of the United Kingdom, born in Simla, in Himachal Pardesh. You?"

"Ah, I'm, uh … from Seattle."

"Oh yeah, what brings you out here? This wasn't a hot spot on the jet-set tour last time I checked the brochures."

"Just curious about the place; I looked at a map and thought, hell, I'm going there."

"Oh." I started to make a pipe.

"So anyone here working?" he asked.

"You need to make your own if you want to smoke Chinese around here; this is Pakistan. You should have bought the balls like those guys." I nodded at the men smoking on the other side of the room. He seemed confused. He started to look around the room, and I could see he was trying to figure out the game.

"Don't worry, man. I'll make you some pipes as soon as I get a few in myself. Relax."

I smiled and lay my head on the rest and smoked. He was clearly uneasy; it dripped off him like syrup. When I'd finished the pipe, I looked up.

"Next time, buy the balls, man. In Pakistan they smoke opium in those hand pipes."

I raised my eyes toward a man lighting up his clay pipe with a hot coal. "In Pakistan opium's made into those little balls so it burns. It's chandu just like this, only cooked down till it gets stringy enough to work into balls. A couple balls are about one of these little cups, give or take. It's OK."

"I was in Calcutta up until two days ago. I've been smoking there, and it's all like you got here. I just flew into Rawalpindi and hired a car to bring me up to Chitral. I just got here. I smelled the opium when I was having tea."

"What were you doing in Calcutta?"

"Looking for watches."

"Watches, what for?"

"That's what I do. I collect antique watches and clocks. Calcutta is one of my regular stops. I got people there. I check in once or twice a year. Amazing how much stuff shows up in that city."

"I can imagine."

This guy's story was like Charles and his inbred premature ejaculators: good but weird; besides, there was something with his English. It didn't sound West Coast somehow.

"Never thought of Calcutta as a place for watches."

"Not many do; that's why it's still good. Plus it only takes one or two finds to make it worth it. Lots of stuff lingering around an old city like that—just have to dig it up." His eyes lit up when he talked. This guy was either for real or real good.

"Put your head down, man. I'll make you up some pipes." I reached over and took a cup from his tray.

"Thanks, man. I really appreciate it."

"Nothing to it, man." I started to warm the pipe bowl over the lamp.

"Don't mind me," he said, smiling, as he took one of the brass cups off the tray and licked it out and chased it with a pull from his chai. He didn't even quiver, and chandu is god-awful stuff. This was hard-core.

"So you sell your watches in Seattle?"

"Some of them, but generaly I sell in New York, London, and sometimes Hong Kong. Seattle, well, they don't like to pay what they're worth. In Hong Kong I trade for other watches or clocks. It's like any antique—you know what someone wants and what they will pay, and then you go out and find it for less, hopefully considerably less."

"I guess," I said, finishing up his pipe. "Never been in the antique business myself. Hard to imagine there's a booming market in old watches out here, though." I looked at him for a reaction as I handed the pipe stem over and held the bowl over the lamp. He didn't flinch or answer—just took the pipe and started smoking.

"School in San Francisco. Where?" he said with a stream of smoke bellowing from his mouth.

"The Bay Area actually—prep school in the East Bay, St. Timothy's." I'd never heard of St. Timothy's, so I figured he wouldn't have either.

"Good school, is it?"

"Good enough to get me into Berkeley. So the clocks and watches brought you to Swat and Chitral?" I wanted to get the conversation off me and back on him.

"Not really. I just always wanted to come up here. I had a good year and had some extra money and time. What do you do here?"

"I'm on break. I'll be heading back to school in a few months." I knew that was a bust the minute it came out of my mouth.

"Oh," he said and smiled. "Look, my name is Jerry, and to tell you the truth, I'm up here because someone told me that the best hashish in the East can be found in Chitral, and I'm looking."

I'd blown it with that bogus line about being on a school break—no way could I pass that one off, lying there in native clothes, making Chinese pipe in Mastuj. I could have kicked myself. I could do better than this. What was I thinking? I should have just started making pipe and not said a word. Now he had that "I got your number" look on his face, and I hated that. But I figured what the hell? Let's get to cleaning it up. I hadn't bought his watch story, and the hashish shopper bit was even worse.

"Is that right? What deranged hippie told you that the hashish is good up here? You're lucky to be smoking—or excuse me, eating—opium up here that isn't half ginseng or pine tar. The hashish is worse! Look, Jerry, if that's your name, this isn't hashish country, leastways not good hashish country. What are you doing up here? People don't eat opium like that for the fun of it. Well, maybe some do—I might—but they don't come to Swat to do it."

"So when you due back in Berkeley?" He took another bowl from his platter and licked it out, this time without any tea.

"OK, that was lame, I'll agree. My name's Skip, and I am an independently wealthy reclusive opium addict. So what's your real story?"

He laughed. "My name's Jerry like I said, and I do deal in clocks. I'm not up here looking for hashish, you're right; I'm up here looking for clocks. One of my connections in Lahore told me that there were a number of very valuable Russian timepieces coming through Mastuj. If I wanted to see them, I needed to get to them en route, before they hit town. So you know anything about that? I would pay you for information."

"Independently wealthy, remember. Look, Jerry, I'm not up on Russian camel herds or what they are carrying—never even heard of any for that matter—and I don't deal in clocks or anything else. I just lie around and do opium. But if I hear of anything, I will let you know."

He picked up his last bowls of chandu, licked them clean, stood up, and left without saying another word.

The next morning, the weather finally cleared, and the sun felt good on my face. I didn't see any sign of Jerry the clock guy when I got my tea and was glad of that. I figured he must still be around though; this wasn't a place for day tours.

I set off for a village Peter had told me to check out. It was about a two-hour walk northeast. That was about as far apart as these villages got up here. I walked the trail out of town up and over the first ridge, and the smell of mint filled the air. It grew wild along the little rivulets that ran down the hillsides, mixed with small wild strawberries that the birds pecked at. In an hour or so, I came to a pass that looked down into a high valley. From there I could see what looked like an old rail track running along the far side against the hills. Peter had said it was there. It came into the valley from a little canyon at one end and then ran out the other side through a wash. In the north end of the valley, facing south, in a kind of half moon, was a village. There were a few small stone buildings, none of them near the tracks, and a few others that ran up the hillsides and were perched alongside terraces of barley and other grain. There was a lot of grass growing around the track and in the valley, so I couldn't tell if it had seen any traffic recently. It was too far away to really tell.

As I headed down the path, just about halfway to the village, a man came around the bend right in front of me. He wasn't wearing his shirt and instead had it tucked in the back pocket of his Levi's; he wore army-issue jungle boots. That wasn't all. I almost stopped in my tracks. Big as shit, right across his chest, he had a tattoo that ran from shoulder to shoulder of a bald eagle with arrows in its feet flying over an unfurling American flag. I couldn't believe it. He had to be nuts walking around up here like that. There wasn't anything even remotely subtle about this guy. Whatever he was using for a mind sure wasn't anything I recognized. He walked right by me, acting like he owned the mountain, without a word or a look. I liked that and breathed easier. I was looking to be unnoticeable.

This was weird for sure, and I hoped it wouldn't get any weirder. As I walked, I couldn't stop thinking about this Captain America guy and trying to figure out just what he was doing out here. It was one of the weirdest things I'd ever seen, surreal and real at the same time.

There's nothing to do in these little villages besides work the fields or flocks, fix your house, or tend to other chores. If you aren't doing that, you're at the chai shop. Everyone ends up in the chai shop at some point. Here it was a small three-sided stone lean-to with a kerosene stove in the back and a woodstove in the middle. It had stone walls and an open front that could be shuttered off if the weather shifted. There were tables and chairs and about six men here and there. A little man was busy making tea on an open fire at the front. I nodded at him as I walked in, and he started right away to make me a pot. I sat down as far from anyone as I could.

There were two men in the place who looked Mongolian; they were squatting on low backless benches in the far corner and keeping their eyes averted while in deep conversation. Mongols never looked you in the eye for more than a short glance. There were three other men all leaning on a table, speaking what sounded to me like Russian. They had bad-fitting suits and were drinking some weird green soda in bottles with Russian on the labels. The table behind me had a single man eating a Kabob. No one in the place looked local apart from me and the guy making chai, not even the Mongol camel herds. Peter was right about this being a crossroads.

The Russians weren't here for the water, that was sure, and the guy I'd passed on the way in, Captain America, wasn't either. I sat there hoping no one would speak to me; I knew only a few Chitrali words. The chai came, and I handed over five rupees and got my change with a nod.

I sat there sipping and listening to the Russians but never looking their way. Whatever they were discussing, it sounded important. Russians usually laugh a lot but not these three. Russians so serious and drinking soda pop almost made me laugh, but I couldn't afford to laugh. I was lucky Mickey wasn't there with me, or it would have been impossible not to. I hadn't expected to see so many different folks in this little village. It was a surprise.

I couldn't make heads or tails out of the jabber from the various tables in the place, but it kept on at a steady pace. I turned my attention to the guy with the kabob who now had a friend who had come in and joined him. They were definitely from somewhere else too. I kept my eyes down so as not to make contact with anyone in the room and my ears open. A chai shop in a tiny village in the lower Yarkhun with not a local in it—this was interesting if not just plain weird. I wondered if Captain America had been here before I'd come in. Somehow I doubted that. But it certainly would have topped things off, a real low-budget Casablanca. Then another man came in and sat down with the other two behind me.

"Is it through yet?" one asked the other in a heavy accented English. It was the first English I'd heard.

"No, not a thing as yet."

"And how long have they been here?"

"An hour or two and still going at it."

"Did you get anything?"

"No, not a twit."

They weren't English, at least not British English. They were dark-skinned and had what sounded like thick Indian accents. This was freaky. I'd heard three different languages now, none of which were local. I knew that all it would take was for anyone to ask me a question, and I'd be flipped in a wink as out of place. Till now, no one had given me any notice, and I liked that. That would hold only as long as I didn't speak, but the quarters were getting close. I sipped the last of my chai while keeping my eyes down and walked out without anyone taking much notice. One of the Russians looked up but turned right back to his conversation.

The sun was shining through low trees that lined a rock wall along a barley terrace. I walked looking for a place to sit. About a hundred yards down, there was break in the wall, and I went through and sat under the trees facing the field. I looked out across the barley and up at the snow-covered peaks. It was a beautiful place, even if it was full of weird people.

I sure wasn't cut out for this stuff I thought, but I had said I'd do the job, so I needed to do it as best I could. I still didn't like it. And when I was done, was it going to be good enough? I wasn't happy with the Russians and that Captain America guy. What the fuck was that all about? I needed to get back to Mastuj and process all I'd seen and get it on paper. I was feeling like this was not a good place to be. No big surprise, I guess. Why would they have bothered to hook me up to come out here if they were willing or able to do it themselves? It wasn't complicated, but it was looking more and more risky. You never knew what might happen with Russians out here; they could be even worse than the Chinese. Both were paranoid as hell and particularly jumpy about Americans or anyone that seemed like one.

I'd made a deal, and I would do what I said. I would, but putting myself in places like that chai shop the way I had was touchy; I needed to focus more. I had to remember that. All it would have taken was the chai boy asking me damn near anything, and I'd have been flipped faster than a chapati on a hot skillet. I needed to be ready for that. And one thing for sure was I didn't want to be made as American by any batch of Russians out here. What were they doing this far east anyway? And Captain America, what was his game, and how did he fit in the mix? He certainly wasn't hiding his colors. More was going on out here than anyone would think.

If I didn't look out of place, I'd be fine; at least I told myself that. But most everyone I'd seen out here so far looked out of place in some way. So if that was true, maybe I wasn't a threat to anyone. Playing my cards right was the key, and I liked that; I could work with that. I just needed to figure out what play was right, hopefully before I needed to make it.

I watched the cloud shadows moving across the mountains. The day was getting short. I could think about this on my way out. I needed to get back on the trail. I had two hours of hard trekking ahead and not much more light than that left in the day.

I got to Mastuj half an hour before the sun set and stopped to get a kabob and some tea. I popped my head into the den to see if the clock guy, Jerry, was in there. I was beginning to think I should start up that conversation again. I didn't know who he was or what he really was doing out here, but at least the score was even on that one. I might be able to find out something about the Russians I'd seen. I didn't think it was such a stretch, his looking for Russian clocks, anymore. But I didn't see him there. The boy brought my food, and I asked if he'd seen him. He shook his head like a dashboard dog and said, "Buy bottle chandu, Jerry. Go room."

"Room, which?"

"Last room, right side" His eyes lit up as he ran off like a young deer, tucking the five rupee note I'd handed him into his pocket.

The next morning I was up early. I wanted to get on the trail as soon as there was light. I pulled on my sandals and splashed icy water on my face and headed to get a chai. The morning was a combination of hazel, blue, and black with the brightest stars still showing. There was a champagne glow pushing up over the mountaintops in the east. Silhouettes of the ranges were layered deep in the sky as the first shot of sun broke just over a mountain, its warm fingers poking through the few clouds in its path and hitting my face.

At the chai shop the fires were already burning strong, and steam was coming off the pots. I thought about going by Jerry's room but decided I'd do it when I got back, I still had things to do in that village and didn't want to get delayed. By the time I arrived at the pass, above the village the sun was full in the sky, and smoke was twisting up from the cooking fires. Below lay the valley full of barley and wheat, green on green. The water running in the little creeks along the trail sounded like whispered conversations.

I sat at a table in front at the chai shop this time. The boy brought me a naan and hard cheese without a word. I took a bite of the bread. It was fresh, hot, and gritty, and the cheese was hard and sharp. Village cheeses were crap shoots; some were good, some were Ok, and some were crap. This one was good.

No one else was in the place now, but there'd been someone earlier. The boy was picking up empty pots and saucers from the table next to mine. It was a different place without the Russians and Cashmeres jabbering at each other. It was like in the Kush, except for the chairs: slow and quiet. I remembered conversations full of laughter and lots of smiles in places like this. I sat there thinking how much I loved the way life happened in these places.

I knew it wasn't like the Kush here, not really; it just reminded me of it. This place was a crossroads for god knows what and who. It could be the whole Yarkhun, Kashmir, Jammu, Wakhan, and maybe even the Pamir, with the Russians tossed in for good measure. I still hadn't seen any Chinese yet, and that seemed strange.

I sat there thinking about all I'd seen so far and heard the day before. Russians weren't uncommon in northern Afghanistan, but this was Pakistan. I would have expected to see Chinese if anyone out here, and I hadn't seen hide or hair of them. Another two or three hundred miles west, Russians wouldn't be so out of place, but here? And just who were the others with their Indo-English accents; were they Indians? Pakistanis? They would have been speaking Urdu if they were Pakistani and from around here. They had to be Kashmiri or from Jammu, Northern Indian of some stripe. What were they doing out here? The only folks I'd seen that looked like they belonged were the Mongol camel traders. They were nomadic and moved through Pakistan, Afghanistan, and Persia. You could run into them anywhere from Jammu to the Sudan.

I guess it didn't really matter if I knew the why or what, as long as I noticed it all and brought the info back to Lawrence. That's what they told me they wanted, and that was fine. But it was feeling a bit squirrelly. I couldn't help but wonder just what this place was all about. Especially with Captain America walking around out there like some surrealist painting. It was weird, all too weird.

I put my feet up on a chair, closed my eyes, and leaned back. The sun hit my face and shoulders, and I nodded off. Sure as shit, poof, there I was back in Baba's little hobbit home, sitting on the low bed and watching him poking at the fire like I'd never gone anywhere since the last time I found myself there.

"Ah, come on—give me a break," I heard myself say. He looked over, but he was not the old man I remembered. His face had turned young and his body straight.

"What happened to you? You look like you're twenty! I'm sleeping, right?"

"Don't be so sure of things." His lips didn't move, but I heard him speak in my head. "Want some chai?"

He was speaking in that language I didn't know but did. "Baba, how come I understand you? This has to be a dream."

"You know why," he said as he handed me a cup of chai on a saucer. He was old again now like I'd remembered him. "I don't know what this is—a dream, a message, a joke—but I don't care much right now. It's good to see you."

"Good to see you too. I didn't know how long you would be away, but it wasn't as long as I thought it might be."

"Away? What do you mean, away?"

"There's a lot before you to understand. It will happen in its own time; don't push. Drink your tea and get some rest."

"What are you talking about, what?"

"Remember the fish, the one you saw in the river behind the rock, pushing its head out looking for a bite? In the end he will get netted unless he knows when to look and when to hold." He turned and poked the fire, and I could hear a wind start to pick up outside. I stood up and walked toward the door.

"Keep the wind out—the dust too. I'd watch for rain."

I stepped out and could see miles and miles of mountains in all directions. When I turned back around, the door was gone.

"Skip, Skip," I heard.

I looked where the door to his little mud shack had been where the voice was calling my name. But all I could see were deep canyons leading off into the mountains. The sky opened then, and a face started to take form. It was round and pale. I blinked my eyes, and there was Jerry leaning over the table and shaking my foot.

"It's morning, time to wake up."

"What the fuck? I was in a good nod, asshole!" I shot back. I was stoked as the line came rolling off my tongue as I pulled out of my dream or whatever it was. Bam! I was on my game. It was like I was sitting inside myself and directing the show. That one line had made up for all the stupid stuff about being on college break, and I smiled inside, feeling on top for a change as I sculpted my best pissed-off look. I was actually glad he'd shown up. I wanted to get more information from him. And I knew I'd nailed him this time. He was hooked with the opium-head story now for sure. This couldn't have been timed better!

"If it ain't Jerry the clock man; you should know better than to bug a sleeping dog.

What you want, run out of chandu?"

"No, just thought I'd say hi."

"What, we're old friends all of a sudden? I was having a good dream, man."

"Look, Skip, I know we didn't get off to the best of starts the other day. I'll go with that, but it doesn't mean that I shouldn't say hello if I see you, does it? Especially out here. I mean, this isn't Lahore."

"Sure as shit isn't … That's why I'm here! You interested in telling me why you are?"

"I just saw you lying back and thought I'd come over and see what was up."

"*I* am up now, thanks very much! It's OK. Forget it."

"I'm for some chai. What about you? Your pot looks cold."

"What the hell, I'm up now. So what are you bugging old opium heads in the morning for? You didn't come all the way out here to see me is my guess."

"First off, it's afternoon, not morning. That must have been a long nod. I'm here to look at the timepiece I told you about."

There was nothing in his face that would give him up on this. Maybe he was a watch dealer after all, a watch dealer with one hell of an opium habit. Stranger things had happened.

"So was it what you were hoping for?"

"Better. The problem is it's not for sale."

"What? Why? I thought you said it was going to an antique store or something, and you just needed to get in between." I pulled my chair back and stretched out my legs on the ground.

"Yeah, I thought so, but it seems it has been paid for already."

"You come all the way out here to shortcut some big city dealer and find they already had your game cut before the merchandise left the warehouse? Been there, man. This is Pakistan; life's rough."

"Yeah, yeah, tell me something I don't know."

"There are over a million hairs in one square inch of a sea otter's fur …" I winked. "Maybe there's something else you can get from 'em—you ask?"

"I'm going to do just that. That's why I'm here—supposed to meet up with one of them. That true about otters?"

"You speak Russian? And yeah, it's true."

"They aren't Russians; they're Kashmiris. They speak English. They've just got Russian stuff…. Damn, that's a lot of hairs."

"Well, I'd love to stay and meet your friends and discuss zoology, but I got things to do and places to go now that I'm awake. Rain check on the tea, OK?"

I didn't want to be sitting there speaking English if any of that bunch I'd seen before happened to show up. As I walked away, two of the Kashmiris that I'd seen before passed me. I heard Jerry call to them as I turned the corner. If they were the clock dealers, then who were the Russians?

I walked out of the village toward the far end of the valley thinking about my dream or whatever it was and what Baba had said in the midst of all this shit. All these folks and the visits from Baba too were too much; I needed to let it go for a while, give it a rest. Things made more sense when I came back to them sometimes. There wasn't much of a picture yet, leastwise one I understood. It just didn't make any sense, none of it. But in the end it didn't matter. All I needed to do was gather the info, not figure out what it all was about. But still I couldn't help but wonder.

I walked out to the far northern end of the valley where the train track came out of the canyon. Broken granite shot up in sharp angles on either side of the canyon. Where the tracks ran, there was an embankment that fell off to a fast-moving stream that entered the valley, twisting like a snake and pooling up in eddies at each turn.

About a half mile up the tracks, well into the canyon I sat down, and opened my pouch. One of the things Charles had in there was a caliper with a note taped to it. It said "rail tracks, three places, 50 yards apart." I took the three measurements while walking up another half mile or so, looking to see if there was any sign of use. I couldn't imagine where this track came from or where it went. The only indication a train ever stopped in the valley was a small, raised stone landing along the tracks about a half mile from the village and three hundred yards or more from the closest barley terraces. But there was nothing there that looked like anyone had been there. If there had been a building there once, it was gone now. Still, the rails were shiny all the way, and the ties were tight, with all the spikes set.

I spotted a wad of paper in the rocks by the creek and slid down the bank to take a look. It was an empty crumpled pack of Russian cigarettes. Someone else had been up here pretty recently. It was dry. It must have been dropped since the rain stopped, and that wasn't more than four days ago. I stuck in it my pouch and looked around for more stuff. I spotted a fair amount of broken bottles and other crap here and there, lots of it Russian.

In this part of the Yarkhun, you would see Chinese and sometimes Indian stuff, but not Russian. Something was going on. And the broken bottles were not normal. People didn't throw out bottles; they were too valuable. They must have been thrown from a train by someone who didn't care. There had surely been train traffic judging from the crap along the creek side. It had been recent and maybe going on for a while. Everything I saw said these tracks were in use and not by locals. The Russians in the chai shop seemed like good candidates to have some connection to all this. Still, I was clueless about where a rail line that should have been deserted in 1948 or earlier had come from or where it went. There were no tracks out here, no train stations I'd ever heard of, at least not operating rail. There was no place for them to go or come from. Maybe there was a mine or quarry, but where? What direction was the destination? There were no answers here, no place to load railcars in the valley.

Tracks like these had been laid in some pretty far out places from Burma to the district of Lai in northern India, but most had long been abandoned and had rotted out or been torn apart for the steel and wood. But this one was working? How had anyone gotten railcars, not to mention an engine that worked out here? And who had managed to keep the rails tight like they were? This place was weird and getting weirder.

I walked the track that ran through the valley, picking up more stuff, and then headed back to the village and the chai shop. When I got there, everyone in the place looked local; that felt good for a change. I got a flatbread for the road and was getting ready to head back to Mastuj when Jerry came walking in. He looked at me but didn't say a word—just sat at another table and put his head down on folded arms. I walked over and sat down.

"What, I'm no longer cute enough to court?"

He looked up at me red-eyed. "Got any 'O'?"

"I might. Not feeling the best right now, are we?"

I did have a little bottle of chandu with me, so I pulled it out of my pouch and wiggled it in my fingers, smiling.

"I got Delhi belly, man. I've been tossing it all day."

"You gonna stay here tonight?"

"Can't. I've got to meet someone in Mastuj tomorrow. Can I get some of that opium, man? I'll pay for it."

"You sure as shit will. You walk in here, don't even say hi, and then you want my stash."

I winked. "This here is my personal stash, man. I boiled it my self. I don't know where you got your habits, but licking out those cups like you did the other day is like bobbing for apples in the local latrine. Bring your sorry-ass self upright here, and I'll give you a dose, but then I want to know what you're really doing here and as much as you know about this place. And you pay for the opium and any chai."

"Done," he said.

I poured about half of my little bottle of chandu in his tea, and he gulped it down like cold water. He leaned his head back and closed his eyes. After a few minutes, the tension started to leave his face, and his eyes cracked open a bit. "Thanks, man, I really needed that."

"I could see. You look like shit."

"Yep." He smiled without moving his head or looking at me.

"OK, its pay-up time. First the rupees; then tell me what your real story is."

He reached into his pocket and handed me a twenty rupee note.

"I don't have change."

"Keep it. I can afford it. Just glad you had something with you."

"I don't have a lot of interest in suffering, thank you. I don't go places without what I need. So now back to our conversation in the den. I don't get why you're out here. You don't even know how to smoke dope out here. I mean, come on, man—what's up? People don't come to Mastuj for the attractions, let alone to hike out to the villages. And shit, you don't even wear a watch; what's the deal?"

I was sure he was convinced I wasn't a threat by now, just another opium head. I knew there was more to him than he'd said, and clearly he had a tar habit, not just a bad belly. I knew the chandu would set the hook; it was good stuff. I always carried opium when I was in the mountains. You never knew when you might need it. One slippery rock in the river or a loose piece of shale at the wrong step, and you could find yourself walking for days with a broken arm or worse.

Jerry was convinced that I was just another addict hanging on a pipe wherever I could, and that was just fine. I sat there and watched him getting more and more relaxed as the opium started to take. I thought about the questions I had and just how I should ask them. It felt dishonest, but then an opportunity like this was too good. I didn't like this guy much. At least I thought I didn't; I really didn't know him. It wasn't like lying to a friend. Still, playacting in this way bugged me, but I was getting better at it. It hinted at some of my old life in Oakland, and I wasn't sure just how much of that I wanted to own. It was a thin veil now that I held at arm's length. More like a costume I used to wear. But now here I was planning to pump this guy for information, and he didn't have a clue. I didn't like working this way, but I needed to find out what he knew. He might know something about the tracks, where they went or came from and why all the Russians around and no Chinese.

"Why'd you come so far off the track without enough stash to hold you through, man? You should know better. I've seen the amount of O you eat."

"It's a toss, man. I never can tell how good the opium is going to be in places like this. I don't use opium all that much, only when I'm out of the city. I use morphine if I have a choice. I need a lot of O, good or bad."

"Licking out those chandu cups like you did is scary, man, and risky. You can seriously get sick from that. Not the opium, but the chandu. Who knows what the water they make it up with is like, and god knows what else slips in when they brew it. Smoke it, mix it with alcohol, or boil it like I do, but don't just lap it up. Even French hopheads that shoot the stuff cook it first."

"Yeah, I get it. I got the shits to beat the band on top of all the rest." He managed a smile; I could tell the opium was coming on. It was time for the real questions now, but I had to do it right. I didn't want to put him off. The opium would help, I knew that. It was better than anything he'd had up here for sure, and I'd given him a good slug.

"Look, Jerry, I went with the clock deal you ran at the den because I know none of us wants to be out on front street, and it was a bad spot for a conversation back in Mastuj. I get that piece. But we're deep in the Yarkhun way off the loop, not a place that draws tourists. There aren't any clocks in the shops here—come on, there aren't any shops! The other day I was sitting in here with three Russians at one table, what I guess was your pack of Kashmiris at another, and then a third batch that looked like camel herds out of the Pamir, all sucking up tea. The only local was the guy making the chai."

"It's interesting, isn't it?" He said, smiling.

"Yeah, you could say that; fucking strange, if you ask me. And get this—coming out here, I passed some guy that looked like a reject from Marvel Comics. I couldn't tell if he was Captain America or Sergeant Fury, but he wasn't hiding his spots. What do you know about this place?"

"It's a crossroads, man; I was sent here."

This was not a good thing I was hearing. Was there some other bunch of spooks in this game that had sent him out here for the same reasons I was here?

"To represent a wholesaler, a broker." He continued.

"Let me guess: it's not in clocks or watches."

"Well, not only. It's true that I do deal in watches and make a good dime at it, but that is not what I'm out here for—you know that. And you're not out here looking for opium; let's get straight with each other."

"I never said I was, and as I recall our deal, I straighten your head out, and you talk to me."

"OK, I'll play; I'm trying to make a sale. The Kashmiris you saw are interested in a large number of M14s and M16s. I happen to have a large number for sale. These particular guns went lost during training on Grande Island in Subic Bay, so they can't go just anywhere. The clocks are, well, added gravy; that's how it works. The Russians out here, as far as I can figure, are my competition. And Captain America is out here doing nothing but looking weird as far as I can tell. But like I told you, I've never been out here before."

"No shit," I said, not surprised and relieved hearing the rest of his story.

"I've been in places like this, man," he continued, "more than most, and that tattooed guy is like nobody I've ever run into before. I can't even begin to guess what's going on with him. Unless he's Navy intelligence looking for the guns, which I don't think is the deal, he's way too obvious. Besides, I don't think anyone knows they're missing yet. And if they do, they're looking in Manila or someplace close."

"Yeah, I can't figure him either. As long as he ignores me, I'm happy. I was out walking earlier and went up a canyon along the north side where train tracks come into the valley. I didn't know there were any trains out here. The rails were clean, the spikes were tight, and all the ties were in place. Got any idea what that's all about?"

"Those tracks come in from the north, from a place called Lasht. Never been there, but I understand it's hot right now; at least that is what my people say. If you follow them out to the south, you end up somewhere in Russia, they tell me. That's all I know."

"You see any Chinese up here? Usually they're all over the place in the north Pamir and the Wakhan?"

"Nope, none, zip. And I hope I don't. I got enough competition with the Russians."

"You're in guns—well, that makes sense—but I still don't get Russians in Pakistan."

"Come on, this isn't Pakistan; you know that. This is the Northwest Territories, tribal. And what I hear through the grapevine is that Russia is making eyes at Afghanistan, and it's just a matter of time before they hook it up."

"Give me break. Afghanis won't marry up with Russia, or anyone for that matter. The Russians must have a death wish. Never happen."

"It's just what I hear, man, and I hear it's already a done deal, just a timing issue. No complaints here. It could be good for business. That's what this rail line's about, I think; somehow, it's part of the deal."

Was this guy Jerry for real? He was coming out like I hadn't expected. Who did he think I was now? Was he just loosening up on the opium, or had he decided I was in his camp for some reason? I was hearing things I really didn't want to know but needed to I guess. This was too crazy—something going down between Russia and Afghanistan? I couldn't imagine that the Kuchi, Pashto, Pacto, Waziri, and a hundred other tribes would ever let any others take up in their lands. He couldn't be right. But there was lots of activity out here that didn't make any sense without some off-the-wall take on it, and his take was as good as any at this point. Even if he wasn't right, he'd given me the keys for my report to Lawrence and maybe the reason they had me up here in the first place.

"I'm heading back to Mastuj. You coming?" Jerry said as he stood up.

"Sure, fine."

"So, Skip, are you going to tell me just what you are doing up here?"

"*Did,*" I answered softly.

The weather had gone bad again, and I spent my time in Mastuj turning up what might be of interest there. Jerry had taken off to some meeting a few days after we'd talked, and I hadn't seen him since. Time was getting shorter, and I needed to get to Rawalpindi and settle up with Lawrence. It didn't look like the weather was going to let me back out in the hills anytime soon. I had plenty enough information to make it worth it. I already knew more than I wanted to and had zero interest in spooking around out here anymore.

I hadn't seen or heard a word of Peter, who was supposed to be watching me. I figured he must be close, but I had no idea how to contact him. I'd sent a message with a goat herd to the hunting camp, but I got no answer.

The weather continued to be bad, and I was ready to get out. I'd walked out to the village a couple times when the rain had slowed. It was cold and wet, and not much was new. There had been a group of Russians in the village each time, but only two were repeat faces. I'd seen a train pass through too, with seven cars behind an old black coal burner: a fuel car, then two boxcars and a flat car with three lumps under tarps, two passenger cars full of Russian solders from what I could see, and another flat car with three more lumps under tarps. I'd walked out to the landing thinking I might make out what was under the tarps when the train stopped, but it never did stop; it just kept right on heading south.

That same day, the boy at the chai shop asked me in broken English where I was from. I couldn't fake it any longer and told him Bombay. Four Russian heads turned in unison like automatic doors right then. I'd managed to keep a low profile up till then, but it was blown big-time now. I didn't know what that meant other than that my usefulness as a pair of ears and eyes in this village was over. I wasn't sure what the Russians were thinking, but they weren't happy thoughts, judging from their faces. I'd been in that chai shop a whole lot while they had been talking. I didn't understand a word, but they didn't know that.

Right then, I realized I didn't want all this stuff in my head. I must have been nuts to say OK to Charles and the others. I hadn't known what was going on out here, and now I didn't want to. I had no plans to return to the States, so why did it matter if old stuff was cleaned up or not?

I'd gathered all this information, and now I was feeling like a quail on a fence post, just waiting to hear the pop and feel my feathers fly. I'd been focused on getting what I needed for Charles and Lawrence and figured I had enough to prove that I'd done the work. I hadn't wanted to get made by anyone, but no luck there. And in no way did I want the Russians to be the ones that made me, but that was history now.

I'd started carrying my little Walther with one in the chamber all the time. I was a few thousand dollars richer with a new passport, and that took off a little of the edge, but only very little. I kept thinking about Peshawar, about Cecile and Amber, and how much I really would rather be there. I wondered about Mickey. Had he gone to Margao like we planned, and what was he up to? I wanted to be anywhere but in Mastuj. It had been more than a few days since I'd figured my message had got to the hunting camp, and still no Peter, and that didn't make me any less anxious.

I went to the den late in the afternoon to try to relax. I hadn't been there because I didn't know when Peter was going to turn up, and I didn't want any more people seeing us together than need be. But I was finished sitting around that little room waiting. When I got there, I lay back on the headrest and made a pipe. I took a long, deep draw and closed my eyes. When I opened them, in walked the two Russians from the village who were always there. They sat down across the little room. One spotted me right away and poked his friend in the arm. They looked over, smiled, and nodded a greeting. I nodded back and started to make my next pipe. I focused as best I could and didn't look up again—just went on with what I was doing while keeping my ears open. They were talking in Russian, and I could hear their voices moving closer. They sat down a few feet away, just out of my line of vision, and started to smoke their hand pipes.

"Hello, hello, Englishman," said one in a practiced and good American English.

I looked up without lifting my head off the rest and said, "I'm not English."

"Not English—American then?" He looked at his friend and said something I didn't understand. I leaned up on my elbow, and my vest fell open, uncovering the Walther in its slip holster. I could see their eyes flash to it and then lift like they hadn't noticed.

"I'm from Bombay, and if you have something to say to me, say it in English, not in Czechoslovakian or whatever it is you're talking. I'm trying to get my head screwed on here and still have a way to go, if you don't mind?"

I lay back on the headrest and started to finish making my pipe, hoping I'd been convincing enough. I wanted them to think I was just another opium head in the back hills, hanging on a pipe. It was weak, I knew, but not out of character for what I'd been doing, and I didn't have any other play. Jerry had bought this play in the end, it seemed, and if he'd had contact with these guys, he might have said something. It was the best riff I could run. I hadn't expected the Russians here. They hadn't been in Mastuj, or at least I hadn't seen them. If they were here for a reason, I didn't want that reason to be me or turn into being me, but I had a sinking feeling about that.

"Mr. Bombay, were not Czech. It's Russian we speak. You know what we say in Russia?"

"Haven't a clue." I looked up. "What do they say in Russia? Piss off as many opium addicts as you can in the Yarkhun? Fifty points for each five minutes you keep them from getting their head straight?"

This set them back a pace or two. A pissed-off addict. At least the idea had wings. Keeping it up was the key now.

"If you don't mind, I'd like to smoke in peace till I'm where I need to be. Give me a half hour or so to mellow, and then we can talk languages and culture and stuff, OK, Russians?" I shook my head and lay down again and proceeded to work on a pipe. I lay there and smoked just about as much as I could take. I was getting nauseous, and my head was swimming. They kept sitting there smoking those little sepses and talking in low voices.

The one who spoke English finally said, "Mr. Bombay, in Russia we speak Russian to our comrades, French to our lovers, and English to our enemies."

"Let me get this right—if I speak French, you'll kiss me? I guess I'm just lucky." I went back to my pipe.

"We'll be seeing you, Bombay." They got up to leave.

"I don't know, mon ami—have to check with my wife." They stared at me angrily. I shook my head, trying like hell to keep up the act, and lay back and started on another pipe. Finally they left.

Sweat was dripping down my side now onto my belly, and my head was swimming from so much opium. I sat up and ordered tea. The last comment, I didn't like. I wasn't interested in seeing either of these guys again. I ate some bread, and my stomach started to settle a bit. I went off to my room, looking over my shoulder all the way. I stopped to take a leak, keeping my free hand on my Walther while I listened for any noise coming up on me. I didn't like this feeling. The Russians had shown up here for some reason, and I couldn't get it out of my head that it could well be me.

I got to my room, closed the door, and slipped the foot of the bed in front of it. I lay down with the Walther out and in reach. I'd smoked a lot of opium. I couldn't keep my eyes open and fell into a deep sleep. Suddenly I felt the bed move and heard the door bang against it. My eyes shot open, and I tried to focus in the dark. I grabbed around for the little automatic. Just then I heard Peter's voice.

"Skip, you in there?"

"Shit, where the fuck have you been?" I said jumping up and sliding the bed away from the door. "I needed to get the hell out of here yesterday."

Peter stepped into the room. "Yeah, I know, saw the Russians. You get what you needed to or do we need to go deeper, there's more of this stuff out in Abi-wahkun?"

"I got all I'm getting. I need to get to Malakand and down to Rawalpindi. Let's get it in the wind now." I stood up and grabbed my bag.

It was dark, and a light rain was falling. The headlamps from the Rover lit up the road like two little spotlights as we passed out of town. The river was high, and you could hear the rumble of water over the sound of the engine. It got even louder whenever we slowed down for a turn or a washout. I was muddy-headed from all the opium, and I drifted off into a restless sleep.

When I opened my eyes, or thought I had, I was in a dimly lit room, and Baba was huddling over his fire again and poking at two small pots of chai in the coals. I started to stand, and the low roof came toward my head. Just then, the roof opened, and a huge raven flapped its wings and lifted me into a deep blue sky. I was carried up into the clouds, where I looked down at Baba squatting at the fire and looking like he was six feet away. The air whooshed passed my ears and tossed my hair as the wings flapped harder and harder. I heard Baba's voice through the sound.

"Some chai?"

He lifted his head and looked me in the eyes, his face young and unwrinkled, his eyes steely gray on white. I tried to speak, but the words couldn't reach my mouth. I reached out a hand for the saucer of steaming chai. I could smell it. It hung there, a swirling mist, free-floating and spinning like a dervish, the saucer misting and trailing its steam into the sky. Then the raven flew off and disappeared. I looked down at my feet, and they were dancing round and round on layers of geometric patterns of reds, browns, and yellows. Deeper and deeper the layers went. The more I looked, the deeper the endless mix of color and form seemed. When I looked up, Baba was sitting on the edge of his little bed, a cup and saucer in hand and a broad smile across his face that was old and wrinkled again. My feet were planted on the dirt floor, and the mist from the saucer faded, and the walls and roof fell silently back into place. We sat there looking at each other.

"Baba, what the hell?"

"Just a visit to see how you were doing."

"How I'm doing? I'm riding downriver in the Yarkhun with Russians on my ass. Then a bird picks me up and drops me here?"

"Sounds about right. How are you? Do you still think the world is predictable?"

"Did I ever?"

"Drink your chai. I spent all the milk on it."

I sipped the chai from the saucer, and it was like ambrosia, like drinking a mountain lake wrapped in petals of jasmine and rose, a taste like a summer breeze up a canyon. There were no words, just taste and smell.

"Baba, what is this?"

"What is it?"

"I can't tell."

"Chai. I want to tell you something, so listen. The world shakes. It will not change. Still, we have reasons for whatever we do. They may not be what you think—this is important. So when the bird comes, go with her and take the gifts. Now drink. That's the best chai you'll be getting for a while, so don't waste it."

I couldn't speak. I wanted to, but no sound came out of my mouth. I couldn't tell if my mouth was even moving. All I could do was sip the chai, each sip getting more and more intense. I looked at Baba, and the walls fell away again. I looked back at my chai, and mist was pouring off the saucer and filling the space all around me. Soon, I was swirling round and round with the brown mist engulfing me, spinning faster and faster. I closed my eyes; my stomach was getting queasy. Then my eyes popped open, and I saw tubes of light bouncing along and rain falling on the windshield. I was back in the Rover. I pulled my window open as fast as I could, stuck my head out, and puked my guts and then turned my face into the rain.

"Too much opium," Peter called out from the driver's seat.

"Seems like it, or that gas heater you got." I reached down and shut off the flame.

"Need to keep the window open when the heat's on—not good otherwise."

We came to the hunting station and pulled in.

"We stopping here for a reason, man?" I looked at Peter, hoping this wasn't about being horny.

"This is it for now. You need to sleep, and I need to say good-bye."

"Look, Peter, you can screw whoever you want, but do it when I'm out of dodge, OK? I just left two very unhappy Russians who were giving me a raft of shit, and I would like to put as much distance between them and me as possible before sunlight; you know what I'm saying?"

"Not to worry. I understand they have their hands full. I don't think they will be doing much traveling."

"And what makes you think that?"

"Lark found out about them when they came into Mastuj. Not a good prospect."

"Lark? Who's Lark?"

"You see a guy with a big eagle tattooed on his chest while you were wandering round?"

"Shit, yes; I figured him for Special Forces or some kind of insanity. I couldn't believe him; wherever he got trained, they need new teachers or smarter students."

"Looks that way, I know, but he's not American; he's an Australian. He's weirdly fixed on the United States—loves anything and everything American. He's got the training though; he was some kind of special military, ranger or something. He lost it in Laos somewhere, and they had to pull him, so he wandered out here. He can't stand Russians because the United States doesn't like them. I happened to see him yesterday and told him there were two in town."

"That's great! But I was with those two not two hours before you came and got me, and they have a batch of friends up the road. Now if some Australian wacko is about to do god knows what, who do you think they'll finger?"

"Sorry, but still can't go until sunlight. The river washed out the road about five miles down, and I can't crawl past it in the dark. We stay here and sleep, then we're off as soon as the light shows. Don't worry—I'll pop anyone who comes round with bad ideas."

There was nothing I could do but wait. Once inside, I nodded off with my Walther in my hand and the dream of Baba chasing my sleep.

Soon, I woke up to the sun starting to lighten the sky and hills. At the main building, smoke was billowing out the stovepipe. I got a tea, and just then Peter stepped in with his little gal two steps behind.

"Ready to go hill climb?"

"Yesterday."

"Already got bread and cheese in the car. Let's move. I don't want anyone showing before we're gone. No telling what Lark did last night. He's nuts."

"So I figured."

We drove south to a big washout. He was right: the road was gone. We never would have made it in the dark. It took a good two hours and some serious shoveling to get past. Once we were on the southern side and moving again, I felt as good as I had in days. If anyone was behind us, they'd have to have four-wheel drive, a winch, and a real hard-on to get past that washout. We bounced along most of the day until we finally came into Malakand.

"I think Ameed is in his shop. You should check in with him before you move out."

"OK, is this the last I see of you?"

"Unless you're headed to India. I'm off for some R&R as soon as Ameed knows you're back."

"Sounds cool. I'm not planning on India right away, but soon maybe. Might see you on the beach. Anyway, thanks for the lift, the cover, and the conversation." I shook his hand through the window, and there was that grip, like a vice. "Really, thanks man."

"Like to be of help when I can," he said and drove off.

Even in this drippy weather, Malakand was a beautiful place. I walked toward the footbridge, passing stone buildings with carved shutters and doors. I wondered how long a place like this could exist. It was a slice out of time. You'd find untouched villages deep in the Hindu Kush, but towns of this size where buses ran were very few now, and this one could be the last of a kind. It was sad, but clearly its days were numbered. I noticed plastic shoes hung in one storefront, marking the beginning of the end—unnatural colors stark against the wood, stone, clay, steel, copper, and brass everywhere else. Just then I heard Baba in my head and could see him standing right in the middle of my forehead.

"You're lucky to see this place. Most have no eyes for it."

Then he was gone as quickly as he'd showed up, and I was standing at the footbridge, looking across to the other side. I walked to Ameed's shop and went in. He was sitting in the same spot where I'd first seen him. The room smelled of black tobacco, and he looked up as I entered and called to his boy to get us tea.

"Al-salaam alaykum, good to see you, my friend."

"Wa alaykum al-salaam, good to see you too."

"So how did you manage? You find what you were looking for?" he asked excitedly.

"Yep, I think so, though I'm still not sure why they needed me to do it."

"They likely didn't need you for what you think, Skip. It's more probable they wanted you to see what they already had an idea about. That's how it works. It's perspective they need more than objects or people. That is easy stuff. They chose you most likely because they wanted someone to put what they were hearing into context."

"That's not what I was told to do. I was told to gather information, and I did. And got a lot more than I thought I would. I wasn't expecting what was out there. I've been in the Yarkhun and never seen what I did this time."

"That's what I meant by context. They don't understand it and need someone who does."

The tea had arrived, and we drank in silence for a time. What Ameed had said started me thinking, and I didn't like what I was thinking. Had I been sent out here in some kind of training or test? Was I going to be able to get away from these guys after I finished this, or were they going to dig their claws in deeper?

"You still have the Walther, Skip?" Ameed asked.

"I sure do. Thanks for the loan. It helped me sleep more than once." I took off my vest and slipped off the holster, folded it up like I had received it, and handed it to Ameed.

He looked at the little automatic still in its slip, and with a smile, he ran his finger across the breach and licked it.

"You fired it?"

"Yep, I fired a clip at the hunting camp, to check it out."

"Did it work? Did you like it?"

"As true as any I've ever fired and as smooth. It made me feel a few feet taller when I needed to, thanks." I bowed my head in a sign of gratitude.

He reached behind into a carved wooden box and pulled out a short silver chain with a Lapis nugget attached. The Lapis was deep blue, laced with thick gold veins. He took the chain and hung it from a small loop on the holster and then wrapped the strap around the holster tight again and held it out to me. "This is a gift, a loan no more. I think you will find it a good possession."

I sat there and didn't know just what to think. That gun was very valuable out here, and the nugget was like nothing I'd ever seen before. Finally I took it from him and thanked him, bowing my head. I knew that offering to pay for it would be an insult, and not accepting it also would be. Still, I wasn't sure why he was giving it to me. For a moment I was worried he might be setting me up to marry his daughter or something.

We had spent very little time together, but I liked him. He was a solid man, and I knew instinctively that I could trust him. I guessed he felt the same way about me. The gift in the end had nothing to do with his daughter, and we sat and talked for a long time and shared a meal.

"I must get a room, Ameed. I need to be on the bus in the morning. Thank you for your friendship and help. I am sure we will see each other again." I got up to leave.

"Please stay here. There is a room in the back with a stove and a bed."

Morning came quickly. I'd slept better than I had for days. It felt not only safe in Ameed's little room but also kind of like home. When I woke up, there was a warm flatbread and chai at my bedside. I ate and drank and then went out into the shop. Ameed wasn't there, but his boy was standing watch at the door.

"Ameed?" I asked the boy.

"Is gone. Coming tonight only." He bowed his head.

I needed to go. The bus to Rawalpindi was leaving in a half hour.

"Tell Ameed thank you, thank you."

"English man, thank you, yes, I tell him." He bowed again, and I left.

I watched the road rolling by and waited for the dirt to end and the pavement to start. The farther down the mountains we got, the warmer it was. Soon, drizzly weather changed to the hot humid haze of the Punjab. You knew you were back in lowland Pakistan by the smell and heat. We'd been traveling about five hours when we hit the main road to Rawalpindi at Nowshera. The bus had been full until we got here. Now we were half-empty, and that meant stopping for everyone until we filled up again. That meant more hours on the road ahead—no idea how many.

We hit the outskirts of Rawalpindi late in the afternoon. I had the bus driver drop me at a road house about a mile from town proper, where I got a room. I went down to eat. The place was filled with truck drivers. Soon there wasn't a seat left in the place. As it grew darker a couple of men came out from the kitchen and hung a sheet from a roof beam in the back of the place and brought out an old 16-millimeter projector and set it up on a table. It was movie night. The film was Indian with Urdu subtitles. The best I could make of it was a story about a Muslim family in Bihar. It was in black and white and looked like it was made before the partition. It had the standard plot about the poor oppressed Muslims in India and evil rich Hindus. I gave my seat to a trucker who was standing there wrapped up in the film and wound my way up to my room.

I lay back in my room and thought about how much I had changed since I had come out East. I wasn't the same street-smart kid I had been. My life had taken sharp turns and twists and dropped me in the middle of a world as far from where I was raised as anyone could be. I lay there thinking, wondering if I was ever going to be able to return to anything that felt like home, or was I home now?

It was different for me now than I'd remembered. It was like being alive inside my own image of self. I'd lost anything I might have called home identity in a way. I wasn't sure if I liked that or not. What I did know was it felt right. I fell asleep thinking about all this, and the next thing I knew, I was waking up as the sun started to shine through the slats in the shutters.

I splashed some water on my face and crossed the room to open the window. The morning air was cool, and mist from the cooking fires was just starting to layer out over the city. I looked down the street at an endless string of trucks and stops and wondered just how Lawrence was planning to find me. Rawalpindi was a big city, half a million people or more, split down the middle between the cantonment and old town.

It didn't take long though. I was looking down the street when I saw a man with a familiar face heading my way; it was Lawrence with another man I didn't recognize. I thought about calling out but decided that wasn't a good idea. If he was this close, it wouldn't be long before he was at the door. I was right; in less then ten minutes, I heard the knock and opened the door.

"Mind if I come in, Tony?"

"Make yourself at home," I said and stepped aside. "How in hell did you find me so quickly? I figured it would take at least a day with all the truck stops in this city."

"I knew the direction you were coming from and what bus you'd be on—that is, if you didn't change in Nowshera. Ameed told me when you had planned to leave Malakand. Put all that in the hopper, and the rest is not all that hard to do."

"I guess."

"How are you, Tony?"

"That depends on what it is you want. If you want information, I'm fine; if you want what I think about all the information I have, well, you didn't pay me for that. But I could consider sharing if I knew that my paperwork was filed in San Francisco?"

"Look, Tony, we said we would do that for you, and we don't say we'll do things we can't or won't, all things being right." He leaned on the window sill and looked at me.

"OK. Everything that you said and your people Ameed and Peter were cool; it all worked fine. I liked both of them. Peter's a little on the line with the women, but who am I to judge? He was there when I needed him. Almost."

"That's more than I can say for your friend."

"My friend? What's that supposed to mean?"

"Your friend Mickey—he's been like a fungus that won't let go of us."

"So Twitch is spooking you? That's something, I bet. How do you like it?" I laughed.

"That's not it, Tony." His voice was very direct.

"He won't believe that you are OK and that we're working together. He keeps showing up at bad times. Look, he's your friend, so we've been cool with him, but it's getting old."

"What's that supposed to mean, man? You can't deal with Mickey? You do anything to him, and everything I found in the Yarkhun will disappear as fast as your last piss! And you can keep the papers. Understand? Did you try to tell him straight up what the deal was?"

"We did—Amber and Cecile even tried—but he wouldn't have it. He was sure we were holding you someplace and was determined to find out where. You have to do something, Tony. Get him on track, or someone will whack him. I don't want that to happen. You know I don't like dopers, but Mickey is not a morphine head just out there, and he's your friend. He's been eating lots of acid is my guess, and it might not be good acid. There is a lot of crud around these days. Believe me—we know."

"Let me get this right: you and Amber and Cecile have some connection? Mickey figured that out, and he started spooking your asses, thinking he can help me? And this is a big issue for you and your do-anything, go-anywhere crowd?"

"Spot on to all of the above. Amber and Cecile—we know them, and we knew you were housed there for a few days. We went by, Charles and me, to check it out. Didn't know what you might have told them. Mickey showed up at the same time, and that's when it all started. He's sure it's some kind of cosmic conspiracy. He's not a risk to us, just a nuisance, but that's not the trouble. He's a risk to himself. Lots of folks know bits and pieces about what we do. It won't be long before someone figures he's connected in some way. The more he gets seen where we are, the more at risk he is. That could be a big problem for someone who doesn't have a clue. And believe me, he doesn't have a clue right now. He might have at some point, but it's gone out the window now."

"So what about the girls?"

"Don't have the slightest clue. They left Peshawar. They were interested in you for sure."

"Yeah, I miss them now and again too. To think I was relaxed and happy not an hour ago." I shook my head. "So where's Mickey, do you know?"

"You bet we do. He's at the Lawrey Hotel in old town, room 9, with a passel of Austrian hippies with bags full of dope."

"OK, how do I give you my stuff so I can get over and see what's up with Twitch? Do I write it out or something?"

"No! The way it goes is you tell me all you found, and I record you, and then we gather and listen to the tape. When we agree it's good information, we file the papers. After that, we meet again and have a conversation about any pieces that interest us. Then when that's all recorded and booked, we debrief you one more time. Then you're done. So the sooner we get the first recording, the sooner you can go and see what you can do about straightening out Mickey."

"I thought you said you had done the paperwork? What kind of bullshit is this?"

"Tony, we were clear when we agreed to work together that we'd do the papers when we were satisfied what you brought was what we asked for. We were all there for that, as I recall."

He was right, but I thought I'd give being indignant a shot.

"Just working my game," I said, smiling.

If the girls were no longer in Peshawar, I had no reason to go back there. That was sad but not unexpected. It was for the best. I wasn't a make-house type anyway, and I knew it.

"So turn on your recorder. Let's get this done."

Lawrence pulled out a little Sony cassette recorder. It took about an hour to put all the base information onto tape without adding any personal takes on how it all added up to me. I was holding back on that piece in case they tried to hold back on the papers. I was hired to gather information, and I'd done that. If they wanted my take on what I saw out there, they needed to fulfill their part first. All in all, Lawrence seemed pleased with what he heard. He told me that he was sure to be back soon, and I should think about details and what I thought might be going on up there.

As soon as he was out the door, I headed for old town and the Lawrey Hotel. It was midday, and the sun was somewhere in the sky, but you couldn't tell just where through the hazy air that made it grayish yellow from horizon to horizon.

I walked through the door at the Lawrey and asked the way to room 9. They pointed me down a narrow hallway that ran straight back to the right of the stairs. The smell of hashish filled the space. There were lots of open doors with people going in and out. As I passed, I glanced in at people laid out smoking hashish, shooting morphine, or god know what all. Some eyes followed me, but most couldn't have followed a bouncing ball without breaking their necks. The ones who did look were trying to figure why a tribal would be walking around in their hotel, and I bet they were worried about that. When I came to Mickey's room, the door was closed, but I could hear voices inside. I knocked and opened the door at the same time. I didn't want any paranoid hippie locking me out. Mickey was sitting on the bed with a set of Aleister Crowley tarot cards laid out all around him.

"How's tricks, Twitch?" I said before he could look up.

"Dance in hell, mate, if it ain't Mr. Skip! I figured those spooks had you chained up someplace. Where in hell have you been, mate?"

"I told you I had to go do work, remember?"

"Look, mate, I got it figured. It's those girls and the two we road with from Landi Kotal. They're trying to take your brain, but it's not theirs, mate. It's all bloody slow like an old bread pudding."

I just stood there looking at him. I didn't know what he was talking about, but he sure thought he did. There were two others in the room—one on the floor against the wall morphed out of his mind and drooling, completely gone, and the other mumbling and looking out into space near the window.

"Come on, Twitch, get a grip. What in the hell are you doing here with these trogs? What have you been taking, man?" I grabbed him by the arm. It felt like he was made of string cheese. He'd always been skinny, but this was bad. "Shit, man, when was the last time you ate?" I pulled him off the bed. "Get your bag. Lets get out of here. We need to talk."

"We can talk here, mate; it's safe." He fell back on the bed.

This wasn't the Twitch I knew—what had happened? "Shit, man, this place stinks, and you do too. And it's the last thing from safe. When was the last time you saw soap?"

"Good to see you too, mate. They let you out, or you skate? I thought you were dead or as good by now. I've been looking all over for you, but I couldn't find where they bloody had you, mate. Been sticking to that Charles and Lawrence like a bad smell but couldn't get a shift or bugger all about where they had you. I tried, mate." He rolled his head, and his eye started twitching. He wasn't tracking. He knew it was me, but that was about it. I needed to get through to him. He had to get that he needed to lay off with Lawrence and Charles. Lawrence was right; acting like he was would get him in serious trouble. He was so gone, I couldn't believe it was him. I needed to get him where he could sleep it off or at least try to. I jammed his stuff in his bag and dragged him out the door. When we got outside, I flagged a rickshaw to the truck stop. I got him a room and sat him on the bed and sent the boy out for a Coke and some kabobs.

"My cards, where are my cards?" His hands wandered over the bed.

"I got everything, man. Cool your jets."

I poured the Coke into a glass and handed it to him. He ate and drank a little, and the twitch in his eye started to slow down. His eyes were like saucers, wide and black, and his skin was pale. It was bad. Finally he lay back on the bed, and I could feel him relax. I put my feet up on the little table and leaned back in the chair. I had been in the Yarkhun almost five weeks, and seeing Mickey, even as toasted as he was, loosened some of the knots in my gut, and I drifted off to sleep.

I woke up with the stove burning and popping. Kerosene lamps were lit, and Mickey was sitting on the bed, his yarrow sticks set out in two neat piles with his *I Ching* open. Next to it was an open copy of the Kabbalah. He was looking out the window, his head sliding to one side in rhythm with his eye.

"You OK, man?" I asked.

"It all makes sense now—I didn't think it would, but it does, mate." He didn't look at me when he spoke; he just kept looking out the window.

"What makes sense, man?"

"I've been looking around places, all the stations on the line, mate. They all have the same bloody destinations. If time was a bit slower, I could see it better, but in the end it isn't a matter. All the stories, they're all the bloody same no matter who tells them: the Kabbalah, the *I Ching,* the tarot, all the same, all the same. It all fits like some key: Vedic astrology, numerology, all of it. It's all a sea chock-full of fish … all the same bloody fish." He looked up.

"What in hell, man? Get a grip! You need to listen to me and hear what I'm telling you. Remember the last time we were together, when I told you what I was up to? You knew I was working for Charles and Lawrence. It was all cool. You're slipping off the rail, man. We agreed to meet in Margao, and now I find you here in Rawalpindi buzzed beyond belief and running some crap George Orwell couldn't follow; what the hell happened with you, man?"

He was so far gone that I couldn't find a space to get to him. I needed him straight; that was clear. Lawrence was right—if I hadn't known the Mickey from the months I'd spent with him, I would have walked away right there and then.

He looked over my way finally, and I could see a spark of the old Twitch behind the sunken eyes.

"Good to see you, man," I said.

"Likewise, mate." He lay back on the bed and fell asleep.

Early the next morning, I went to his room to see if he'd slept it off yet. He was sitting on the bed again, with his tarot cards out on the table, and smoking Hashish in a hand pipe. The room was full of smoke. I stood at the door.

"How you doing, man? Let's get some chai?"

"Sure, mate, chai. Good to see you're back."

He had clean clothes on, and his hair was wet. "You washed up, man—good idea; it will be easier to sit at the same table with you now," I joked. "What the fuck has been going on with you, man?" I pulled up a chair and sat next to the bed. He started right off.

"I did a lot of reading, mate, while I was looking for you. I finally got it; I figured it all out. But I couldn't tell you about it—didn't know where you were. I figured Charles and Lawrence had you locked down somewhere, and it was all making sense, and I couldn't find you to bloody tell you."

Looking into his good eye was like looking down a deep, open well full of black rocks. Wherever he was, I wasn't. "Look, Mickey, you are not in the best shape, man. You need to get out of town, go to India like we planned. Remember I was going to meet you in Margao? If you keep hanging here in Pakistan, it could be a bad thing, trust me. What I'm doing with Charles and Lawrence is OK—it's mellow, really. But I need to finish up, and you need to stay clear, understand?

"Skip, I've got the key. Nobody is going to do bugger all to anyone, anything. Look, I've figured it all out. It's real simple. Let me tell you."

I cut him off. "Twitch, you've got to get out of Pakistan and soon. I'd love to hear what you've figured out and all that—I'm sure it's real—but tell me about in it Bombay, OK?"

I pulled a fistful of rupees out of my pouch and stuck them on the bed. "There's enough money here to get the train to Bombay and get a room there. Do that and wait for me; I'll be there in a week or so. Understand?" I looked at him, waiting to see if what I had said connected. He looked down at the money and looked up with a sad face. He picked up the rupees.

"OK, I'll see you in Bombay in a week. Don't bugger off, mate, or be bloody late."

"OK, man, and don't shadow Charles or Lawrence anymore, OK?"

"OK, if that's what you want, mate."

I heard a knock down the hall and Lawrence calling out my name. "Mickey, look, I have to go. You get some food and then the train, and I'll catch you up in a week. Get a room at the Rex."

"All right, mate, the Rex."

I got up to leave, and he reached out and handed me his worn copy of the *I Ching* and his pouch of yarrow sticks and said, "Skip, I've figured it all out, mate, I really have—bloody simple, bloody simple. You take this and bring it with you to Bombay, and I'll show you how it all works when you get there."

"You keep it. I'll do the *I Ching* when I get to India."

He smiled a strange smile. "Skip, you know I don't need the book, but you might. I know it word for word, front to back. You take it."

It felt weird, but I had to go. I took the book and the yarrow sticks worn smooth and dark from years of use. "See you in a week—or so." I stood up and headed off to meet Lawrence.

t the meeting all I could do was take their word that the paperwork had been filed. We all knew there wasn't any way to tell short of my going back to the States, and that wasn't anywhere near what I was planning, and they knew it. At the meeting I sat on one side of a table while five men, two of whom I'd never seen before, asked me questions about all the stuff on the tape, about the trains, the tracks, the Russians, the Kashmiris, and all the rest. I'd decided not to tell them about Jerry or the gun deals, that was one card I wanted to keep to play later if I needed it.

After all the questions had been asked and answered more times than I could count, they all stood up like someone had turned a switch and in unison started to leave. I stepped up in front of the man who'd directed the questioning.

"So why'd you send me to do this?" I asked, looking him directly in the eyes. "From what I saw out there, at least two people could have got this information for you, two who were already in place."

"Well," he said, smiling, "in a way you're right, but there was no one out there who was going to see it like you, and that's what we wanted." He stepped to the side to leave, and I stepped back in front of him.

"Then it's my take you wanted, not the information?" He waved off his friends, who had moved in.

"Look, Tony, we both know you're no slouch. That could be good luck or bad depending on how you see it. But you and I both know you got a brain. That and your ability to blend in and still use that brain add a perspective we appreciate that benefits us all. Your money belt, not to mention the passport and the papers, should indicate how much we appreciate it. We work with people like you if we can find them because you're a finite resource. We keep an eye on folks who have the lights on out here; there aren't that many."

I stepped back, thinking about what he'd said, and watched the room empty. When they had gone, I grabbed my pouch off the back of the chair and headed out the door. Charles was waiting with a guy I didn't recognize.

"You're almost done, Tony. How are you feeling about it all?" Charles asked reaching out a hand.

"Fine, if you folks are telling the truth."

"We are." He smiled. I shook his hand.

"And thanks for talking to Mickey. We didn't need to spend time on that. He's on a train to India as we speak."

"Good. I wasn't sure I got through to him. I guess I got him moving. What's he been taking, you know?"

"No, but I can guess. There's a lab in Kabul—we're not sure what all's being made there, but word is LSD and some other designer stuff. We hear Timothy Leary, you know Mr. 'turn on tune in and drop out' is involved, but that's all we know. Mickey was hanging with some of those folks. There is some strange stuff getting mixed up there from what I hear. It's good that he's heading east. Word is they're setting up a grab on Mr.Leary and the brotherhood people that are there; it's not a good place to hang right now."

"Who's doing that? Afghanistan doesn't care about that crap, and they don't have any extradition, right?"

"They don't, not with any nation. But that's not an issue. Baksheesh will get you anything in Kabul. For what it's worth, I think it's Interpol and the DEA heading the show and paying the bills. A little bird says U.S. Air Force choppers and DEA ground boys. They plan to be in and out before anyone can spit. Strictly gossip, you understand? But if you have any friends around Kabul, it would be good to pass the word that Leary's scene is not a good place for the next few weeks."

"Thanks, but anyone I know hanging in Kabul will have to deal with it on their own. I'm heading east."

"Good plan." Charles smiled.

"I hope the stuff Mickey's been into wears off. I'll tell you, weird doesn't cut it. He's somewhere I couldn't get to with a spaceship."

"Yeah, I know, and every time we turned our heads, he was there, nut city. There are folks out here who would pop him just because he was seen lurking us. And that's not what we want."

"So where does that leave me—do I still work for you, or are we done?"

He looked up and smiled that smile. "That's a good question. Maybe you should ask the next Russian you run into—see what they think?"

"Right."

I headed back to the truck stop and sat there in the chai shop. I couldn't help thinking about Mickey and how gonzo he'd gotten. I'd seen him toasted before, but never so completely. I couldn't figure just what had happened with him to get him so crispy. He was a real space general when I saw him.

Didn't matter really. None of this changed anything. If I'd learned anything over the years, it was that you start where you are. I was done with the job except for the last meeting. I needed to figure where I was going next. If Mickey was still tripped out when I got to Bombay, I could head south and lie around on the beach for a while. If I knew where Amber and Cecile had gone, I could head there. I had plenty of money and a good passport. I could go to Europe.

Night came like a fast train, and I lit the fire and sat back to read the English newspaper. The big news was all about India and Pakistan tooling up for another war. East Pakistan was very worried, with good reason. If war did happen, they'd have real problems. East and West Pakistan, with India in the middle, never did make any sense. Besides, all the money and the power were in West Pakistan. If there was another war, this time, chances for East Pakistan's survival were worse than slim. It would be easy takings for India, but India had enough problems of its own with the Sikhs and their northern tribes. They had no reason to add a passel of desperately poor Muslims into the mix, not to mention thousands of square miles of malaria-ridden swamp. It was crazy, the politics out here, for sure.

Buried in the back pages was a small article on a riot in some Indian village outside Darjeeling. It had been kicked off by the burning of a temple full of people, some two hundred. In the end several thousand were killed on all sides, Hindus, Gurkhas, and Sikhs—just another day in India. I laid the paper down and went to sleep.

orning came as the noise of trucks vibrated through my room. The sun was almost visible through the haze, a yellow indistinct sphere in the sky. I went down to the chai shop, and Lawrence and Charles were sitting there. I pulled up a chair and asked, "Mind if I join you?"

"Not in the slightest," Charles replied.

"So when's the last gathering with the big wigs so I can get on the road?"

"Tomorrow morning—you ready?"

"As ever."

I had dreamed about Amber, about walking with her in a market somewhere. She didn't have any clothes on, just her tattoos. Somehow that seemed OK. No one noticed she was naked except me. It seemed normal, like dreams do.

"What happened with the girls—do you know?" I asked.

"Nope, don't know," Charles answered. "They were there the day we visited, and then about three weeks later, we got word they were packing up. They had a Mercedes camper van—don't know whose it was, but it wasn't Johnny Johnny's; different model and color. Next day, they were gone. That's all I know—that and Mickey visited a couple of times."

"Did they drive out of town? Anybody see what direction?"

"Don't know," Charles said and shook his head. "But my guess is yes. What direction, haven't a clue. We could look into it, but I don't imagine we'll be seeing much of you for a while?"

"Yeah, right. Shit, I could enjoy their company right about now."

Lawrence cut in. "I'm sure it was good and all, but they struck me as pretty settled with each other. You think you could fit in there for the long run, really?"

He was right. My life wasn't about keeping house. Even if Amber and Cecile had been willing to bring me into their world, it wouldn't have been enough in the end.

"Guess you're right, man, but I'd still like to see them; they're friends, as good as I have."

"They may still show. There's nothing to say they went west. Could be they headed to Delhi. The biggest textile markets in the East are there."

"So let's get the meeting over so I can go to Delhi?"

"Soon enough," Charles replied.

I t felt weird having the Russians, a tattooed Australian nut case, an American gun dealer and his Kashmir buyers, and now Timothy Leary with acid labs in Kabul all dancing around in my head. As much as I didn't want it, I was now in a loop that was privy to pieces of world information only a select few had any idea about.

The following morning, I paid for my room and caught a rickshaw to the hotel in the cantonment district where the last meeting was set to happen. After that, I figured I'd catch the first bus east to India. I'd had enough of Pakistan and all the rest. Mickey was supposed to be in Bombay by now, and the girls might be in Delhi if I was lucky. If nothing else, there were warm beaches, lots of sunshine, and cashew fenny in Goa and the south.

The meeting went pretty much like I expected it to, questions about how I understood what I'd seen and heard. I almost lost it at one point when they asked me if I thought it was a "significant number of Russians coming in or through the Yarkhun," enough to "warrant more observation."

"If that means you want me to go back out there, then the answer is shit no. What's a train or two full of Russians now and again? I mean, what's there to worry about? I haven't noticed anyone giving a crap about what's going down in Afghanistan these days. And it's all heading that way, far as I could tell. Now, if you're asking me whether you should find some other joker to set up out there and keep an eye on things, well, only a fool wouldn't consider that from what I saw. But I'm no longer working for you after this meeting, and I have at least two Russians out there who would just love to be practicing their English on me right about now, and that's not my idea of a fun afternoon on the Yarkhun."

They didn't push right then, and that was smart, but I could tell they were working up to it. They had a hot one in me, someone who already knew the lay of the land. I could see two of them sniffing around with each other how they might manage to get me back out there. I looked over at Charles, who right at that moment was shaking his head and looking at them with a "don't even think about it" glare. I hadn't seen Charles show this side before; in fact I wouldn't have figured he had the bite. But now it was clear that he did.

I put my hand on his shoulder and smiled. "Should have known. Thanks, man."

He turned to face me and said, "You did what we asked—did it well. You can go now if you want."

"I want. And thanks, Charles. Maybe I'll see you again. You too, Lawrence." I nodded over where he was leaning his chair against the wall.

I headed straight out the door, half expecting a hand to grab me or someone to call after me, but it didn't happen. As quickly as I could get there, I was on the street. I needed to get down the road before I could really sing out. The thought that this was history was like a monsoon ending, with cool sunny days ahead. Of course, it wasn't over, and inside somewhere, in my bones, I knew it wasn't. Still, for the moment it felt good to think it was.

The bus ran all afternoon and into the night, with short stops every few hours. We hit Lahore just after sunset, and I bought some potato patties and a leaf full of rice from a street vendor. From there we headed across the border to Amritsar. At the border crossing they didn't even take the time to speak to me, or anyone on the bus. There were two Sikhs in uniform who walked up and down the isle, looking here and there, and then they walked off the bus. It was the fastest I'd ever crossed the Indian frontier and the only time I'd ever done it without having to show my passport.

We'd been on the road in India for a while when I heard someone talking across the aisle. Seems we had a load of betel nut leaf on the bus—a major commodity in India used to make beedies, Indian cigarettes, which consisted of a small amount of flaky, cheap tobacco wrapped in a betel nut leaf and tied up with a thread. The leaf was also used as a wrapping in a little treat they chewed all over India, betel nut and calcium with some other spices all wrapped in the leaf and sold on the streets. It was a mildly addictive stimulant. Trade in Pakistani betel nut leaf in India was illegal and had been since the last war between the countries. But Pakistani leaf was considered the best, much better than Indian. It crossed the borders by the ton all the time. Even when the war raged, the leaf got through.

We pulled into Amritsar after dark, but instead of heading to the bus depot, we turned down a side road where a truck was waiting. Passengers started to unload the bales of leaf from off the top of the bus. I didn't want to get mixed up here and find myself in an Amritsar jail. I didn't know who knew about this bus, but it was sure someone did.

I slipped out of my seat as soon as I saw what was happening and went up front and told the driver to open the door. He was pretty shaky and didn't want to let me out. I grabbed him by the shoulder and pulled my vest back so that he could see the Walther tucked under my arm. He opened the door, and I stepped down and out of the bus. Without looking at anyone, I started to walk as fast as I could. I heard someone start yelling at me, but I just kept walking, and eventually it stopped.

I came to the corner and turned toward town. I had a choice: I could get a room for the night or catch another bus to Delhi. The bus meant riding all night and the next day sitting up, and hell, it finally came to me—I had money and no good reason to look like I didn't at this point, so I caught a rickshaw to the train station and booked myself a first-class sleeper compartment to New Delhi.

I got to my cabin just as the train rolled out, locked the door, and sat down on the bunk and opened my pouch. I set the Walther on the fold-up table and emptied my money belt next to it and took a count. I tucked all the Pakistani rupees away and stuck a fistful of Indian rupees in my pouch. The rest I folded up and put back in the belt. It felt good not to think about money for a while. Delhi was an expensive city, doubly so if you had to hustle rupees.

I woke up to the sounds of the tracks rumbling below and the porter at the door with chai and samosa, a little potato dumpling. I sat there looking out at the early morning. We were traveling through poppy fields. There were women all through them making shallow cuts in the pods and scraping off the raw opium with short flat blades. Heads and shoulders moved just above the poppy plants. We must have traveled through eighty miles of poppy fields. I knew India grew most of the opium in the world, but I'd never realized just how much. I sat there amazed as the fields rolled by my window like a movie.

Delhi was as busy as ever, people going each and every direction, all focused and looking important; it was funny. I walked around

Connaught Circus, the big business plaza and shopping area in the heart of New Delhi. I thought I'd look around on the off chance I might see the girls.

New Delhi is set up in circles like Paris, with streets fingering out. The textile market happened on the second circle off the Connaught Circus, and it happened only on Thursdays, and it happened to be Wednesday. I didn't have much hope but I figured I'd look anyway. After a few hours I went and booked another sleeper to Bombay for Friday. That way, I could look for the girls Thursday. If they were in Delhi, they'd be at the market. But Thursday came and went without a trace of them. I wandered through blocks of fabric dealers all morning, and the same in the afternoon, asking everyone if they had seen the girls, but no luck.

I decided to get some good food at a place in Old Delhi I liked, a Sikh restaurant that had a butter chicken to die for. It took some coin to eat there, but I had it, and I wasn't going to miss one of those chickens while I was in town. I got a three-wheel Harley-style rickshaw like they had in Delhi and headed off. I'd forgotten how much fun it was to ride around in one of those with no direction or commitments and money in your pocket. I told the driver to just drive all over Old Delhi until I told him to stop and leaned back and watched the old city turn to night. Old Delhi is a smorgasbord of color and smell and sound, with narrow, winding streets meandering like traveling lines in a time machine, opening up on wide boulevards and then moving down another narrow street. The deeper you got into Old Delhi, the further back in time it seemed to go. I loved this old city and had wandered it for hours, day and night, and never tired of it and its secrets.

Eventually I had the driver drop me off a little ways up from the restaurant. I walked through the little archway in the wall just down the narrow street and onto another snakelike road only wide enough for a rickshaw; I turned off it onto a narrow cobblestone foot lane with two-story mud walls on either side. Every fifteen feet or so was another old carved wooden door. Finally I came to the large set of double doors I'd been looking for. I stepped over the threshold and into the open courtyard of the restaurant. There were tables and benches set in circles around a raised center stage that was covered with a thick layer of rugs and just high enough for all to see. Like always, the place was full of people laughing and talking, and the smells of tandoori and naan filled the air. I sat down at a table close to the stage, and as soon as I did, a pitcher of water and another of lassie with two glasses were set in front of me. I poured the lassie and drank it down in one breath. "Eck"—one—"butter chicken," I called to the boy standing at the end of the table. He nodded and headed off toward the kitchen.

There were covered lights along the outside walls. There was no moon, and you could see the stars in the open air of the courtyard. The Milky Way cut the sky in half, and as I looked up, a shooting star drew my eyes to the south. The star lit the sky, and a collective moan swept through the crowd when it flared out in the sky above us. A few minutes later, musicians made their way onto the stage and started to set up. A tabla, sarod, sarangi, and sitar.

My chicken came to the table with a basket of hot naan just as the musicians were beginning to play. After about five minutes, a young woman came out and started singing and dancing. The music was infectious Punjabi pop that had everyone in the place swaying and moving their arms and hips to the rhythm. Old gray-hairs in their starched white turbans, wives in colorful saris, and young children, with their eyes painted dark with bright gold rings in their ears—they all moved to the music. It was a good night at Cana Mahal, and like always, the butter chicken melted on the tongue.

Morning came, and I headed south. I needed to get to Bombay. Mickey was so gonzo the last I'd seen him that I was worried. I put my stuff in my sleeper and headed to the dining car: a first-class diner with a bar and a reading area with overstuffed chairs and side tables. I loved old dining cars. These kinds had been built for the British and the Maharajah classes during the occupation. It felt a little weird at first, but I got over that fast. Hell, I had the coin. I settled into one of the chairs and sipped my English tea and read the *Times of India.*

The situation between India and Pakistan was getting worse. The paper was full of it. It was just a matter of time before the whole thing blew. It felt even better now to be out of the Northwest Territories. There was no news about anything where I'd been. Still, I knew that when things went off—and it looked like it wouldn't be that long before they did—the Northwest Territories were the first route into Kashmir and Jammu from Pakistan. There would be lots of troops heading that way. I'd gotten out just in time.

I wondered why I hadn't seen more Kashmiris out there considering what was going on. The situation with India and Pakistan was right on the edge, with both countries doing their typical "I dare you" crap. What I did know was that it wasn't my job to figure any of it out. Still, I couldn't help thinking about those Kashmiris up in the Yarkhun buying guns. That much I knew, and there could have been a lot more I didn't see. How did the Russians fit? Competition for guns like Jerry had said didn't add up—there needed to be more payoff than that for the Russians to be out there in the numbers I'd seen. Russians and Indians were pretty tight; it didn't figure. Still, it was clear the peace between India and Pakistan was about to crack—how wide was hard to tell, but peace wasn't going to last a whole lot longer, and for that reason alone it was nice to be out of Pakistan.

The day passed like dripping tar as the train moved slowly south. We were in Rajasthan when daylight faded. Evening light on the red rocks and cliffs made them look like old postcards of the Painted Desert. Night came, and the windows turned black, and the focus shifted to life in the car.

Alcohol was illegal in India, and you had to have special papers to buy it. Like prescriptions, you got them from a doctor, or you could get them from the counsel when you got a visa. That way, you paid the fee, and you were issued a permit to buy alcohol. But a British or UK passport allowed you to buy alcohol without permits. So I had a gin and tonic.

The car was built with dark rose wood and ebony trim. All the hardware and table utensils were silver, even the ashtrays. Polished cotton window curtains framed the dark glass, and its reflections showed the bar, the people, and the window across the car. Night was full on now, and the club car filled with wealthy Indians and some foreigners, all saddling up to the bar. Soon all the dining tables were filled with folks in their finest saris and suites. It was surreal and out of time in some way.

While in Delhi, I had picked up a nice shirt, vest, and pants so as not to look out of place in India, but in this crowd, that was dressing down. Still, I must have looked Indian enough as an older man in a Nero suit, who looked like a government bureaucrat from an old movie, came and sat in the chair next to me and started talking in Hindi.

"Niee niee, Hindi jiaga niee," I said, meaning "No, no, I don't speak Hindi."

"You are not Indian?" He looked at me curiously.

"No, I'm not, and I don't speak Hindi, at least not well. What is it you would like?"

"I was thinking you were Hindustani and not supposed to be in here or drinking that." He nodded at the gin and tonic in my hand. "Please accept my apology, Mr. ...?"

"You can call me Skip."

"Mr. Skip. It is a privilege to drink in our country, sir. I hope you understand."

"Oh, I do, and your name is?"

"Rashid Ram."

"Rashid, I've been sitting here all day watching the country go by and haven't had a chance to dress for dinner. There's no more room at the tables, so I decided to order a drink and wait."

"Are you American?"

"No, British subject, most recently in Kowloon. And you are you from Bombay or heading there on business?"

"Business, no, not business—a wedding. I am going to my sister's wedding. She is marrying a merchant, a very wealthy merchant in Bombay." He wobbled his head in that way Indians do.

This guy had to be fifty-five if he was a minute. I wondered how old his sister was. Most middle-class Indian women were married off by the time they were eighteen. If not, they were considered spinsters, and they turned into house servants with little hope of a marriage.

"Your sister's wedding? How old is your sister?"

"She is twenty-six, very old, I know, but still my little sister. It was difficult finding a husband for her. We advertised in the *Times* for two years before we found a possible match.

She is a doctor of medicine. She didn't want to take a husband until she had finished school. We are all very proud of her, but it has made finding a husband difficult because she is so old now. But with a large dowry and her potential to bring income we did find four men and families, but only one who had the proper astrological chart and offered the life she is used to living." He smiled and shook his head. "Mr. Skip, would you like to come to the wedding?"

This was just polite banter. From what he'd said about his sister, I knew he was Brahman, high-caste, so that meant that everyone of high caste or above the caste system, such as foreigners, got invited to weddings, the expectation being that if they are not family or friends, they will say no. I thanked him for the invitation and declined, saying I had pressing business to attend to as soon as I got to Bombay. For a minute there, I felt like saying, "Sure." Brahman weddings are a weeklong celebration, and I could use some celebration. Then I imagined how his face would look if I had said that. I didn't want to put him on the spot, even though he'd only approached me to tell me I wasn't "privileged" enough to be in the club car drinking. What the hell—he was just another upper-caste snob, and there were plenty of them in India. I needed to get on with what I said I would. I had to meet up with Mickey, and I wanted to check around and see if the girls might be in town. Who knew? They might be.

"I'm sure the wedding will be wonderful, Rashid. Sorry to miss it." I turned back to reading the paper to signal conclusion to the conversation.

"Well, I must join my brother and his wife for dinner, Mr. Skip," he said politely. "Have a good journey."

"I will. Good luck with your sister's wedding." I winked, raised my glass, and then took a sip. He smiled and turned and went over to a table where family had held his seat.

We pulled into the station the next day just before evening, after hours of rumbling through the deserts of Rajasthan and Gujarat. The hot, dry landscape had been pulling at my eyes and making my head vibrate like an electric razor. Bombay, like always, was hot and muggy. Still, it was nice to have solid ground under my feet, even though my head hadn't caught up yet. I walked up the long stairs at the station and out onto the street. I stood there, the humid air falling over me like hot, wet tissue paper. My air-conditioned sleeping compartment was just a memory now as the coastal Indian air filled my lungs. I knew the sticky feeling wouldn't last, that I would acclimate in a day or two. But that didn't make it any better.

I got my bearings and headed west toward the water and Mariner Drive. I stopped as I got to the water and looked out across the bay at the Boats moving slowly in the distance, their leaning sails filled with the winds of the Arabian Sea. Then I turned south and walked the wide boulevard along the mud flats at the shore.

It had been a while since I'd been in Bombay, and it felt good to be here, even with the heat and muggy air. If anyplace in India was cosmopolitan, it was Bombay. This was my favorite city in India, and I was happy to be back after so many months in the mountains. I walked the shore wall covered by the smell of the bay from the hot breeze. Slimy fingers of mud reached out under green-gray water in the ebbing tide. Black and white crows swarmed in pockets, popping up like fluttering gangs searching for anything that looked like food along the muddy shoals while dull, small brown birds filled the trees along Mariner Drive.

After a mile or so, the road turned to the left and into the heart of the city, where I was going to meet up with Twitch, at the hotel Rex. The Rex was a little place just off the water wall, a few blocks up from the Taj Mahal Hotel and the Gateway of India, which sat right across the street. An arched buttress jutted out into the water where ferries landed. Both were Bombay landmarks, legacies of the British colonial days.

The Gateway was a landing for slow diesel passenger ferryboats that hugged the west coast. They plowed up and down the coast, stopping along the way to pick up and drop off people, mail, and some cargo. The boats ran the whole length of west India from Gujarat to Bombay and right to the tip of India and then back again, never more than a half mile offshore. It was a great way to see the west coast if the weather was good. It was also the cheapest route south, barring third-class trains, which took forever or at least felt like forever. On the boats you had fresh air and a place to lie down if you claimed deck space. Anywhere else, on the benches or in the common-room cabin, the lice would eat you alive.

The Hotel Rex was just a couple blocks from the Gateway, but some would say a world away from the Taj Mahal; the Rex had cheap rooms filled with all kinds of expatriates, outlaws, and dope heads from all over the world.

It had been a long walk from the train station to the Rex, but I'd needed it. The rumbling in my head had settled now, and my gut was following along. I hit the corner just up from the Hotel Rex and turned down the street. Just then, a voice shot out from the little juice shop.

"Tony, is that you, man?"

It was a voice I didn't immediately know but somehow I recognized in the back of my mind; I just couldn't put a person to it. I wasn't interested in playing name games anymore so I stepped up into the juice bar to check it out. I knew the place, a small, open-fronted shop with two little tables that looked out on the street and two booths along the inside wall—that was it. It was a hangout for low-key foreigners and various hustlers. The voice called out again from the back of the shop.

"Tony, is that you?"

I turned slowly and saw a smiling face looking at me.

"Eric, what in the hell are you doing here?"

He laughed. "Shit, I live here, Tony. What in hell you are doing in India?" He stood up and came over. "I did two years in the Peace Corps here in a little village in central Maharashtra, Parbhani district. When I finished up, I shipped out of Bombay on a slow Norwegian freighter to the States, stayed for a few months, and decided I'd rather be out here and came back, so here I am. What's your excuse—how'd you end up walking around the corner looking like an art dealer from Gujarat? Shit, if I didn't know you, I'd have thought you were some kind of native; you got the look. This is the last place I ever expected to run into you."

"Good to see you too and all, but I'm not Tony here; I'm Skip."

He broke in. "Don't tell me—you're all hippie now and found your real self. Skip what? Rainbow–Sunshine–Dream Dancer or some shit? Come on, man—we both come from Oakland!"

"Cut me some slack, Eric, I'm Skip, just Skip, 'cause Tony's not such a good name for me anymore, too much baggage."

"Well, that's a relief; I thought I'd lost another to Never-Never-Land. Should have known you'd be in the real world. I'm glad some of us still are. You remember Carol Levinson, that cute little Jewish thing at Oakland City College?"

"Yeah, I remember—had a nice shape and other attributes, as I remember."

"Well, she came through on her way to Goa a few months ago, and she is now "officially" called "Mosquito Hawk"—can you believe that one, Carol the piano player? Took all I had not to laugh right there.

"So the word is mucho baggage with Tony? I understand how that gets. Skip it is. Just don't ask me to call you June Bug Pixy River, OK?" He laughed. "I'm cool with Skip, really; from now on, that's it."

"Thanks, man, glad you approve," I said as sarcastically as I could muster. "I've been in and out of India for the last few years. I wonder why I haven't I run into you."

"Just how long has it been, man? The last time I saw you was in Oakland—must be four years, five? You were playing blues at that Panther rally at Oakland City College, and now you're decked out in raw silk with a pouch on your shoulder and a bulge under your vest." He looked down where the dirt and dust had made a clear little outline of the grips on the little Walther 32.

"A long, dusty train ride," I said, brushing the outline off as best I could. "I walked from the train station." I grabbed a wet rag from the counter and tried to wipe the rest of the tracing off. "I had some concerns back home and had to leave, the biggest being the war. Kathy left me for Daniel, and the government decided they wanted me instead. I decided to make my own decisions, so I got out of Dodge and headed east via Mexico. So you live here now, in Bombay?"

"Yep, I live in the city most of the time, though I still keep my house inland; I visit Pune now and again—best whores in India. I'm loosely employed. I speak Marathi, Hindi, Urdu, and some Rajasthan. I do some guiding, but basically I hustle hippies."

"Guiding and hustling hippies?"

"Yeah, I work with a money market, a large syndicate here. They give me protection and mobility, and I supply them with traveler's checks."

"Travelers checks, how do you get those?"

"Most kids coming through—Europeans, Canadians, Americans—don't know how the check guarantee policy works. I explain to the more receptive the subtleties of the system. If they lose their checks out here, they can get them replaced in a day or two, if you know the right place to report it. I offer a percentage of value above the replacement checks. They get the replacement checks in two days or so, and I get up to 20 percent of the value of the lost checks from my people, give or take, depending on the market for dollars and marks that day. Loss reports don't get through the system to the home banks sometimes for weeks or longer, and by that time, my people have floated the checks in the market and turned them into dollars or whatever.

"The checks don't surface for weeks, months, or sometime after that, and usually when they do, it's in Kabul or Moscow in the money markets there. It turns out to be way too much for the check people to deal with, so they just write it off. It's written into their profit and loss line. So the kids get their money back and then some, and I make a living."

"What if the system goes south, and you end up looking like you're screwing someone who takes it seriously? You might wake up real damn sore."

"Could happen, I suppose. But I guess I could ask you the same question without knowing anything about what and how you do your thing, other than that stain on your vest."

He had a point.

"I'm hooked up well in this part of the city, Skip. Here and Dungari both. I'm too valuable to lose, so I count on that. There are parts of the city I don't go to, but in the parts I can go, I go anywhere."

"For each his own man. Good to see you."

We'd been good friends in the States. I wondered about the crud he was involved with, but who was I to judge it? We sat there and talked for about and hour until the conversation slacked off.

I needed to get a room. The Rex was right across the street, and I figured I'd get a room and look up Mickey in the morning.

"It's good to see you, man. I'm off to get a room at the Rex. See you again, tomorrow maybe."

"You're staying over there? Let me take care of it." He waved at a boy selling palm leaf baskets on the corner. When he came over, Eric spoke to him in Marathi.

"What was all that?"

"Just getting you a room."

Before I could drink the last of my juice, the boy had run across the street and was back, handing Eric a room key.

"Here you go, man. Just wave your passport for the guy at the desk when you go over. He won't look at it or ask for it; he knows you're my friend, and I'm good in this part of town. It's third floor center, room 33. Balcony looks right out over the street and the water. I get you the room, but you pay the bill." He winked. "Best room in the house."

"Best room in the house? Shit, Eric, they're all the same."

They were all the same inside, a couple beds and little bathroom and a balcony. But a room on the top floor and in the center was as good as it got at the Rex, and I knew that. I smiled at Eric and put the key in my pouch.

"How about a pipe or two—you smoke?" He looked up trying to figure if I knew what he was talking about.

"Where do you smoke, down in the cages?"

"No, man, I try to stay away from places where I work, unless I'm working. I go to a den in Dungari, a little Muslim place where they smoke Chinese-style. With you it will make a grand total of three foreigners who know about it, and one of them is the friend who turned me on to it."

"Let's go."

As soon as our feet hit the sidewalk, a taxi pulled up in front of the juice bar, and the driver ran around and opened the door for Eric.

"Your cab?"

"No, but my driver." He smiled

We drove out toward Dungari, the largest Muslim district in Bombay. It was about a thirty-minute drive in evening traffic winding along the back streets. Finally the cab pulled up on a dark corner. We got out, and Eric said something to the driver, and the cab drove off.

"We are walking back?"

"No, just done with him for the day. Didn't know when we would leave—figured we'd take a horse cart back, easier to puke off." He laughed.

We walked down the dark road between four- and five-story buildings that leaned on each other like drunks. If it wasn't for them supporting each other, they'd have spit their mortar. In fact some had. There were old Chinese tenement buildings towering on either side of the street with rusted cast-iron railings on the porches and windows. There had been a Chinese exodus from India sometime in the 1950s. Now this part of the city was a Muslim ghetto surrounding the Bombay city jail.

We came to a narrow doorway. It opened to a path between two buildings, a little alley maybe thirty inches wide. You had to duck and turn your shoulders to go through. Then you went two steps down and entered a narrow hall lit with a single yellow light bulb at the far end. The floor was damp, and the smell of opium was in the air. About halfway down the hallway was a stone archway, and another two steps down took us into a small stone basement room. There were two pipe makers there laying on cardboard on the floor and a hobbit-like little man squatting at the far end.

The room was about ten-by-ten with a small, short loft at one end, about three feet off the floor and four feet deep. Eric stepped in like he owned the place. The little squatting man stood up and started frantically laying out fresh newspaper on the floor for us to lie on. He signaled us to lie down as soon as the paper was out. We both lay across from one of the pipe makers, our heads on the hard wood rests. Eric leaned up on his elbow.

"Joseph, this is my friend Skip. Treat him like you do me."

Joseph moved across the little space in a crab walk, never standing, and then squatted there in is his plaid lungi and tee shirt. He shook my hand while teetering his head back and forth like it was on springs. "Very pleased, Mr. Skip. Very pleased."

"Good to meet you too."

He indicated with a turn of his hand the old man across from me. "This, Mohammad Sap, he make your pipe." He smiled again, reaching over and setting two cups of chandu in front of the lamp. "Free, first smoking." Two free cups of chandu for the first-time smoker who was new.

"You train them well here," I said across to Eric.

The chandu was what you'd expect in Bombay. A city like this with hundreds of dens meant lots of competition, so the opium needed to be strong to keep a den in business. Joseph sat there collecting the ashes from the pipes and putting it in a can that sat by his side. That was the trick; the more ash you mixed in, the higher the morphine content and the stronger the opium. Personally, I liked the pure opium without the extra kick, but that was next to impossible to get in a city where opium smoking was like corner bars in the States. And everyone drank bourbon; no one even knew about single malt whisky.

We smoked for about an hour, and then I started to bottom out. I was getting nauseous from the strong opium, but Eric seemed like he hadn't even noticed.

"You're pretty used to this stuff, are you? " I asked, signaling Mohammad Sap to stop making me pipes. I was at the point between a dream and tossing my guts.

"Yep, suppose so. When I was out here in the Peace Corps, I asked my cook if he could get me some hashish. He said yes, but he needed to get it in Bombay. I bought him a bus ticket and gave him some money. He came back with what he said was a kilo of hashish. I didn't know hashish from cow shit—I'd tried it once back in Berkeley at some party but had never seen it. Anyway, it turned out to be opium, and by the time I finished the kilo, I was pretty used to it. When I went back to the States, it became clear that I needed to live in India, so here I am. Answer your question?"

"Yep, nice that there still are places in the world where people who care to can make those kinds of choices. Why didn't you head to Nepal? There's a whole community out there for the same reasons."

"Come on, Tony—I mean Skip, sorry, won't happen again—for the same reasons you aren't in Nepal, I'd guess. I'm here, in Bombay because I'm a part of the place and the people. I don't want to hang out with a bunch of hippies. If I wanted to do that, I'd go back to San Francisco, not Nepal. Don't get me wrong—I like Nepal, and I spent lots of time there, but Maharashtra is home for me."

"I get it, man. I like Bombay as cities go too, but I'd rather hang on the beaches if I'm spending any time in India. You're right though— more jet-set hippie types each year, true, but better than half of them are women!"

"I don't get south or even out of the city at all that much. As for women, I prefer the cages."

"You hang at the cages?"

The cages were a district along Falkand Rd with prostitutes by the thousands. It was a string of six-story buildings that went on for blocks. All the windows and doors on the buildings had metal bars on the outside, typical of the old architecture in that district. Bars kept people from falling out and thieves from getting in. But it gave rise to the nickname "cages" because in every window and doorway were girls from everywhere in the subcontinent, from Nepal, Nagaland, Burma, Kashmir, Ceylon, and everyplace in between. All waving and calling out from behind the bars for business.

"I'm about topped off here, man. I'm going to head back to the Rex. You staying?"

"Nope, I'll head back with you. I have a room up the street from the Rex myself, at the Colonial. Much lower-key and cheaper."

"Cheaper than the Rex? I don't believe it. How much cheaper?"

"Thirty rupees a week with bigger rooms and Gurkha guards and a gated courtyard, the works; I can get you a room there if you want."

"No, I'm supposed to meet a friend at the Rex and head south. I don't plan to be in Bombay more than a day or so."

We left Joseph and walked for a while in the night streets of Dungari. Eric was dressed in a Nero jacket and Western-style pants. Every now and then, kids would come out of the alleys and throw rocks at his feet, and he'd spin around and yell in some dialect I didn't understand.

"Forgot I was all dressed up. Kids don't like strangers. Think they're devils."

I laughed while looking at a table surrounded by six roughly eight-year-old boys, all smoking and watching five others gambling with an old, worn deck of cards. They were spitting and talking like a bunch of old Italians in San Francisco's north beach.

"Yeah, they grow up quick in Dungari." I could see sadness in Eric's eyes for the first time when he said this. It was the old Eric I liked so much, still there. My head was swooning, and so was my stomach.

"Man, let's get that horse cart. I'm about to toss my cookies."

"It's a lot of money from here. If we walk another fifteen blocks or, so we'll be on the route, and it's cheaper.

"Fifteen fucking blocks? I don't have fifteen blocks in me, man. My stomach is flipping around like a fish. Get a cart or a cab or whatever. I'll pay. I got money. I need to get to a cold drink soon. I need something inside to toss. OK?"

He laughed. "Feeling a wee bit queasy, are we?" He stepped out into the street and flagged down a horse carriage and started into haggling with the driver over the price. The guy was finished for the day, and Eric clearly didn't want to pay the extra rupees to get him back to work. All I wanted was a place to sit that was moving toward home! Eric started to walk away, but I didn't feel good enough to take another step.

"We'll take it!" I cried out and stumbled up into the seat behind the driver.

We stopped at the first place that looked clean enough to get a drink. I downed two iced Coca Colas one right after the other. The cool soda calmed my stomach some, and the sweat stopped pouring down my forehead. Back in the carriage, I was just about to say how much better I felt when, wham, up it all came. I hung over the edge of the carriage tossing my guts for a couple minutes. Finally things settled down a bit, and I was OK, and we headed off in the Bombay night toward the Gateway of India and the Rex.

T he next morning, I went down to check at the desk. The guy who was there had been asleep when I got back. When I got there, he looked up from reading the paper and stared at me, waiting. I told him my name and room number and offered him my passport.

He just sat there.

"Not needing passport," he said. "Signing book is all." He pushed the registration book at me and went back to reading the paper. All the hotels in Bombay held your passport until you paid up, so this had to be because of Eric. I signed next to my room number and checked the book to see what room Mickey was in. Sure enough, there was his scrawl on the previous page, next to room 8. I headed down the hall toward the room. What in the hell was he getting a room on the ground floor for? I'd given him plenty of money. All the first-floor rooms were snake pits. Their balconies were more like sunken porches that opened out below the street. You were just a few feet from the sidewalk and three feet below it, separated only by an old rod-iron fence that kept people from falling in. At night you had an eye-level view of the rats that were everywhere, and during the day, you could watch feet go by or peek under skirts. The wind, if there was any, blew dust and crap in swirls and into your room if you left the porch doors open. During the wet season, you'd bail. These were not good rooms. Still there was a crowd, Italians and French hippies for the most part, that seemed to like them. I could never figure that one out.

I came to room eight and heard music inside. It sounded like Big Brother and the Holding Company—there was that distinct Janis Joplin voice—but I didn't recognize the song. I knocked, and the door opened. There was a beautiful Oriental girl standing there, hippie-looking for sure but beautiful. She was Korean or maybe Japanese, five feet if that, and wrapped up in multicolored layers of cloth. Her hair was tied up in a series of interwoven knots with glass beads here and there, and it was thick and hennaed red-black. Almond eyes looked up.

"Who are you?" she asked in light New York accent.

"Skip, a friend of Mickey's. Is he here?"

"You mean Twitch?"

"Yeah, Twitch. We're friends. We're supposed to meet up here."

"You're Skip?"

"I already told you that." I didn't have time to chat her up or wade through whatever fog she was in. I wanted to know where Mickey was.

"I told you who I am. Where's Mickey? And who are you?"

"My name's Naomi. Twitch and I are old friends. He told me you were coming. He's not here. I don't know where he is—hasn't been around for days. He left with some guy, and I haven't seen him since. It had something to do with a bust in Kabul; you hear about that? They came in helicopters and took Leary right out of his house and trashed up a lab. People were hopping fences and running every which way, he said. It was DEA, they say. Seemed like it was Leary they were after. Anyway, this guy was there and told Twitch and me about it, and then they left.

"So where'd they go?"

"I don't know." She stepped back from the door. "Come in."

"You say Mickey told you about me?" I sat down on the bed. "Nice music, but we need to talk."

"Yeah, I recorded it a few years ago." She turned the tape off.

I could see one bed hadn't been used at least in a while; her clothes were folded and stacked neatly on it. It reminded me of Cecile and Amber's. "So when did he leave with this guy?"

"Four days ago."

"He tell you when he was coming back or where he was going?"

"No, but he did say you'd pay for the room when you got here. I guess he was out of money." Her mouth turned in a little, and her eyes lowered.

"Don't worry, I'll get the room," I said. "How is it you know Mickey?"

"We met in Afghanistan couple years ago. I knew his wife, when they were together. I was doing some business for a friend in Kabul a year or so ago, and he turned out to be involved. We liked each other and spent a couple weeks hanging out together before I went back to the States. Then about a week ago, I was sleeping at the Gateway, waiting to get the boat to Goa, when he spotted me. We got to talking, and he bought me dinner and then brought me back here. Said I could stay in the room—use the spare bed—until you got to town or until I could get the boat."

"Sleeping at the Gateway? You're nuts or harder than you look. This is Bombay, not Berkeley. Strange folk prowl these streets at night, not to mention in the day. New York is kindergarten compared to parts of this town!"

Her face turned up with a look that would make a Bangkok taxi driver apologize.

"I've slept in lots of places," she said, putting her hands on her hips and setting her feet apart like a Korean Annie Oakley, "and with lots of people. When I don't have the scratch, I don't have lots of choices but I know how to use the choices I have. I'm not a fool, Skip, and I'm not one to claw my way through when there are other ways. Lots of Europeans sleep at the Gateway. You have to be there when the boat hits the dock to get deck passage, or you're shit out of luck. Deck space is the only place on the boat there aren't any bugs! " She looked me up and down, and I wasn't about to say shit. Then she slowly turned her eyes away and shook her head. "I was expecting money when I got into town, but the situation in Kabul put a chink in that plan."

"Yeah, I've had times like that myself."

"I do believe you may well have," she said softly. "Now I've got to get to Goa."

"You plan to leave when?"

"Yesterday—shit, last week—but they don't seem to be down with my plans. I'm always catching the next ferry. I got a friend in Goa who owes me and has the bucks, so the first deck passage I can buy or screw for, I'm on it." She raised her eyes, shrugged her shoulders, and sat down on the bed. "I've got money enough for a ticket and to rent a motorbike one day when I get there. Enough money, that is, if I don't have to spend any on this room, which I will do if I have to. Twitch is a friend, and I won't hang him out, and I can find more money if I need to; I know how."

"I'm sure you do, but I'll take care of the room; you get your ticket. Anything else you can tell me that might help me find Twitch, or figure out when he might come back?'

"I don't know much. I expected him back an hour or so after he left, at least that's what he said. But you know him and time. After three days and four nights, I'm not counting on seeing him soon. I hung in here hoping you'd show up."

"You know the guy he left with?"

"They called him Diamond in Kabul. That's all I know. I saw him a few times, but we never talked. He was one of those Laguna Beach brotherhood guys. None of them liked New Yorkers much, or girls as far as I could tell. When he showed up here, he seemed out of it like Mickey's been, but he remembered my name—that was a hit. I figured they were off with friends to talk about the bust. Twitch isn't like I remembered him, Skip. He's pretty out there."

"Yeah, he's been weirder than normal."

"Ain't that the truth." She rolled her eyes.

"I'm going to check around and see if I can't find him. You work on your ticket.

I'll pay for this room now. I don't stay in the snake pit if there's an option. You can move up to room 33 with me; you can stay there until you get a boat or we both get a ride south."

"Twitch said you were righteous."

"Well, that might be stretching it."

I watched as she gathered her stuff. She really was beautiful. It was hard imagining her sleeping at the Gateway. She was so exotic, I bet every male in smelling distance was playing knight in shining armor. Twitch showing up must have been a gift. She wouldn't have to play anyone against anyone else or make friends she didn't want to. She struck me as smart.

"Look, Naomi, at the moment I'm flush and trying to do right by my friend. That's it."

"I know," she said as she finished gathering up her stuff.

We went up to my room, and she put her stuff on the extra bed and sat down next to it. I wanted to sit and talk, but I needed to find out about Mickey. I was worried something might be up.

"I'll be back," I said. "And don't worry—I *will* be back. I'll pay for the room when I go out; you just stay here. You got the key for the old room?"

"Yeah, but I don't have Mickey's."

"That's OK. I'll deal with it. I'll have them bring you up a key for this room. Here are the rules: no guests. I don't want anyone in the room but you and me. No one knows I'm here except you, got that? Don't bring anyone back, and you don't tell anyone where you're staying even if you're screwing them, got it?" Her head turned up, and she stared at me with a look I couldn't read. "That's the deal, Naomi, if you want to stay here—you OK with that?"

"I'm on with it all, Skip. I'm not saying anything to anyone, you have my word, and I'm not going out. I would like to sit on the balcony if that's OK though." She looked at me for a sign of permission and then added, "I'm not screwing anybody for my ticket, or fun, and I don't have any plans to either, yet. And for the record, Mickey and I are friends. I knew his ex-wife." She got up and opened the balcony doors. A soft breeze came in off the water and swept the layers she wore back against her hips. Her breasts rose up like a swell on a still sea while the sun shined through the layers, cutting a dark silhouette of her sculpted body. *Sometimes you are just damn lucky,* I thought to myself.

"Go ahead and sit on the balcony and enjoy; just don't flag anybody down or draw attention up here. I'll be back in a while."

I went by the desk on my way out and dropped off the key and paid Mickey's tab. The guy reached under the desk and handed me his passport.

"You take."

Mickey had to be coming back; he wouldn't leave his book behind—that is, unless he'd got another. Maybe that's what was going down and why he was out of money. I'd given him plenty of rupees. The Kabul deal might have been too close for some reason. Maybe he needed another passport? I took the passport, figuring I'd give it to him when I found him. He could trash it, sell it, or whatever.

I told the guy at the desk to take a key up to the room for Naomi along with a lassie and some chicken and rice. I didn't know the last time she'd eaten, but she wouldn't have told me she was hungry even if she was, I could tell.

I headed down the water wall at the end of the street and toward the Gateway. It was busy and full of important-looking Indian businessmen and women all going this way and that. On the breakwater about halfway to the Gateway were three hippie types smoking hashish.

"Good shit?" I asked as I walked up. They all turned at the same moment, like their heads were on one neck. *Weird,* I thought.

"Any of you know Mickey Twitch?"

One of them mumbled through red beetle nut–stained teeth in a thick French accent. "Who?"

"Twitch —Mickey Twitch. English, skinny, smokes lots of hashish, long matted brown hair?"

"No, man," he said in slow motion and looked at his friends, who just sat there like they were trying to figure out if this was planet Earth. I stood there a while thinking maybe something more was traveling up to their brains on a very slow train, but they just drifted back into another universe. I said thanks, might as well been speaking to myself, and went on down the road toward the Gateway. When I got there, I saw Naomi was right. There were about thirty people out there all lounging around on blankets and bed rolls.

I stepped across the street quickly on the off chance someone might recognize me. In my time around India, I'd run into a lot of dopers, most of whom I really didn't want to shoot the shit with right now. I knew if the guys on the wall hadn't seen Twitch, none of these others likely would have either. After all, he'd pulled Naomi out of there.

I flagged a cab and headed across town to the Chore Bazaar. There was a den there that Mickey and I both knew. It was an old Chinese den. It was the only place I could think of other than the Rex that we both might go. It was stashed away in a third-floor attic. There were two other dens on the third floor there where you occasionally saw foreigners, but not in this place. It was one step further up. You'd go into an open room where a Chinese family lived. They would tap the ceiling, if they knew you, and an attic door would open. A ladder would lower, and up you went. When you got up and inside, you were in a room covered with Chinese carpets, with two little windows with songbirds in cages hanging out side. There were three old Chinese men, skin and bones and working ornate and beautiful pipes. No one got in here unless they were invited. Mickey and I had a mutual friend who had invited us both at different times. I stuck my head up through the trap door but didn't see Mickey. I couldn't just leave without smoking, so I had a couple pipes and then left.

I walked down the street wondering why Mickey had told Naomi what he had, that I was coming. He didn't need to tell anybody that, and he was savvy enough to know he shouldn't. Unless, like she said, they were good friends, and he knew he could trust her, and he didn't have enough money to cover stuff. But I'd given him a fistful of rupees, more than a month's worth, I'd thought. Why was he out of money, and when had he told her about me, and that I had money? Was it when he left with Diamond after hearing about Kabul or before? Had some connection to the Kabul deal given him the jitters? It seemed she was connected to what went down, or at least it sounded that way, so why not take her with? Maybe this guy Diamond had something to do with that. Naomi didn't have much interest in him, it seemed. And she was right about some of those brotherhood guys; they could have spent more time picking a gender. But all that didn't really matter. I knew that the last time I'd seen Mickey, he was so out of it he couldn't hold a thought longer than it took for a piece of dust to cross his sight.

I had no idea where he could be, and I didn't want to leave Bombay without at least hooking up and making sure he was OK. He knew I was coming, so he shouldn't have left. Then it hit me—I should go see John Berret, a friend we'd discovered we both knew during one of our conversations. He might know where Mickey was, so I flagged a cab and headed to Mariner Drive and his flat.

I stepped into the old lift in the hall and slid the iron gate shut, pulled out the number 4 knob and swung the worn brass handle over to the "up" label. John lived on the fourth floor of this old Edwardian apartment building along the water. His place looked out over Mariner Drive and the Arabian Sea; it was very nice, right between Baliwood and old downtown. The building had numbers of old British still living in it, military types who'd stayed on after the partition. John had been a child in London during the German blitzing and had moved to India with his family right after partition in 1948. The rest of them had eventually gone back to England, but he'd stayed.

I knocked on the door and heard light footsteps approach. The door opened, and there was a young girl, maybe sixteen, in a plain blue sari with a silver chain running from a large ring in her nose up to her right ear. She had a distinct set of tattoos on her lower lip and chin. Her eyes were big and set inside thick black liner. She must have been from Nagaland, judging from the Oriental features and long straight nose. John always did have young pretty house help.

"John?" I asked, and she stepped back and put her hands together and bowed her head slightly. "Namaste," she said.

It was just like the last time I'd been here, as if nothing had moved; John was sitting in front of the window, looking out over the water with a gin and tonic in his hand.

"It isn't even noon yet, man; I hope that's a soda pop."

"If it bloody were, I would be looking for a new girl Friday!" He turned his head my way, smiled, and lifted his glass in greeting. "Have a slog, will you, Skip?"

"A bit too early for me, thanks. But I'll take a tea."

He waived a hand at the girl, and she was off into the kitchen.

"Bugger all, Skip, what lost tribe of smelly goat herds you been hiding out with? Haven't seen you in a couple years, I think." He looked me up and down with a smile.

"I've been in Afghanistan, in the Hindu Kush, and up in the Northwest Territories, the Yarkhun. Just in town for a few days."

I didn't want it to seem as if I was just there looking for Mickey. John had been a good friend to me. Introduced me to layers of Bombay I would never have known had I not known him. He was a good man with an interesting mind that surfaced occasionally, popping up from under a deep sea of gin.

"So what you been up to, anything new and exciting, besides the new help?" I smiled as the young girl brought my tea.

"Oh, Jotry is new to you, isn't she? She's been here for months now; cute, right? He sister was even cuter, but she found a husband. Jotry took her place. Very good cook and all."

"She lives here? "

"Six days of the week. One day with family, working twice as hard as she does here, I'd venture. She's always eager to get back. Her sister gave better massages, but she's learning." He nodded, and she turned and went back into the kitchen.

"Like all young pretty girls in Bombay, she's hoping to marry a British passport. It makes them very agreeable indeed. Not a chance of course with me; my family would disown me. But they don't know what they don't see." He winked and raised his glass and took a long drink. "As to actual efforts, I've been doing a series of shirts. They've been a bloody hit in Europe, actually. They are very nice, seven colors on silk. Good silk too, from Mysor. I'm doing six designs: a white and green Tara and some Tibetan tonka art. I understand there isn't a girl in Europe that doesn't want one, or so my buyers tell me. Business was fine at first, but now I can't fill all the orders, and they have to wait, and they don't like that. Bloody foreigners just don't get it. And now I understand through a number of ears that there is a plan to take my designs and make the shirts in Bangkok."

"Sounds like bad business partners, John. I happen to know someone who might be able to help. An old friend of mine who I just ran into knows lots of the right people, I understand. I'm sure he could get some folks to visit your associates and clarify how wrong it would be to steal your ideas."

"I know all the right people in this town—you should know that! But I do appreciate your thoughts. I'll deal with it as I always do." He smiled and stared out the window.

"It's your call. Glad you had a good run with the shirts even if it was short."

"Bloody well isn't over yet. I'll squeeze their dandy asses blue! I'm selling them all the bloody designs. I've a meeting set up tomorrow. They'll pay for what I copied." A smile broke across his face, and a sense of satisfaction swept over the room like a wave. Just like John to hustle the hustlers.

"I'm sure they'll see it as money well spent, as I know you will," I said. "By the way, I met somebody you know in Kabul last year, Mickey, Mickey Twitch."

"Mickey, you knew Mickey—he's dead, you know."

My heart sank to someplace deep, someplace dark. "Dead? When? How?"

"Less than a week now. When did you get into town?"

"Yesterday."

"I wasn't there of course, but people told me what happened. They knew Twitch and I went back a long time. From what they told me, it was thankfully quick. Stuck in the neck is what they said—bled out in just a minute or two. He was cremated the day before yesterday, I think. Don't know who if anyone collected the ashes."

"Stuck in the neck—what happened? We were supposed to meet here in Bombay. I looked for him at the Rex but found a gal named Naomi in the room. You know her? Did she have anything to do with this?"

"God no, Skip, Naomi is bloody family. She's been in and out of here since she was a baby slung across her mother's back—a damn good woman that one, as a friend or anything else. She was rooming with Twitch, was she? You saw her, and she didn't know he was dead?"

"No, or didn't let on. What the hell happened? Was it an old debt, what?"

"As I understand it, no. It was just a bad place at an extremely bad time. From what I'm told, Mickey had been spouting some of his mystical mumbo jumbo with a room full of Danish hippies, taking the floor as always, I'm sure. He'd dosed them all, or some of them, on acid he had gotten apparently through a lab in Kabul. Seems it was much stronger than anyone had expected.

"It was all just fine at first, or at least that's what everyone thought. Then one of the younger ones, a Dane, I believe, started getting antsy and went to use the loo or something, and when he came back, he went nuts. Jumped Mickey, saying something about spells and Satan and that Twitch had put the cree-cree on him or something like that. Apparently, Mickey tried to talk the kid down, but his eye started twitching, and before anyone could do a thing, the kid stabbed him in the neck.

"They all jumped the kid as soon as they figured out what had happened. They were all very stoned, it seems. They got the kid to the floor, but he'd stuck Mickey real good. No one knew what to do. Nobody there had any training. Dandies, most of them, of course, toasty pops all blitzed out of their minds, as you well know—not the cream of the crop. One fellow there, a kid from Laguna called Diamond, apparently did try to put pressure on the wound, or so it looked, but by the time clear heads arrived to help, Twitch had bled out."

My gut turned in a twist, and I could feel the swell of tears in my eyes start to push. My head was spinning, and my heart was weeping. "Nobody had the moves to stop this guy? Who was there?"

"Look, Skip, it happened; it's over. Twitch was my friend too, but he's dead; really, he is. The kid is in jail, and they're planning to send him back to Denmark. It seems he still believes he killed the devil or god knows what. He's clinical, Skip. It's a shit of a deal for sure, as you Americans like to say. It was a shark bite, a lightning strike—nothing you or I could have done."

I didn't know how to answer. Part of me wanted to run to the jail and see who'd done this to my friend—and then do what, I had no idea. I was bursting inside, and I needed to do something. I had no words. Mickey was dead. Shit, I should have been there. If I'd only been there, it might have been different. I could have kept him alive or nabbed the kid before it happened. But the reality was it had happened, and Twitch was gone. After a while, my insides started to settle back, and I asked, "Who got his stuff?"

"No one I know; most of it was burned with him, I'm told."

"I have his *I Ching* and yarrow sticks. Said he didn't need them anymore last time I saw him, that it all made sense, that he knew the *I Ching* by heart." I laughed softly, thinking how true that was. And he really didn't need much of anything anymore. "I'll miss that crazy-ass fool."

"I already do, Skip. Sorry it was me that had to tell you. I would have rather it been someone else, and we could have just shared stories. But someone had to tell you I guess it's good it was me. What say to that gin and tonic now?"

"Yeah, sure."

" Jotry," he called.

s I walked back to the Rex, the sun was setting over the city. All along the waterfront, there were fires burning and people cooking their evening meals. The street communities were setting up their sidewalk homes, and the birds were singing their last songs of the day, and I was as sad as I'd been for a very long time. I'd known Mickey and I were heading in different directions—I'd know it for a while—but I'd never expected this. As I turned the corner past the juice shop, Eric called out to me, "Skip, how's it hanging?"

"Hey, Eric, could be better."

"Come have a juice; it's on me."

I stepped up into the shop and sat down across the table from him. "You here every day?"

"My office away from the office." He shrugged his shoulders. "A bad day, was it?"

"Yep, real bad. My friend, the guy I told you I was supposed to meet, is dead. Some Danish asshole stuck him. We were good friends. I just found out. It's been a bad day, and I'm pissed."

"Sorry, man. I heard about that deal—happened a few days ago. I hear they burned the guy yesterday or the day before. The kid who did it is in jail waiting to get deported. I could get you in to see him if you wanted."

"No, what's done is done; as I hear it, he's full nuts and getting worse. I got no reason to see him. Besides, I might not do myself any good if I did. I'm pretty pissed."

"I get that for sure. So you were close, this guy Twitch and you?"

"Very."

"Sorry, Tony; shit, I mean Skip."

"That name shit doesn't matter to me much anymore, Eric, but thanks for remembering. You going to Chor Bazar tonight? A few hours in the den sounds pretty good right now."

"I could. I've been there already this afternoon, but I don't have any reason not to go again." He smiled, and freckles on his cheeks rose up under his eyes like a bunch of red-brown grapes. I looked over toward the Rex and up at my room. Naomi was sitting with her feet up on the little table and watching all the happenings along the street, She spotted me looking up and waved and smiled.

"Eric, I need to tell someone what's happened. I'll meet you here in an hour or so—that all right?"

"OK, fine with me, Skip. Bring your friend if you want."

I headed across the street and up to the room. As I stepped through the door, the smell of sandalwood filled the air. Incense was burning in a small ceramic dish in the middle of the table, and right next to it was a pineapple and two mangoes in a brown clay bowl and two blue glass bottles of water with their hard rubber stoppers tight. The beds had richly colored cloths over them, and the windows on either side of the door to the deck were hung with thin red and brown paisley cloths. I picked up one of the waters and pushed the rubber ball down with the butt end of my knife. The water bubbled out and dripped on the floor as I walked out on the patio. Naomi looked up at me. "Hope you don't mind that I fixed up the place a little?"

"No, it feels good, thanks." I took a long drink from the bottle as I sat down in the chair across from her.

"Here's the deal. I got no idea how to say this any other way. Mickey's dead."

"Dead? Oh no! I thought maybe he was hurt when I didn't see him for two days, but dead—I didn't want to think that. How?"

"Some kid stuck him in the neck, and he bled out."

"Oh shit, not him!" She threw her head back and closed her eyes. After a long few seconds, she sat back up and looked over at me.

"A couple days ago, I was out getting some food and heard about that, but I never thought it was Mickey." She sat there shaking her head.

"Apparently it was. A good friend of both of ours told me about it." I didn't know what else to say. I sat there looking at her. I could see her sadness was real and deep. Her eyes filled with tears that started to roll down her face.

"Did you get something to eat? I asked them to bring up some food when I left."

"Yeah, Skip, thanks. I ordered water and fruit, I hope that's OK. I'll pay for it if you want."

"No, it's fine."

We just sat there for a long time without saying anything. Night had come, and the lights from the boats on the water moved up and down out across the bay. I closed my eyes and drifted off.

"Tea?" I heard a thin voice ask. I opened my eyes, and there was Baba, standing right across from me in his low little room, his hand stretched out with a steaming cup on a saucer.

"Baba?" I sat up and reached out to take the cup. "I'm back here again? OK I'll bite, this is somehow real, or I'm totally off the ledge, and it doesn't matter either way. So what's this visit about?"

"It's about what you need to know," he said, still talking in that strange language. But like every time before, I understood. "It is new time now—none of the old roads—and that's good. I'm here to tell you that the ravens have their eyes on you—that is good too, you know that?

"I saw your heart shrinking, so I thought I'd give you some tea. Drink. It's good, strong black tea. The past is sour right now, but tomorrow demands attention."

"Look, Baba, I don't understand any of this. Will I wake up and be right back at it like before? Will all this make even less sense? If I'm losing it, I really would like to know so I can do something about it. Is this a hallucination of some kind, a dream?"

"Tomorrow is not a dream; it is a possibility. You are always awake; you just don't notice. Drink the tea and remember about the ravens. They'll call, and you'll go, and tomorrow will know that you are there when you arrive."

I was totally confused now. None of this made since. In one sense, I knew I was sitting in Bombay, and in another, I knew I wasn't. I could smell the musty dirt on his floor and the smoke in the room and the tea.

I took a sip, and my mouth felt like a vast cathedral of taste and smell. My whole body was filled with ambrosia like before, but it was not the same—it was a taste of spring in the early morning on a high mountain in the sun.

"Baba, what is this? This is great!"

"Just tea. Do you want more?"

I opened my eyes and saw Naomi looking at me and holding the blue glass bottle of water.

"Do you want more?" she said

"No, no, I'm fine," I answered as the patio and her beautiful face came into focus. She tilted the bottle up and drank the rest of it. "I figured it out, Skip. I'm pissed that Mickey's dead, and I'm pissed that he didn't come back, but most of all, I'm pissed that shithead Diamond didn't tell me. Was he there, do you know?"

"Yeah, he was there. He's the one who tried to stop the bleeding, they say."

"Crap, he couldn't pour piss out of a boot with the directions on the sole. Damn it, Mickey was my friend." She just looked out over the street, her hands on the railing, and started to cry.

I stepped up next to her and put my arm over her back. "Yeah, I know. He was my friend too." She looked up at me with eyes filled.

"God damn him, I'm tired of losing friends!"

"Me too, Naomi, but what's done is done and over. Twitch is dead. John Berret was the one who told me—he says you know him, so you know it's the truth."

"John's a good friend of my mother's, and mine, so why didn't he come tell me?"

"He didn't know you were here, or that you knew Twitch."

"Yeah, that's true. Shit, I don't want Twitch to be dead!"

"I get it, but he is. I'm heading over to Chor Bazar with a friend, to a den there, to smoke some of this out of my head. Want to come?"

"I don't smoke opium, but I'd like the company, and I'd like to get out of the room. But what about being seen with you—that could blow the whole 'don't tell anyone we're together here' bit, no?"

"I'll be out of town before that matters; hopefully both of us will. John says you're good people, and that's good enough for me. I'll make sure you get to Goa. Besides, you're awfully pretty. I can think of a lot worse things than to be seen with you." I winked, trying to play it off as a joke, even though I suppose I meant t it. She was beautiful.

She smiled, looked me in the eyes, and reached up and pushed my hair back from my face and said, "You're cute too."

No one at the den had ever seen anyone like Naomi that was sure. We were deep in the Muslim ghetto of Dungari where Western women almost never went, and Naomi was an exotic example of women anywhere. Mohammad Sap kept looking down at the floor while Joseph made a place for her up on the little raised portion in the back, never looking her in the eyes. He shuffled here and there, covering it with his freshest newspapers, and then ordered her a pure milk chai and ran out the little door and came back with a large embroidered pillow from somewhere for her to lie on.

I called over to Joseph, "I don't get pretty pillows; what's the deal?" He looked embarrassed and started to get up. I raised my hand to stop him and signal him to sit back down. "Just a joke, man, just a joke."

I could see he didn't understand and was getting more uncomfortable. "It's fine, thank you, it's just fine."

Eric started speaking Marathi, and the heads started to wiggle, and smiles came back to the faces. After things had settled, he looked over. "It's OK now, but be careful, man. They are good guys and thought they'd insulted your wife."

I looked up at Naomi and shrugged.

"Always wanted to marry a Scotsman," she called down.

We lay round in the den until I couldn't smoke any more. Eric could have stayed indefinitely; he had that hop habit real deep, it seemed.

We caught a horse carriage back to the hotel like before, only this time I didn't puke. Naomi and I talked about Twitch, trying to get our heads around what had happened. Eric said he'd run into him once, but that he was so out of it, he didn't want to know. "But," he added, "sorry I didn't know him in better times like you did."

We both knew that he was just being nice to an old friend, to me, and that he really didn't give a crap about Twitch, and why should he? It was nice that he'd said that, but he didn't need to. What was done was done. If the history between Mickey and me hadn't been what it was, I'd have avoided him like the plague, like anybody else I'd run into who was as toasted as he was the last time we were together.

The hardest part was that I knew I'd already cut ties with Mickey when I left Peshawar. I likely wouldn't have hung with him when I got back. But his death made it harder. Easier, I guess, too. It was lucky he'd lasted as long as he did. Some edges are just too steep and the fall too far to climb back up from. Twitch had lived a good life, at least some of it. I knew I had been with him and had been a good friend. I'd remember him that way.

On the long ride back from the den, Eric ran a string of stories about Bombay. He held up his right hand, and you could see his pinkie finger all curled up in the palm, stuck there by thick layers of scarring running halfway down his hand. "I jumped a Gurkha from behind one night," he started. "He was beating a friend of mine with a bamboo stick. Before I knew it, this happened. And get this—right after he cuts me, he grabs my hand and wraps it up with a piece of his own shirt. Then he spends the next half hour apologizing. He was a night guard at the hotel. Didn't know the guy he was hitting was a friend of mine. That night, I found out that the story about Gurkhas pulling their knife, that they can't put it back into the belt until blood is drawn, is true. He really was sorry.

"Anyway, I came down with some jungle fever from the cut right that night and ended up on the loft at Joseph's for five days, sweating it out and drinking opium tea. By the time I went to see a doctor, the tendon was lost up in my arm somewhere. Goes to show, don't fuck with Gurkhas." He laughed and lit a beedi.

When we got back to the Gateway, Eric headed off to his place, and Naomi and I walked down along the water.

"Tomorrow we'll go down and get cabin passage to Margao. If we get it, we can board early and stake out a prime place on the deck. And we'll have our own bathroom. I'm going south myself, so it's on me. That work for you?" I stopped and leaned against the water wall and looked out at the lanterns bobbing on the boats in the distance.

"Works fine, but I need to know why you carry that." She reached up a finger and touched the tracing of the grips on my vest.

"It was a gift. A friend in the Northwest Territories gave it to me. I needed it there; everyone wears them like shoes. Guess I got used to it."

"Shoes? I suppose I shouldn't have asked. It just makes me a little nervous, especially when you can see it through the vest like that." She raised one eyebrow and gave me a curious look. "You got money, right? Get a dark vest." She smiled.

"You're on, right after we book the cabin tomorrow."

"OK, but I'm washing that vest tonight."

Morning came, and the smell of coconut oil from Naomi's hair rose up off my chest. The fancy knots had loosened, and her almond eyes were looking up at me.

"Sorry about the hair," I said.

"Not to worry. I'll just tie it back up. I know how," she said, winking.

"I know you do. I need to get moving soon; the booking office opens early. If we're lucky, we can get on today's boat." I sat up and reached over to the other bed for my pants, and Naomi wrapped herself in her sari and went out on the patio to get my vest.

"It's dry and sort of clean," she said as she held it up for me to see. "At least you can't see the gun handle on it. That'll do for now."

We bought tickets for a first-class cabin with a bathroom and fan. There were only two cabins on this boat; the rest was deck passage. We went back to the Rex, gathered our stuff to take down to the boat, and paid for the room. I told Naomi to go ahead and get our stuff into the cabin and to stake out a spot on the deck before the other passengers were let on. I was going to get a dark vest, change some dollars into rupees, and then join her.

I caught a cab to a tailor who I knew was in the money trade. I figured I'd get a vest and change money both. I changed a hundred dollar bill for rupees and bought a dark cotton vest he had hanging in front. He spotted the Walther when I was changing and asked if I wanted to sell it. I thought about it but decided not to. I told him maybe when I got back to Bombay. Always good to keep your options open with the people you do business with. On the way back, I stopped at the juice shop to say good-bye to Eric and pick up a few bottles to drink on the trip. but Eric wasn't around.

After telling someone at the counter, "I need two big bottles, one pineapple and one strawberry," I sat down at the front and looked down the street toward the water. The wind had picked up, and the trees shook overhead and made a rustling sound.

"Tony, glad I found you."

I turned to look. Right there in front was Tom standing on the sidewalk. "Tom! Fancy seeing you here! What you been up to? Been a long time since Mexico."

"I know. Saw you in Kabul and in Peshawar too, but figured you were busy, and I knew I was, so I passed on the howdy. I knew we could catch up later. Eric told me I might find you here or at the Rex."

"You know Eric?"

"Yeah, we work together now and then." He smiled. "Speaking of work, that's why I'm looking for you."

"Look, Tom, I don't have any work for you. I'm just starting vacation, actually. Sorry."

"No, not for me, man. I'm not looking for work; I got plenty. It's Charles who wants you to do some work for him." He looked at me with that whiskerless Mexican Indian face of his, waiting for some response.

"Charles? I did my work for them; I'm paid and finished."

"Yeah, I know, I know, but he said I should offer it to you anyway. He said you might like the money. Also, he said he was sorry to hear about Mickey."

"Yeah, that was a bad deal. How did he know about that?"

"Don't know. I guess news travels fast on the right wire. Anyway, seems like Lawrence and Charles liked your work and want you to do some more."

"Fuck no, I told them I was made by the Russians, and I wasn't going back in the Yarkhun, and I'm not. They can pull whatever rabbit out of the bag they want. I don't give a shit. Going back in there is like asking to be popped. There is no amount of money worth it."

"They're cool on all that, believe me. They don't want you to go into the Yarkhun; they want you to go into Northern Jammu maybe into Tibet just a little ways, but way up north, east of the Yarkhun. They will give you five grand for a month's work out there; the clock starts here in Bombay and includes meeting up with them in Simla to get instructions and maybe three weeks in the field, if that. All they want is for you to keep your eyes open and tell them what you see like before."

"You know these guys pretty well?" I asked as the juice walla brought out my first bottle and set it down in front of me.

"Shit, yeah," he said, throwing up his hands like a Jewish diamond dealer.

"Is this going to go on forever? I can use the coin, sure, and I can do the work, but I also have a friend who just died and a beautiful girl waiting for me on the boat to Goa, and in case you think I'm tight-wired, I also have an old Afghani baba that keeps dancing in my head with vague messages. Sometimes I'm not sure if I'm living or dreaming or what the fuck is reality. Do they really want me to bring them information? Maybe you could do it. I'm not kidding, man. You know me, and I'm telling you the truth here. I really would love to spend some time in Goa with this gal." I did my best to raise one eyebrow.

"It's good money, Tony, and she'll wait if you ask her, won't she?" He smiled.

The second bottle came to the table. I pulled out a twenty rupee note, handed it to the walla, and waved him away to keep the change.

"She's not a puppy, man. Ask her to wait? Look, I'll think about it, but right now, I need to get these to the boat." I stood up and headed toward the water.

"Five grand," I heard him call out behind me.

When I got to the boat, Naomi had the room all fixed up with colored cloth on the windows and the fan going.

"I thought we might like these on the way." I held up the bottles of juice.

She was silent for a minute and just looked at me and then said, "My friend in Goa is an old boyfriend. I thought you should know after last night. I wasn't planning on meeting you, like this, and he and I have been over for a few months now, but he still owes me money, and I intend to collect it. How's that going to be with you?"

This wasn't a big surprise. A woman as beautiful as she was not being taken or having recent history with someone would have been the real surprise.

"Look, Naomi, I enjoyed last night a whole lot, and you don't owe me for anything. Are we straight on that? The boat trip, that's a gift. You need to do what you need to do right now. I get it. I can afford it. I'd like to spend more time with you, that's for sure, maybe even more time than that. Who knows."

I looked at her sitting there on the bed, her hair tied up tight in those knots. Damn, she was pretty, but she had business to attend to in Goa; she'd had it all along. I'd shown up in the middle of it all.

Did I really want to go and deal with an old boyfriend and a bunch of Laguna brotherhood types? Not really. She was worth a lot, but not with all that baggage attached. And as nice as she was, I still hoped I might run into Amber and Cecile someplace.

"Look, Naomi, I ran into an old friend just now, and I have some work I need to attend to. Can I meet up with you in Chapora in about six weeks? If that doesn't interest you, I get it—just say so. That's fine."

"It does interest me; let's do it. I have stuff to clean up before I can try something new the way I'd like to with you. I would guess your life is not that much different. At least we both know how we might feel. We both lost a good friend this week, and last night made it better for both of us. That matters, and I think I really like you."

"Yeah, it more than matters, and I know I really like you. I'll be on the beach in six weeks."

I watched as the boat pulled out and headed south. Naomi waved to me from the deck. As I watched her, I saw two ravens land on the railing right next to her, almost as if they had taken my place on the boat; she reached over and fed one something out of her hand.

I walked along the road toward the corner and the Rex. The afternoon sun was radiating up from the street like a furnace, and the humid air made it hard to take a breath. A layer of exhaust and dust lay over the city, and the sun was lost in the grayness. Just then, two ravens landed in the tree overhead and called out. I looked up and saw the face of Baba reflecting in their blue-black feathers. I shook my head and wondered when the train north to Simla was going to leave Bombay.

LaVergne, TN USA
16 June 2010
186293LV00003B/4/P